THE REPENTANT MORNING

Chris Paling is the author of five previous novels, *After the Raid*, *Deserters*, *Morning All Day*, *The Silent Sentry* and *Newton's Swing*. He lives in Brighton.

D0765953

Chris Paling

THE REPENTANT MORNING

V

VINTAGE

Published by Vintage 2004

2 4 6 8 10 9 7 5 3 1

Copyright © Chris Paling 2003

Chris Paling has asserted his right under the Copyright, Designs and Patents Act, 1988 to be identified as the author of this work

First published in Great Britain in 2003 by
Jonathan Cape

Vintage
Random House, 20 Vauxhall Bridge Road,
London SW1V 2SA

Random House Australia (Pty) Limited
20 Alfred Street, Milsons Point, Sydney
New South Wales 2061, Australia

Random House New Zealand Limited
18 Poland Road, Glenfield,
Auckland 10, New Zealand

Random House (Pty) Limited
Endulini, 5A Jubilee Road, Parktown 2193,
South Africa

The Random House Group Limited Reg. No. 954009
www.randomhouse.co.uk

A CIP catalogue record for this book
is available from the British Library

ISBN 0 099 28755 2

Papers used by Random House are natural, recyclable products made from wood grown in sustainable forests. The manufacturing processes conform to the environmental regulations of the country of origin

Printed and bound in Great Britain by
Bookmarque Ltd, Croydon, Surrey

So, at a given moment, he resigned himself to the joys of alcohol, wisely telling himself that if there was to be a hateful and repentant morning after the night before, he would at least see that the pleasure of the night before was not marred by the hatefulness of repentance – so that the night before and the morning after, the one in its pleasure, and the other in its pain, might, from the true perspective of a long-distance view in time, seem to cancel each other out.

Patrick Hamilton, *Hangover Square*

July 1936: London

Meredith Kerr was sitting between two men at the table closest to the saloon-bar door. Her younger companion, the elegant Billy Royle, was competing for her attention by surreptitiously stroking her thigh beneath the table. He was watching her face for the sudden blush of pleasure, the first indication that she would allow him back to her flat at the end of the evening. Meredith had already repelled the other man's bullying advances and was now smiling to placate him through the pall of cigarette smoke. Harry Bowden was not smiling back at her. None of the three had taken off their wet coats. They were waiting for the rain to slow and another man to join them before going on to the Paradise Club.

Meredith's attention drifted towards the high grey glass of the saloon-bar window; she saw acid blue sparks flashing from the wet overhead lines as a tram passed by along the street. Then she heard the tinny hiss of rain on the pavement which signalled the door opening. The first to come through it was Arthur Lawler, whom they had been expecting. The second man Meredith didn't recognise. But it was because of him that she pushed Royle's hand from her thigh, sat up straight and tugged her damp sable coat round her shoulders.

'What can I get for you?' Lawler offered. He leaned over the table, tall and thin like a gallows.

'Later,' Bowden said.

'Good evening, Kit. Good to see you.' Royle stood and offered his hand to Lawler's companion. Kit Renton shook it, then turned and went up to the bar.

'Well . . .' Lawler was embarrassed for Royle, who was still standing and smiling hospitably. 'I must have a few words with Kit, then I'll come over and join you.'

'Please introduce us properly,' Meredith said.

'Yes. Yes, I will,' Lawler said, and followed Renton to the bar.

Harry Bowden was now staring sullenly into space in the way he often did after the first few drinks of the night had diluted his habitual sourness into melancholy. Only when the bar door swung open again and caught the back of his chair did he come to life, clumsily rise to his feet, nudging the small table as he did so, and set off unsteadily towards the gents'. At the lavatory door he paused and glared into the mirror. He blotted the sweat from his brow with a large blue handkerchief, smoothed his moustache and, unsettled by what he had seen in the glass, auditioned a smile. As he pushed open the door of the gents', the light above the mirror briefly glossed the dome of his broad bald head.

Glad to have been freed from Bowden's stifling presence, Meredith Kerr faced Royle and said, 'Quickly. Tell me who he is.'

'Who?'

'Arthur's friend.'

'Kit?'

'Yes. Kit.' She tasted the word for the first time and felt the delight as it softly exploded against her teeth.

'Why, what's the hurry?' Royle said and laughed.

'Before Harry gets back. Come on, Billy, you know what a misery he can be when he gets jealous.'

'Well, Kit was at Lancing with us; with Arthur and me. I'm surprised you haven't seen him around.'

'In here? No. I would have remembered.'

'No . . . actually, come to think of it, Kit's never really been one for the pubs . . .' Royle pursed his lips, considering, then said, 'As a matter of fact, I think it's probably a year since I last saw him. Though it doesn't seem that long . . . No, it must be a year. Perhaps more.'

'Is he married?'

'No. Well, I say no, but I very much doubt it.'

'And what does he do?'

'Bits and bobs. He used to write for some political rag – in fact he started all that when he was at school – he was an Anarchist, or a Communist, or something – a Red, anyway. He was one of those boys who spent too much time on his own. A loner. You know the kind I mean?'

When Bowden rejoined them from the gents', Meredith was soon talking and laughing with the two men – and they were glad of her new mood because it infected their own. But her attention never entirely strayed from the broad shoulders of the man who was standing among but aloof from the cheerful crowd at the bar.

Lawler hadn't failed to notice that Meredith was captivated by his drinking companion. Reaching irritably to remove his trilby from a saturated bar towel, he returned his attention to him, saying, 'Do go on. I'm sorry, I am listening to you . . . Italian planes. Did I hear you say that two went down?'

'They were bombers. Savoias. Mussolini sent a squadron of them as a present to the Fascists. Actually, three apparently went down. Two in French Morocco, one ditched in the sea. That's how we heard about it.' Kit Renton had a habit of picking carefully through his words as though he was afraid he would be called to account for them later.

'So now the Italians are involved in Spain, are they?'

'Yes. And the Germans; it's Adolf Hitler's Junkers which are ferrying Franco's thugs in from Morocco. Do you know what they call him?'

'Hitler?'

'Franco. "Miss Canary Islands 1936." He was practising his golf there when he was collected.' Renton sensed that Lawler was struggling to conjure up even the smallest curiosity about his plans. With some annoyance he went on to say, 'Anyway, what I came here to tell you, Arthur, is that I'm going out there.'

'To Spain? Are you serious?'

'Of course. We have to make a stand.'

'We?'

'Yes. We should all make a stand.'

'And what makes you imagine that the Republicans want us over there fighting their battles for them?'

'Because it's not simply their battle. Besides which, we're already involved: non-intervention is an act of hostile involvement.'

'When do you leave?'

'As soon as I can arrange it. Certainly within a month.'

Kit Renton too had now been caught up in watching Meredith Kerr. In the mirror behind the bar he studied the diamonds of rain jewelling the fur of her damp sable coat, her harsh, side-parted auburn hair softening into curls, her porcelain skin, bright red lips and clear, unfathomable eyes. He could see why the men were paying court to her; she was a real beauty and she seemed to know it. But Renton would have preferred to have encountered her in a different context – to have glimpsed her in a park, or walking alone, unselfconsciously, along a street. He would not have approached her, for he was not a man who had any confidence in his appearance, but he would have regretted not having done so, and the vision of her would have stayed with him for a long time.

'Who's the woman with Royle and Bowden?' he asked Lawler. 'Is she tight?'

'No. Not really. Her name is Meredith Kerr . . . She's an . . . well, she's an actress of sorts.'

Renton hoarded images like that of the group around the table and took them with him to meetings in draughty halls. That way, he knew that if they ever turned to him and asked him whether he remained committed to the cause he could draw on such moments and use them to remind him why he was there. The wealth of crooks like Harry Bowden angered him. Bowden's lieutenant, Billy Royle, was an old school friend, but Renton had always dismissed him as a chancer who would lose his allure when the drink took a toll on his looks. Until it did, however, he remained secure because the women, drawn to him via their attraction to the wealthy Bowden, would protect him. And that, in Kit Renton's analysis, was a model of how the world worked. It was all there, in all of those tiny transactions and huge compromises: Harry Bowden wanted Meredith Kerr. Meredith Kerr, Renton could see, found Bowden physically unappealing but gave herself to him because he was rich. Perhaps she needed beautiful jesters like Billy Royle to take the taste away afterwards.

'You disapprove of us, don't you?' Arthur Lawler said.

'Why should I disapprove?' Renton leaned on the bar and reluctantly took his eyes from the woman's beauty and quiet desperation.

Seeing she had lost Renton's attention, Meredith chose that moment to lift her empty glass and call, 'Get me another gin, Arthur darling. A large one. And one each for the boys.' Her look sobered as it snagged on Renton for a second when their eyes met in the mirror. Renton saw her mask slip and a momentary dimming of her pride.

'Will you take another one?' Lawler said, tilting his empty glass towards Renton's pint mug.

'. . . I'm sorry?'

'Another drink?'

'No. This one should see me through.'

'Yes, please,' Lawler called towards the barman. 'When you have a moment, please.' Arthur Lawler's voice warranted attention though it belonged to a class he had never felt fully qualified to be a member of. He boarded in a commercial hotel and existed frugally on what was left of the proceeds from the sale of his mother's house. Meredith Kerr's sable had accounted for much of his contingency fund and the evening was looking set to cost him what remained of it. But Meredith, more than anything else, hated it when he complained of being short. Bowden was never short but only rarely did he ever see fit to pay for anything. As for Royle, the question of him putting his manicured hand into his pocket rarely arose. 'That's Billy for you,' Meredith always chided whenever the subject was raised: Billy Royle, Meredith's penniless pet.

From the table by the door Meredith called, 'Hurry up, Arthur, we're getting terribly thirsty over here,' and Renton saw the weak, placatory smile as Lawler conceded his attention to her again. The call, though, he knew was for his benefit.

'Do you want to go over and join them?' Renton said.

'No. Not yet.' Lawler had sensed a danger in Meredith's attraction to Renton – one which he had never felt from Royle or Bowden or any of the other men who wanted her – the danger of losing her entirely.

'Tell me, how will you travel?' Lawler asked after hurrying the barman. He had just recalled the earlier topic of conversation – the uprising in Spain and Kit Renton's future role in it.

'It's all arranged. I go to Paris first to establish contacts and collect the papers. I understand the best way in is to cross the border in the south at Cerbère, although apparently the French are now making it as difficult as they can. A few of us are over there now.'

'This is your lot, is it?'

'Yes. And others. We can operate together when it's absolutely necessary.'

'Aren't you afraid?'

'Of what? The fighting?'

'No. The dying, I suppose.'

'The only thing I'm afraid of at the moment is not getting there in time.'

'You really believe this is important, don't you?'

'How can anyone with a soul not feel that way? Come and

see me before I go. Please.' Renton picked up his long umbrella. 'You know where I am, don't you?'

'You don't have to leave yet, do you?'

'Yes.'

'Look, Kit. If you're looking for a loan, I'm afraid . . .'

'Don't worry. I'm not going to touch you for cash.'

'You're going to try and convert me. Is that it?'

'Perhaps.'

'You're wasting your time.'

'Time spent with an old friend can hardly be called wasted, can it?'

'But you haven't finished your drink.'

'You finish it. I'm afraid the company is too rich for me.'

Regretting now that he hadn't awarded sufficient attention to Renton, Arthur Lawler turned his back on the group by the door and, for the first time in the evening, faced him. His friend was thinner and more pale than he remembered from their last meeting. There was now little differentiation between the pallor of his skin and his fine fair hair. The collar of his shirt was frayed and his tie was knotted lopsidedly. Beneath his tweed jacket he was wearing a green woollen sweater.

'Please take care of yourself,' Lawler said, feeling a genuine, deep-seated affection as he shook Renton's hand.

'I do.' Renton spent a smile from his meagre store. From somewhere inside him the light came up and showed in his eyes and he looked young again. 'You do have my address?'

'Are you still on the corner of Berners Street?' Lawler could hardly bear to think of the sordid room, the smell of stale fat from the filthy cooker in the corner, the stench from the shared lavatory at the end of the corridor.

'Yes. Second floor. Please come.'

'I'll try. Good to see you, Kit.'

'You too.'

As Renton made to go, Lawler said, 'Before you leave . . .'

'Yes.'

'Meredith asked me to introduce you to her.'

'Next time.'

'If you're sure.'

'Yes.'

'Cheerio, then.'

The barman was wiping his palms on his long white apron when Lawler turned back and said, 'Two. No, you'd better make it three gins, large ones, and a Scotch.' The barman nodded and reached beneath the mahogany counter for clean glasses. He was staring at Meredith in the way that men often did and Lawler felt a deep sense of pride. He watched Renton pass the table by the door, and saw Meredith tense and prepare herself for him. But Renton avoided meeting her eye and chose not to acknowledge Royle's half-hearted farewell. When the door shut behind him Meredith seemed to shrink within the second skin of her coat.

'Get a move on, Meredith's sobering up.' The bulk of Bowden docked beside Lawler at the bar.

'I've ordered,' he said.

'What did Renton want?'

'Oh, you know Kit.'

'Yes, I know him. I was asking you what he wanted.'

'It was a private conversation.'

Bowden's interest tarnished everything it touched. It was Lawler's belief that Meredith had never been the same since he started driving her out of town on Sunday afternoons on 'runs' in one of the new Rileys from his Great Portland Street showroom, all the time making promises to her about the men he could introduce her to.

'What do you make of Royle?' Bowden asked, taking out a cigarette case, opening it, then seeming to think better of it and clipping it shut again.

'What is there to make of him?'

'Does Meredith see through him?'

'Of course she does,' Lawler said, looking fondly towards her. 'She sees through everybody.'

Billy Royle was fluttering his long eyelashes at her now, mimicking an acquaintance. He was trying to chivvy her out of the gloom that seemed to have descended on her the moment Renton left the bar.

'If that man had money he'd be dangerous,' Bowden said, then immediately called, 'Hurry up with those drinks, will you!' His shout provoked a startled laugh from a drunk woman standing beside the mechanical piano. Her gin-baffled eyes slowly shifted their focus to the door as a dapper man came in from the rain, shook his head without removing his hat and dashed water from the gutter of the brim across an old man reading the *Evening Standard*. The new arrival, realising immediately what he had done, reached inside his jacket for his wallet, saying, 'Oh, I am sorry, you must let me buy you a drink.' And the old man silently handed him a warm, empty whisky glass.

'Last night . . .' Bowden said.

'I'm sorry?'

'Last night Meredith said she hated being a woman. What do you make of that?'

'That sounds like her. Ask her today and she'll tell you she loves being a woman more than anything in the world.'

While Lawler paid the barman, Bowden corralled three glasses into the triangle formed by his thumbs and first fingers and carried them over to the table. By the time Lawler had collected his change and joined them, Meredith had already thanked Bowden for the drink by granting him a passionless kiss on his cheek. Lawler waited for the three of them to make space for him round the table. When none of them moved he fetched a chair from beside the unlit fire and forced his way in next to Meredith, who immediately protested, 'Be careful, Arthur, you'll tear my lovely coat!' She tugged the hem away from him and elbowed herself some more room.

'Clumsy,' Royle said stupidly, the drunkest member of the group.

'Finish these up and we'll take a taxi,' Bowden announced.

'Of course we shall,' Meredith said. 'I'm not traipsing around the streets in this weather.'

'What did Kit want?' Royle asked Lawler. The mention of his name sparked Meredith back into life.

'Why is everybody so interested in Kit all of a sudden?'

'Something to talk about, I imagine,' Royle said, smiling at Meredith and silently mouthing a question at her.

'He's going out to Spain.'

'Christ,' Bowden said. 'God help them with Reds like Renton getting under their feet.'

'I think it's the "Reds" he's going to help,' Lawler said.

'When is he leaving?' Meredith asked, pushing Royle firmly away with both hands.

'As soon as he can get away,' Lawler told her. 'He has nothing to keep him here.' Finishing his drink, he turned to Bowden and said, 'Did you say you were going to find a taxi?'

'Did I?'

'Look, Meredith,' Lawler said. 'Kit is an old friend. But he . . . he's not like us. He's not interested in pubs and . . . getting tight and going to clubs and . . . that turns some people against him. Billy, here, for example. Billy dislikes him not simply because he's considerably cleverer than he is but because he believes in something.'

'I don't dislike him, Arthur. Not at all.'

'And Bowden dislikes him because Bowden distrusts anybody who isn't motivated solely by financial gain . . . yes?'

Bowden laughed and said, 'Well, don't expect me to deny it.'

Lawler tried to discern what Meredith really felt about her benefactor. A glimmer of cold hate directed towards Bowden was quickly shrouded by her smile.

'You promised you'd introduce us, Arthur,' Meredith said.

'I know I did. I tried, but he had to leave.'

'Well, perhaps you didn't try hard enough.'

'Perhaps I didn't,' Lawler admitted, and Meredith chose to back down.

Royle was looking away towards the bar. Something he saw seemed to prompt him to ask, 'Do you remember when Kit ran away from school, Arthur?'

'On which occasion?'

'When they found him living under the railway bridge at Shoreham. God knows how he slept with those trains rumbling overhead every ten minutes.'

'What was he running away from?' Meredith asked.

'Who knows,' Lawler said. 'Kit was a law unto himself. Once, he . . .' But he broke off and took another sip of his drink. He felt suddenly disloyal, as though every piece of information he offered about his old friend weakened him.

'Please tell me.'

Lawler selected a safer memory. 'Once he disappeared for a couple of weeks. The school called his father down from . . . Hoxton, wasn't it?'

'Yes. That's right,' Royle said. 'He came on a motor-cycle.'

'That's right. A Douglas Twin. Lovely machine. He was wearing a long leather coat, goggles. There's very little family resemblance in any respect – his father was tall and thin with rather narrow shoulders. Like a bird of prey. I think he was some kind of marine engineer, though none of it rubbed off on Kit. He's hopeless at mathematics. All sciences were entirely beyond him. Languages were his forte. I seem to remember he was learning Russian a few months ago.'

'His father borrowed an Austin from one of the masters and drove us into Hove for tea,' Royle added. 'He didn't seem at all concerned about Kit. He told us he was sure the boy could look after himself. He called him a . . . what was it he called him, Arthur? A forager. That's it. Kit's a good forager, like his mother, he said. I don't think we knew anything about Kit's mother, did we?'

'No. She died. I think.'

'And when he came back to school,' Meredith persevered, 'where had he been?'

'He said he'd been staying in Brighton; lodging with a railwayman and his family close by the station. He didn't consider it at all out of the ordinary.'

Bowden came to life and announced, 'And now he calls himself an Anarchist, Meredith. I'll tell you what an Anarchist is, shall I? An Anarchist is a fellow who borrows money from you to buy the gun he then comes back with to rob you. When he's done that, he tells you that, as far as he's concerned, he refuses to live by any rules drawn up by any government. Then he throws you out of your home and moves into it with his friends who call meetings to plan how they can steal the property of everyone else in the vicinity. Needless to say, you won't come across an Anarchist who has anything worth stealing.'

'Anarchy,' Lawler said. 'After the Greek. *An*, an absence of. *Archos*, a ruler. I think Kit, had he been here to defend his position, would have argued that being without a ruler doesn't necessarily imply that one should live without rules.'

In reply Bowden belched loudly on to the back of his hand.

'I want to meet him,' Meredith said and immediately all three of the men fell silent. 'Why are you looking like that, Billy? You look as though you've swallowed a fly.'

'Why do you want to meet Kit? I wouldn't have imagined he was your type.'

'And how do you know what my "type" is?'

'Well, I rather thought . . .'

'No. All right. You should meet him,' Lawler conceded.

'But why? I simply don't understand,' Royle asked again, this time looking towards Bowden for an explanation.

Meredith said, 'You grant me your permission, Arthur? That's terribly nice of you.'

'Of course not, Meredith darling, I hope you don't imagine I meant . . .' Lawler blushed. 'I'll take you round there. We can stand him lunch at Bertorelli's. Or Schmidt's. He's always strapped.'

'No. I'd like to meet him alone.'

'Well, well,' Bowden said. 'Meredith is smitten.'

'Of course she is.' Royle tried to take her hand but she pulled it away.

'But then Meredith often wants what Meredith can't have.'

'Perhaps,' she said, smiling at the three men and picking up her handbag, 'that's because Meredith rarely gets what Meredith really needs. Excuse me for a moment, boys. Why don't you find us that taxi, Harry.' She turned and immediately the men standing around the bar made an honour guard to let her through.

'But what does she see in Renton?' Royle asked out loud to nobody in particular.

Dancing with Bowden, with Royle, with Lawler; there had been an unbroken relay of men in Meredith's arms. Bowden clung to her clumsily and tightly; he sweated and seemed to know how it repelled her. There was just enough self-loathing in Harry Bowden to make him tolerable to Meredith. She couldn't have endured so much time in his company without it. It was always a pleasure to take the floor with Royle; he had finesse. As he guided her round the crowded room their bodies barely touched. He danced to show her off to the other men. Drunk or sober, Royle would always cut a decent figure on the small dance floor of the Paradise Club. When it was Lawler's turn, he drew her to him like a father; gentle and encouraging. She reciprocated by holding him with the formality of the old friend he was, not the lover he had always wanted to be.

None of the men spoke to her while they danced and Meredith did want to be spoken to. Tonight she ached for an intimacy beyond the physical, which was unusual for her. One day she knew it would be different. But nowadays so many of her thoughts seemed to begin with this plaintive, fading hope. Her mind took her back to the bar three hours before and the man standing beside Arthur. His clothes were terrible. There was nothing conventionally appealing about his looks. Perhaps she had held his gaze for two seconds, but now she wanted to be with him and only with him and she wanted it with a sudden fierce hunger.

The Paradise Club was full. The men in the small humid room outnumbered the women by four to one. One of a party of smart Italians was now moving eagerly towards Meredith, pulling a metal comb through his hair.

'The music goes round and round oh oh, oh, oh, oh oh, and it comes out here,' Lawler was crooning in her ear.

'Kiss me, Arthur. Please,' she said and after the shock of her request, Lawler did, and she enjoyed the soft union of their lips because, in closing her eyes, she pretended she was kissing Kit Renton. When she pulled her head back, the man who had been approaching her had walked on to the gents'.

'Are you all right?' Lawler asked her.

'Yes. Why do you ask?'

'You don't seem yourself tonight.'

'Don't I?'

'Just say the word and I'll walk you home.'

'And have me all to yourself?'

'That's not what I meant.'

They continued to dance until the music stopped. Nobody applauded the band.

'Shall we sit down?' Lawler said.

'If you'd like.'

'Well, would you?'

'Yes. I suppose so,' Meredith said and Lawler led them back to the table where Bowden and Royle were sitting silently, their ties loosened, their faces flushed by the drink. Having allowed herself to acknowledge her feelings for Kit Renton, Meredith felt her misery dissipating. As it did she was happy to take back the burden of responsibility for the mood of the men she was with. She smiled and told them how much she was enjoying herself, but the words sounded hollow. Kit

Renton was crowding her mind and she felt guilty for the lie.

Two hours later, at the end of a short, stinking alley close by Oxford Street, Meredith Kerr knocked three times on a green door. A hatch immediately slid open and the cropped face of the man inside looked out at her without recognition. Meredith could feel the cold stone through the soles of her shoes, the rain like a needle drilling into the skin of her hands. Tiredness lay heavily over her. She was now so sober that the world had become too real to bear. The practicalities of her existence had once more begun to weigh her down, anchoring her dreams. Alcohol was no good to her now. She had reached the point at which her body ached with the saturation of the gin but her mind needed something stronger to quieten its call that she go immediately to Kit Renton and express her feelings to him.

It was too soon. That much she knew.

Occasionally, when she reached such moments of crisis, she went to visit the Chinese boy on Poland Street.

'Come on, you know who I am,' Meredith said impatiently. The thin hatch slid shut and the door opened. Meredith crossed the threshold and quickly took the narrow stairs without looking back at the doorman, now sitting on his stool again and reading a newspaper by the light of a candle. Halfway up she stumbled and snatched at the rope banister, which saved her fall.

A heavy door was wedged open on the first landing. Walking slowly through it into the dim, familiar room, she saw that three of the low metal cots bore sedated figures. Another was empty. The room was lit by torn red paper lanterns. The pale glow softened the sordidness of the bare floorboards and oily rattan mats, the paper peeling from the damp walls. Currents of cold from the open window stirred the thick sweet soup of opium smoke. On a mat at the centre of the room a man in a dress-suit sat cross-legged, leaning back against a heavy oriental cushion. A Chinese boy of delicate beauty in sky-blue silk passed him a long ivory pipe. The man took it solemnly in both hands, put it to his lips, drew on it and, after a moment, handed the pipe, like fragile porcelain, gently back. The boy placed it on the stand and, bearing the burden of care, he watched the opium take effect. The man breathed deeply and laid his hand on the boy's shoulder. Using the support to pull himself to his feet he took three careful steps to the last empty cot where he lay down on his back and crossed his wrists against his chest. He peered through the door that the opium had opened and saw the vision that the narcotic had painted for him. The boy took the pipe across the room to him and offered it again. Still lying prone, the man took another draw. After a third he seemed to lose the will to hand the pipe back. He nodded slowly and slipped away. Satisfied that the man was at peace, the boy gestured to Meredith to take the cushion. He smiled, the boy's repertoire of expressions limited to polite or happy subservience.

'How are you?' Meredith whispered and held out her hand. The boy smiled again and took it like a gift. Instead of shaking it or kissing it, he turned her hand over and examined her white palm. The boy had never spoken. The only communication between them had been the ritual passing of the ivory pipe.

'Make me a good pipe tonight,' Meredith said, gesturing towards the flame of the lamp. 'I need to go far away from here. Do you understand?' She was talking solely for her own benefit as she watched the boy dip a needle into the treacle and pull it free. 'Do you mind the rain?' Meredith asked. 'I don't imagine you feel the cold in this room, do you? The cold. Do you feel it at all?'

At the far end of the room another man shifted in a cane chair. The chair creaked, the man was still. It was too dark to make anything out beyond the vague outline. Meredith assumed him to be the proprietor and his shifting in the chair a gentle reprimand for her hounding of the boy.

'One day I expect I'll arrive here and you'll be gone,' Meredith said. 'I'll knock on the green door and nobody will be there to open it. Then what shall I do? . . . It's not that I couldn't do without it, no, it's not that at all. It's simply that knowing this place is here has become . . . Could we close the window? Would you mind?'

The figure in the chair turned and slid down the sash.

London: Two Weeks Later

'How do I look?' Meredith, standing beside the black marble mantelpiece of her living room, set down her gin glass and took a cigarette from an inlaid ivory box.

'I'm sorry, did you ask me for the time?' Lawler asked and lowered his evening newspaper. 'It's five and twenty to five.'

'God. Is that all? Why don't you do something useful? Why don't you go and fetch another bottle?'

'Of course.' Lawler put aside his *Standard* and struggled to his feet from the low chair.

'I hope you're going to dress.'

'I wasn't intending to. I'll wash when you've finished in the bathroom.'

'Sponge your jacket down. Try and make it look a little newer.'

'Yes. I will.'

'. . . Well, what are you waiting for?'

'I'm sorry, I'm a little short of . . .'

'And what do you expect me to do about it?'

'I thought you might lend me three or four pounds for the evening.'

'That's two days running, Arthur. This has to stop.' Meredith rummaged in a small bag, found a man's wallet, unfolded it and thrust a five-pound note towards Lawler.

'That's Bowden's, isn't it?' he said.

'Yes.'

'Won't he miss it?'

'Don't look at me like that, Arthur. He left it here, I didn't lift it. What do you take me for?'

'No. I wasn't suggesting you stole it.' In an effort to sober himself, Lawler took three deep breaths before attempting to negotiate the route from the chair to the door. He carefully avoided the table, the radiogram, a pile of back issues of the *Sketch* stacked under a standard lamp which was tugged to the extent of its plaited flex and Meredith's tangled pink dressing-gown which lay hugging itself where she had discarded it, beside the door to the chilly hallway.

Lawler had arrived at Meredith's flat just before three, having left the pub at two and then taken a sobering walk across Piccadilly, through the park, along the Mall, and then down to the river where he had leaned against the wall and passed a happy half-hour watching a tin-legged screever rendering Big Ben in chalk on the pavement. When the cripple had finished, the image of the clocktower looked like a reflection caught in a puddle. Lawler gave the man a shiny sixpence which he could ill afford and then found a taxi which cost him his last few shillings. His knock had fetched Meredith from the bath. After letting him in and swearing at him, she had relented and rewarded him by shrugging off her dressing-gown and walking glistening and naked back into the bathroom. Afterwards, listening to Meredith in the bath and trying to visualise her white marble body, all he could seem to call to mind was her face. She had looked at him as he imagined she would look at another woman in a dressing-room; she felt neither threat nor thrill at being seen naked.

'Bitch,' Lawler had said out loud.

'What?' Meredith had called.

'Stupid bitch,' Lawler said louder. But it was lost beneath the racket of the clanking geyser. In a sudden fierce fury he stood and kicked away the chair. It slewed against the wall. He stamped on the floor and the dusty chandelier above him rattled. He clenched his shaking fist and slammed it against his palm. He did it again, again, again, each time mouthing an oath. He imagined Meredith in front of him, sitting naked on the chair. He booted the seat cushion where her knees would have been, raising a cloud of dust. He launched his fist against the grease spot where a thousand heads had lolled. A tired spring threw him back.

'Arthur!' he heard. 'What are you doing?'

Instead of answering, Lawler walked to the bathroom door. This time he would have it out with her.

'Arthur,' she called. Then, more shrilly, '. . . Arthur!'

'. . . Yes?' He waited at the door.

'What are you doing?'

'I'm . . .'

'What?'

'. . . I'm straightening up a bit.'

'Well, do it more quietly.'

Arthur laid his forehead against the cold varnish of the door. He looked down the line of his thin body at his scuffed shoes. He flexed his right fist again and felt the power in it. The sinews in his wrist tightened. He clenched the fingers of his left hand and squeezed as tightly as he could, but he couldn't feel any pain. He straightened up and went back into the living-room and pulled the chair away from the wall. He knelt down, unruched the filthy rug and laid it over the silhouette of dust on the dull parquet. He sat in the chair and gazed at the cigarette stubs which lay among the sooty asbestos honeycombs of the gas fire.

And now he was calm again and standing at the hallway door with Bowden's five-pound note in his wallet and nearly three-quarters of an hour to kill before the pubs opened.

'What *is* the matter with you today?' Meredith Kerr was watching herself lighting a cigarette in the overmantel mirror. Her hair was fastened up. She smelt of powder and French perfume, which armoured her. She was wearing a backless sequinned evening-dress and the pair of long black gloves she had only just found after searching for them for three weeks. Fastening the cigarette holder between her teeth, she smiled at her reflection and offered herself a light.

'Did you say gin?' Lawler asked.

'Yes. Of course. Of course, gin.' In the mirror she saw the tall shabby figure by the door: the manservant to a household which could no longer afford one. The man was staring at her, stupid with obedience.

'Yes, Arthur? Was there something you wanted to say to me?'

'Do you hate me?'

'How can you say that?'

'Because that's what I feel.'

'You need a drink, darling.' Meredith went to him, linked her arm through his and kissed him on the cheek. 'Have you been boozing on your own again?'

'Yes.'

'Well, you mustn't. You must always ask me or Royle or . . .'

'Bowden? No, thank you.' Lawler felt his anger returning and, with it, some of his strength. 'Besides, I did ask you, Meredith. I telephoned this morning as we'd arranged and you told me to leave you alone. So I did.'

'And that's why I love you, Arthur. Because you always do as you're told. Now go and fetch some more lovely gin and everything will be all right again.'

As she opened the door and pushed him gently through, Lawler turned to kiss her cheek but the door was closed in his face. He walked along the short hall corridor passing the bedroom door, the small, little-used kitchen, and out through the front door into the stone-floored hallway. The flat next door was unlet, the door unlocked. Lawler went in and found his suitcase in the pantry where he had hidden it. A moment later he heard a brisk parade of footsteps along the hallway. There was a pause and then the door was tentatively pushed open.

'Arthur! What are you doing here?' It was Royle. His eyes were rheumy with beer, and he was holding a small bunch of pansies.

'I'm checking on my suitcase.'

'I see . . .' Royle said and came in, pulling the door shut behind him. 'No, I don't.'

'Look. I'm in a bit of a spot. I've been kicked out of the hotel and I haven't found a way to break it to Meredith. Besides, surely more to the point is what you're doing here.'

'I can never resist peeking in through an open door.'

'I'd appreciate it if you didn't mention it to her.'

'Of course I won't.' Royle filled an abandoned teacup with water and stood the small, bruised posy in it. 'Everything in order?'

'Yes.' Lawler shoved the suitcase back into the pantry and closed the door.

'You could take this place,' Royle said, looking round the grim room with uncritical eyes.

'I can't afford it.'

'Really?'

'The truth is, I can't afford anything.'

Lawler followed Royle into the sitting-room where dirty nets greyed the view of the Euston Road.

'I don't suppose you've heard from Kit?' Lawler said.

'No. Have you?'

'No. I meant to call in on him. I think he's leaving tomorrow.'

'And did Meredith ever get round to seeing him?'

'No. I don't think so . . . I imagine we're expecting Bowden's company tonight.'

'Yes. We're due to meet up with him at Meredith's. Around nine.'

Through the wall they heard the slow muffled bump of jazz from Meredith's radiogram.

'God.'

'What's the matter, Arthur?'

'I'm not sure I can stand seeing him tonight.'

'Here.' Royle passed over his hip flask. 'Harry's not so bad when you get to know him. Besides, he's come up with a scheme to make us both a few bob.'

'What?'

'Racing.'

'Horse racing?'

'No. Motor racing. Apparently one of his contacts is looking for a driver. Harry recommended me and now I'm down for a try-out.'

'It's rather dangerous, isn't it?'

'Not in the least. There's nothing to it. Well, it all seemed pretty straightforward when a pal let me have a go last summer.'

'When are you going to do it?'

'A couple of weeks' time. At Brooklands. It's not a formal meeting, though doubtless there'll be some wagering. You should come along.'

'Is Meredith going?'

'Of course.'

'Yes. I might just tag along.' Lawler lifted the hem of the net curtain and said, 'Is it still raining?'

'No.'

'Good. I promised Meredith I'd go and fetch some gin.'

'I'll come with you.'

'There's no need.'

'I could do with the fresh air. I've got a bit of a head on me. I only called in on the off chance. Meredith's not expecting me until later.'

'In that case, perhaps we could have a quick one before we come back.'

'Good idea.'

Having set off towards Great Portland Street, Lawler stopped off at the booths in the Underground station to telephone Meredith to explain the delay. She answered the call quickly; her voice was uncharacteristically light, borrowing something from the timbre of the bright tenor saxophone which was tooting a solo from the radiogram.

'All right, Arthur,' she said. 'Don't feel that you need to rush straight back . . . but don't be too long.'

'You sound happy,' Lawler accused her.

'I am. Sometimes it can hit you like that, can't it? When the rain stopped and the sun came out again I found I was happy.' She didn't go on to say that the sun brought images of Spain to her mind, and Spain and Kit Renton now nestled in the same chamber of her heart. For two weeks she had thought of little else but him. But as the time went on she became increasingly afraid of going to him. She had invested so much that their meeting could only be a disappointment.

'When you're happy, I'm happy,' Lawler said.

'Don't say that!'

'It's true.'

'That's a terrible responsibility to bear.'

'Don't tell me you didn't already know.'

'. . . In that case I suppose I should try and behave better towards you.'

'Well, I don't blame you,' Lawler said, his spirits rising.

'Perhaps you should. Perhaps you should shout at me rather than taking it out on my furniture.'

'You heard?'

'Yes.'

'All of it?'

'Most of it.'

'I'm sorry.'

'I know what I must seem to you sometimes.'

'I am sorry.'

'Don't be. You do know how much you mean to me, don't you?'

'Most of the time . . . but sometimes I find it difficult.'

'I know.'

'. . . We won't be long, darling.'

'Good. You know I can't bear my own company for too long.'

In the pause that followed Arthur listened to the music from the radiogram, then Meredith cut the line.

As she often did when she was alone in the flat, Meredith now found herself thinking of Arthur Lawler. He had once (one long, drunken afternoon at Schmidt's) confided to her that when he came home for the school holidays his life was entirely solitary except for the silent meals taken at the long table with his mother, who was invariably reading the newspaper. He was an only child and his mother rarely organised any expeditions. But he had been at pains to point out to Meredith that he wasn't asking for sympathy; he was not unhappy. This world of comfort and silence changed in his fifteenth year when his father died while he was away on business in Hamburg. At the sparsely attended funeral Arthur took his lead from his mother and shed no tears. Another woman cried throughout the entire service. A month later his mother sold their home in north London and they moved their furniture into a tidy set of rooms, which always felt borrowed, on Russell Square. They remained there until his mother died quite suddenly of a heart attack four years later. Orphaned at nineteen, Lawler's aimless life barely seemed to change, except that he now took his meals entirely alone and developed a habit of drifting out afterwards in search of camaraderie in the Fitzroy Tavern. In time he wandered further. He began to frequent the Coal Hole in the Strand and then, overhearing a mention of it in a conversation between two men in paint-specked coats, went out looking for the Rising Sun in Chelsea. It was here that he developed a taste for tenpenny glasses of port.

It was a week after his twentieth birthday that Lawler suffered an extended and debilitating period of unhappiness. Port and whisky alleviated his misery, but he always felt worse when he returned alone at night to the empty flat in Russell Square. One morning he awoke feeling so wretched that he was convinced there was something in the fabric of the building which was affecting him. He packed a suitcase with his clothes and locked the door, leaving all of his family belongings behind. By the end of the morning he had moved into a commercial hotel and returned to the rooms in Russell Square only once to let the auctioneer in. He considered his adulthood to have begun on the day he moved out. In celebration, he began to drink at lunchtimes as well as in the evenings and stopped visiting the public library where, since his mother's death, he had taken to spending his afternoons.

Meredith had always had the facility for manufacturing an interest in the self-pitying histories of men. But in Arthur's case, as the afternoon in Schmidt's wore on and he revealed more of his story to her, she became genuinely curious. Her father had also died when she was young. When her mother agreed to marry a friend of her husband (with little enthusiasm, Meredith felt) and Meredith told her she was going to live in London, she seemed not to care. Meredith had had no intention of going to London. She had made the statement for effect, so convinced was she that her mother would beg her to stay at home. Because she didn't, Meredith chose to see it as fate and left home.

Meredith Kerr met Harry Bowden on a park bench two days after she arrived in the city. She had been dressed, she thought appropriately, for an interview at a secretarial college on Charlotte Street (this, at least, her mother had arranged for her). Perhaps her make-up was overdone, but she had learned how to apply it by watching her mother, who sat at her dressing table each night, a bottle of Heering's cherry brandy in front of her, getting herself ready for dinner.

Bowden had been drunk. Meredith laughed at the absurdity of his clumsy approach but she detected a kindness in him which she had not felt since her father died. She missed the appointment at the college, choosing instead to drink the day away with Bowden. When they stood at the bar and he asked her what she wanted, her eyes ranged across the unfamiliar labels on the bottles on the glass shelves. Then she saw the Heering's cherry brandy, and Bowden bought her a large one. And soon, like Arthur Lawler, she was part of a world she didn't much like but didn't want to leave.

It provided her with the dubious comforts of a family and gave her life a structure which revolved around the opening hours of five or six public houses and clubs, all of them within a half-mile radius of Oxford Circus.

Royle and Lawler were halfway down Great Portland Street, and well on their way to one of these pubs, when Royle asked Lawler, 'What will you do for money?'

'I expect I'll have to look for a job.'

'I could speak to Harry.'

'No.'

'Suit yourself. Oh, incidentally, I knew there was something I wanted to mention to you. I was talking to Quinn – the motor-racing chap – and he gave me some sterling advice as far as money was concerned. I'd be happy to pass it on to you.'

'Go on.'

'He told me that when he makes a new friend he always makes a point of borrowing a few quid from him.'

'I don't understand.'

'That's because I haven't finished yet.' Royle had been distracted by a blonde woman crossing the road.

'Go on.'

When the woman turned a corner, and Royle caught sight of himself in a shop window, his own image immediately supplanted that of the woman in his affections.

'Well,' he continued, 'he leaves it for a few days to make the chap believe he's forgotten, then, at the moment he knows the chap is going to ask for the money back, he returns it. The point being that the new friend is eternally grateful not only for the return of the money but also for having been saved the embarrassment of demanding its return. Quinn, therefore, is firmly ensconced in said friend's good books. The financial cost to him, nil.' Royle's smile clouded. 'Unless, of course, through force of circumstances, the money is spent and repayment becomes difficult.'

'In which case I expect the opposite applies – said friend financially inconvenienced, embarrassed and angry.'

'Yes. It's a strategy not without its risks. Unless one has sufficient money at the outset.'

'In which case I doubt such a scheme would even be considered.'

'No. I doubt it. Though Quinn suggested it was foolproof.'

'Good old Quinn.'

'Do you know him?'

'No, but I feel as though I do.'

They walked for a while in silence until they reached the huge and pristine plate-glass windows of Harry Bowden's car showroom. A long, low stone trough ran the length of the inside of the window sprouting ivy and midget ferns all of the same height. The five cars parked side by side, bonnets forward, looked like glowing monuments to a new age. Under the engine of each car was a sand-filled tray to catch the oil. A gloomy-looking man in a neatly pressed brown overall was slowly sweeping the gleaming aisles between the vehicles with a new broom.

'Aye aye, it's Wilson,' Royle joshed, nudging Lawler in the ribs as they entered the cool, tall vault of the showroom. 'Where's the boss?' Royle called.

'He went off,' Wilson told him without looking up from his work.

'Where?'

'Dunno.'

'And how's the missus today?'

'No better.'

'I'm sorry to hear that, Wilson,' Royle said, smiling. 'Are you in the process of locking up?'

'What do you think?'

'Mind if I show a chum round?'

'Do what you like.'

Royle winked at Lawler and led the way across the glossy floor towards the glassed-in salesman's booth. 'Wilson's an

Esperantist,' Royle whispered from the corner of his mouth. 'But for Heaven's sake don't ask him to talk to you about it or you'll be stuck with him jabbering away for hours in wog at you.'

Outside the door of the booth were two modern comfy chairs and, between them, an ashtray on a stalk and a table with a few flimsy catalogues on it.

'I have a suspicion that Mrs Wilson takes to her bed to avoid having to listen to her husband talking to her in a language she can't understand,' Royle said as he opened the door and wafted his way through the capsule of cigarette smoke. He took out a large key from a desk drawer and leaned down to unlock the rusty padlock of a wooden ship's chest.

'Scotch or gin?' he asked Lawler.

'Scotch.'

The action of raising the chest lid triggered a mechanism which elevated a platform of gin and Scotch bottles, a jar of cherries, a plastic pineapple-shaped tumbler of cocktail sticks, a miniature wooden barrel of cigarettes and a brass ice bucket, half full of stale water. Royle kneeled down, poured two generous measures and handed one to Lawler, saying, 'Here's how.'

'Cheers.'

'Besides which, Harry said that Wilson's missus is a moral re-armer – so I suppose at least she has something to keep her happy.'

'. . . Good grief!'

'What?'

'I've just seen it!'

'Seen what?'

'You're jealous.'

'Of Wilson? I should think not.'

'I believe you are. And I'll bet you've been round to his place.' Royle sniffed.

'Well?' Lawler pressed him.

'I'll admit that Wilson has invited me south of the river on more than one occasion.'

'I thought so.'

'More for his sake than mine, I might add. I'm happy to share a trough of gruel with any man, as well you know, Arthur, particularly when I find myself a little short of the wherewithal. But I have to say . . . I have to say I found Mrs Wilson rather alluring.'

'Oh God . . .'

'It's not what you think. I mean, I might once have dropped in to see her when Wilson was otherwise detained, but I have to tell you that absolutely nothing untoward took place.'

'She sent you packing, did she?'

'I really can't remember the finer details. There seemed to be any number of children tugging at her skirts . . . What do you think?' Royle said, gesturing towards the cars. 'Want to try one for size?'

'Why not?'

Royle locked up the chest and Lawler followed him out of the booth to a neat red two-seater.

'What is it?' Lawler said.

'Try it out.'

Lawler climbed into the driving-seat, put his glass on the leather seat beside him and tested the steering wheel. He flicked a switch which clicked on and off solidly, and pressed one of the stiff foot pedals.

Royle leaned in over the door. 'It's an Imp. A sports tourer. They brought it out a couple of years ago to replace the Brooklands. Very popular with the motor club – and the ladies.'

'I don't know, I think I'd prefer something more . . . substantial.'

'Of course, sir. If you'd like to step this way.' Royle bowed and opened the low door. They passed another tourer which Royle patted fondly on the radiator, finally coming to a halt by a black saloon with a long vented hood, a shining silver radiator, spoked silver wheels and sleek sweeping mudguards which put Lawler in mind of Meredith's plucked eyebrows.

Royle hooked his thumbs in his braces and declared, 'This is a Riley Kestrel. One and a half litres. A substantial and supremely comfortable four-seater.'

'I'll take it.'

'Of course. Unless sir would prefer it in the "special series".'

'What does that mean?'

'Uprated suspension, engine and gearbox – for the more discerning customer.'

'No. I'm sold on this one. Send it round, will you.'

'Of course, sir.'

The Scotch had lifted Lawler's mood. With luck, and depending to a large extent on his alcohol intake and Meredith's frame of mind, he knew he also had a reasonable chance of a real spell of happiness at some point in the evening.

'Would Meredith like it, do you think?' Lawler asked.

'I'd say it might get her down the aisle but you'd always lose her to a chap in an Alpine Tourer.' Royle was looking fondly at the last car in the line. 'This is the girl I'd take.'

'What do you do when it rains?'

'You get wet.' Royle climbed agilely in, sat behind the wheel and took possession of the machine in a way Lawler knew he never could.

'And what about the winter?'

'What about the winter, Arthur?'

'Yes. Of course. You're talking hypothetically.'

'Am I? How do I look, Wilson?' Royle shouted towards the tall showroom door.

'Eh?' Wilson was standing on a stool, reaching up to push the long bolts into place.

'Suit me?'

'You'll catch it if Mr Bowden finds out you've been in his whisky chest again.'

'I'm making a sale, man. He won't begrudge me a measly measure of Scotch for that.'

'I'm off home. Have you got the keys for the back?'

'No. You can let us out, Wilson. We're on a mission of mercy for a damsel in distress.'

Wilson tutted and wearily undid the bolt.

'Come on, Arthur. Let's go and seal the sale.' Royle handed his empty glass to Wilson as he passed him. Lawler, embarrassed, did the same.

'Good night, Wilson,' he said, feeling some camaraderie with the man.

'Good night, sir,' Wilson replied, feeling the same.

Outside, Lawler sprinted to catch up with Royle who was rushing after two young nurses in identical blue macs, their arms linked. When he reached them he raised his hat and smiled. They declined to join him for a drink and Royle didn't press them, but Lawler could see that with a little encouragement they would have come. The thought for some reason depressed him into a moody silence which didn't lift until he had drunk two large Scotches in quick succession in the Posts. The vagaries of the licensing laws meant that the pubs on the other side of Oxford Street didn't open until half an hour later. This led to them both considering the first half-hour's drinking as 'the magic time' in which the alcohol would have only a benevolent effect on them.

'That's better,' Lawler said, rubbing his hands. 'One more before we get back?'

'It's my go.' Royle pulled out his wallet and flourished it at the barman. 'Same again, Geoffrey. Two large Haigs.' The good-hearted, habitually happy young man in the long leather apron smiled broadly and poured out two more measures.

'Here you are, gentlemen.'

'Oh,' Royle said, crestfallen.

'What's wrong?'

'I thought I came out with . . . no, hang on, I paid for Harry's beer at lunch, didn't I?'

'You're telling me you don't have any money?'

'Not a bean.'

Lawler handed Geoffrey a ten-shilling note while Royle lifted and set down his fresh glass.

'So how many motors does Bowden sell?' Lawler asked, the alcohol tripping him up over 'motors'.

'In a week? Or a day? Or, indeed, an hour?' The notion struck Royle as hilarious and he yodelled a laugh.

'An nour,' Lawler pronounced carefully.

'An nour!'

'Yes. In an nour.'

'How long's an nour?' Royle asked and winked at Geoffrey who had become infected by the mood of his regulars.

'It's approximately sixty ninutes.'

'Ninutes! And how long's a ninute? No, wait, I know this one. It's sixty . . .'

'Approximately,' Geoffrey put in.

'. . . Approximately sixty . . . well, what was it? Sixty whats?' Royle turned to Lawler and hammered him on the back. 'Well, come on, man. Sixty whats?'

'Sixty . . .'

'Yes?'

'Seconds, I suppose.'

'Oh. Of course. Of course. What time is it, George?'

'It's Geoffrey, sir. Ten minutes before six.'

'Except,' Royle announced. 'It can't be, can it?'

'Can't be what?'

'Seconds.'

'I expect not,' Lawler conceded, at which point the door swung open and the Fells twins swanned in theatrically, with their matching crimson velvet jackets, silver wigs and poodles.

'Ah. Boys!' Royle called out and swooped on them. The waxy, apple-red faces of the ticket-agency men recoiled in unison. 'A question for you – if an *nour* is sixty ninutes how many . . . now, what was the question? Arthur, what was the question again?'

The riddle was passed from the twins to Boy Merrell who had just closed up his jeweller's shop on Great Titchfield Street and from him to another of the regulars, a young bank clerk called Gregory Swift. Each time an old or new face appeared through the saloon-bar doors the din intensified and the pace of the evening picked up. Arthur edged his way to the far end of the counter and watched it all. He saw Royle, his face flushed and his tie loose, moving virilely through the growing crowd – throwing an arm round the wide shoulders of a soldier, offering a brisk respectful handshake to one of Bowden's thugs before vaulting up on to the bar to kiss the young barmaid on the cheek. A bark from the door drew him towards a portly man in a houndstooth suit. When Royle had broken through the crowd he pumped the man's hand vigorously up and down, then he led him over to Lawler's corner of the bar where he introduced him as 'Johnnie Quinn. You remember don't you, Arthur? The man with the advice.' To Lawler, Quinn looked like a half-inflated version of Bowden. The only straight line in his butcher's face was the plane of his long nose. They shook hands but Quinn's crude interest had already slid past Arthur, finding nothing to detain it.

'Mind my beer, will you,' Royle said and lurched off towards the gents'.

Lawler's foot had gone to sleep. He lifted it from the brass footrest, shook it, set it down again and stumbled as he tested his weight on it. As he did so, he caught sight of himself in the bar mirror. Only then did he recognise the distance between the man he was and the man he appeared to Quinn. With the absolute clarity that drink can sometimes bring he suddenly knew that nobody could guess all that he was capable of: a man with an appetite to see and enjoy all of the colours the world had to offer, who could love and laugh and be kind and gentle and generous. Instead, they were confronted by a grey statue standing silent and malevolent at the end of the bar.

One of the Fells twins, standing close at his back, called, 'What's a fellow got to do to get a drink round here?'

'Blast and damn him!' Lawler heard to his left. When he turned he saw three men standing on chairs looking through the window at somebody going off down the street. 'Look out!' one of the men shouted as his flimsy chair toppled and he fell heavily on to the floor. The other two men stood over him and applauded like performing seals.

Lawler looked at his watch. A quarter to seven. Another hour lost. Meredith came into his mind. He remembered saying, 'I'm sorry, did you ask me for the time?' and Meredith lighting a cigarette. This was shortly before he went out on an errand with some money she had given him. Lawler reached into his pocket for Bowden's five-pound note and pulled out instead a crumpled ten-shilling note, a half-crown and a handful of coppers. He had been robbed, he was sure of it; fleeced by Royle or Quinn or Boy Merrell or one of the thugs by the window.

'What's all the trouble about?' Royle asked him when he had lurched back from the gents' and seen the expression on Arthur's face. Quinn whispered into his ear, then moved off to join Bowden's men.

'I've been robbed,' Lawler told him.

'Never mind. It was worth it, wasn't it?' Royle said, draping his arm round Lawler's shoulder. 'Time to go, old chum?'

'Yes.'

Somehow, suddenly, they were outside in the cool evening and Royle was re-fastening his collar and tidying his tie. Lawler felt sluggish from the drink but he was already beginning to sober up. Bowden's men followed them out and, a moment later, Quinn.

'So,' said Royle. 'Everybody on?'

Bowden's lead man nodded, the two behind him deferred and stood with their arms crossed. A line of command had already been swiftly and silently drawn: Quinn was at the head, then Royle and Bowden's lead man. Below them, the two pasty thugs.

'What's going on?' Lawler asked.

'Never you mind,' Royle said, looking towards Quinn and asking, 'What time were they due to leave Chelsea?'

'Six-thirty from the barracks,' Quinn told him and then they all stood and waited silently until one of the men announced, 'Here they come,' as a green Austin van turned out of a side street and pulled up in front of them. Quinn climbed in beside the driver and Royle went to the back and swung open the doors. Along each side of the interior were wooden benches. Between the benches, a crate of rubber truncheons. The two men sitting inside shuffled up towards the front of the van and Bowden's three men distributed themselves two to one side, one to the other. Lawler smelt the sweat and smoke of the bar on them as they climbed in.

'In you go, Arthur,' Royle said.

'What's all this about?'

'I think you know, don't you?'

'I promised Meredith I'd get back.'

'And so you shall. After we've done a little job for Harry.'

'I told you. I don't want a job with Bowden.'

'But we need all the help we can get. In you go.'

'No,' Lawler said. 'No. I won't. And neither should you.'

'You'll be sorry.'

'I doubt it, Billy.'

Royle climbed in and slammed the door. Somebody inside banged twice on the back of the cab and Lawler watched the van pull away towards Tottenham Court Road.

Later, at Meredith's, they celebrated. The radiogram was turned up as loud as it would go. Bowden had stood them eight quarts of beer and six bottles of gin. When the young woman in the flat downstairs came up to complain at the noise, one of Bowden's men tore open her dressing-gown and her nightdress and tried to drag her into the bedroom. Lawler pulled him off and managed to bundle the woman out of the door. Royle's lip had been cut and Meredith bathed it for him. Quinn's knuckles were raw. Bowden, puce-faced, wearing a bow tie and tails, was pushing a child's toy pram round the room, singing madly as two women joined the impromptu conga. Lawler heard Royle explaining to Meredith that he didn't want the pram in the room. He'd seen Quinn take it from a child and use it to batter an old man round the face.

'Where are we going?' Bowden, who was at the head of the conga, called.

'We're going to Bow!' Quinn shouted in reply and took one of the women round the waist.

'And what are we doing?'

'Kicking the Jews!'

'So what are we doing and where are we going?'

'We're kicking the Jews in Bow. Kicking the Jews in Bow . . .' The conga progressed round the flat and threaded out through the hall, down the stairs and out into the street, leaving Royle and Meredith intimate on the sofa and Lawler standing alone by the door. He reached to turn down the radiogram. The glowing green glass behind the dial burned hot. He saw Royle leaning down towards Meredith's face, forcing his bruised lips against her. She didn't respond; but kneeling across her, holding her down, he hitched up the velvet hem of her dress to her thighs. Then Royle slipped the straps of her dress from her shoulders, freeing her breasts. Meredith held her right arm across herself, to protect herself from him, but he pushed her arm aside with only a gentle force. Royle couldn't understand why recently she had taken to resisting him.

When the conga returned they were locked together on the sofa. Lawler stood by the radiogram and watched it all, disturbed and aroused. But now Meredith's eyes were dead, as though the body Royle was spending himself into belonged to somebody else.

Madrid Telephone Exchange: The Same Night

'Good evening, *New York Post*. To whom do I have the pleasure of speaking? . . . And good evening to you, Alice. This is Theodore Goss filing from Madrid. Shall we get this over and done with? . . . That's fine, and if young Ramon who I assume is listening in to our conversation chooses to interject, please ignore him. You don't mind, do you, Ramon? . . . No, I will not deviate from the text I presented at your office. Alice, here we go:

As the world turns its back on the trials of its youngest Republic, what began as a *coup d'état* is swiftly assuming the proportions of a civil war. But as those of us who lived through the last great conflagration know, all wars enjoy their moments of absurdity as well as horror. News reaches us here in Madrid of an incident that combines both. It took place in the appropriately named Boca do Inferno – the 'Mouth of Hell' – and concerns the death of rebel leader General Sanjurjo, who was, until last week, living in exile in Portugal. Two rebel generals are now detained in Republican jails, and Sanjurjo was to be a key player in the insurgents' battle plans. The General, a large and reputedly vain man, is reported to have been overcome with emotion when he was greeted as the Spanish Chief of State by the airman sent to Estoril to collect him. The pilot in question, playboy air-ace Juan Antonio Ansaldo, suggested that they set off without delay for Burgos, a city in the north of the country, currently serving as the rebels' HQ. The Portuguese authorities, however, intent on maintaining at least the pretence of diplomatic relations with the elected government in Madrid, intervened, and Ansaldo flew off alone in his tiny, two-seater De Havilland. The plan was that he would land at a race-track nearby where he would collect his passenger diplomatically out of the sight of the authorities and fly on. The General, meanwhile, instructed his staff to pack a large case with his dress-uniforms and medals so that, on his arrival at Burgos, he would be suitably attired. Later that day the rendezvous was made at La Marinha race-track, Boca do Inferno. Despite the pilot's concern over the combined weight of the suitcase and the corpulent General, Sanjurjo insisted they take off without delay. Witnesses say the Puss-moth struggled to leave the ground, the undercarriage caught a line of trees and the plane crashed. Sanjurjo was killed instantly. Ansaldo walked unhurt from the wreckage. The fate of the dress uniforms is not known. Only two men in Spain now have use of them: generals Mola and Franco. Franco is the senior officer and his is the name you hear in every bar and on every street corner across this city.

'. . . Did you get that, Alice? . . . Good. And Ramon, you may now remove your headphones and return to the bar. Goodnight to you both.'

London: The Same Night

Meredith Kerr looked back over her shoulder before turning in through the wide door of the tall, red-brick mansion block on the corner of Berners Street. The man charged with following her was watching from the vantage point of the canopied hotel doorway opposite, where he had taken refuge from the rain. It was Royle, his face shadowed from the meagre night-porter's light by the wide brim of his hat. He had seen Meredith twice walk past Renton's tiered corner block before finally finding the courage to go in. Royle was drunk but his senses were sufficiently sharp to be alert to trouble. He was concerned she would be taken for a tart straying three hundred yards from her beat on Wardour Street. At two-thirty a.m., as the West End enjoyed that brief few hours of quiet between the clubs closing and the early workers arriving, few respectable women walked the streets alone.

The five-storey block was dark. Royle's attention dogged the jagged line he imagined Meredith would be taking up the wide stone flights to the second floor. As his eyes reached Kit Renton's window he saw the thin curtains shimmer. Royle looked at his watch and caught a bitter taste of the cigar smoke spilling from the dining-room window behind him. He found himself longing for the sparse comfort of the small room Bowden allowed him above the car showroom in Great Portland Street. The room was granted to him for services rendered. Services such as following Meredith to her assignations and reporting back.

Kit Renton had not been asleep when he heard the knock at his door. He was listening to the rain. Tonight, bright rain fell that sounded like a chain dragging and sparking across dry streets.

The knock did not surprise him. He was often called on late at night and slept fully dressed for such an eventuality. When he opened the door, Meredith walked straight past him into the flat, tugging off her long gloves and offering only a curt 'Hello'. Renton followed her in, found the matchbox and lit the gaslight. It stuttered and popped, then settled to an even hiss as the room was illuminated by a dull green glow.

'I expect you're wondering why I've come to see you,' Meredith risked.

'Well, yes,' Renton said.

'You know who I am?'

'Yes. Of course.'

Finding herself embarrassed and overwhelmed by Renton's presence, Meredith stooped to pick up a magazine from the bed. She read out the title: '*The Adelphi.*'

'. . . Yes.'

'Do you know the editor?'

Renton could see that her hands were shaking. 'Jack Common? We've met once or twice.'

'An attractive man with an odd accent. Arthur introduced us. Sometimes he acts like a pimp. Arthur, I mean. It's almost as if he seeks out those who are most unlike him and offers them to me – or the other way round, I'm not sure which – in the misguided belief that he'll benefit in some way.' She laid the magazine carefully down on to a table cluttered with overlapping books and newspapers and pamphlets. The weight of opinion intimidated her into focusing her attention towards the far end of the room: the Bulle shelf-clock, a circular tin ashtray with four spent matches at the compass points, the gas ring, the small geyser above the sink and the single plate and cutlery laid on an upturned beer crate. In front of the crate there was a packed suitcase.

Renton said, 'Arthur is a very good and a very old friend of mine.'

'I know. And you won't hear a word said against him.'

'I won't.'

'I wouldn't expect you to,' Meredith said, and smiled. It was an invitation to Renton to do the same, but he declined.

'I suppose you don't have any gin, do you?' Meredith had so much wanted to do this sober, but now she needed to shed some of her fear.

'No. But I might have some beer.'

'It doesn't matter. Should I sit down?' She gestured towards the chair drawn tight to the table.

Renton took a cautious step away from the door. The room was sufficiently small for any move to be invested with significance. 'Why don't you take the bed,' he said, allowing his voice to soften. 'It's more comfortable.'

Meredith sat down, then stood again and shrugged off her fur. She looked round the room for a clothes hanger and, seeing none, draped the sable carefully across the foot of the bed. She caught sight of Renton watching her and saw herself through his eyes. Feeling a little disgusted with herself, she said, 'I don't suppose you approve of this, do you?' and Renton remembered Lawler asking the same. The room had filled with the smell of her perfume.

'What *are* you doing here?' Renton asked her. He had pulled the chair out, intending to sit. Instead, he turned it round and straddled it, using the flimsy wooden back as a brace against his breast.

'I think you know that,' she said.

'I don't think I do. Does Arthur know you're here?'

'What has Arthur got to do with it?'

'I understood you two were set up together.'

'Really? Well, I can see why he wanted you to believe that. The truth is . . . the truth is . . .' Meredith lay back on the bed, kicked off her shoes, and rested her feet on the cushion of her damp coat.

'Go on . . .'

'God. I don't know what the truth is. I don't know what the truth is at all.' She sighed. '. . . Beyond the fact that . . . All right,

I'm just going to say this to you, I don't know why I feel I have to apologise for it, nevertheless . . . the fact is that when I saw you in that saloon bar last week and you smiled at Arthur I thought it was . . . I thought I . . .'

'Yes?' Renton said.

'Tell me why you ran away from school.'

'What did Arthur tell you?'

'Please don't blame him. Or Billy. I was curious about you. That's all . . . I'm rarely curious.'

'I thought you were an actress. At least that's what Arthur told me. Actresses are expected to be curious, aren't they?'

'He told you I was an actress, did he? Well, that's Arthur trying to be kind.'

'You're not an actress?'

'Not quite. You know I've become quite poor at judging people. I used to be quite shrewd. I think Harry has tainted me in some way.'

'Bowden tainted you? You surprise me.'

'Yes,' Meredith said. 'If you're always in the company of someone who judges people harshly all the time it tends to rub off on you. It hardens you in some way.'

'But Arthur's not like that.'

'No. Arthur's quite the opposite. He can find the good in anybody. I'm surprised he hasn't been robbed blind.'

'Would it matter to you if he was?'

'Of course it would! What do you think I . . . ?'

'I'm sorry.'

'No. No, don't be sorry. I . . . I mean what little you know of me . . . from . . . the outside I expect you think I'm rather cold-hearted. Yes, I expect that's what you think, isn't it?'

'Well, I don't know you. All I do know about you is what I've seen and what Arthur has told me.'

'And from what he has told you you've made up your mind that I'm only interested in taking him for all he's got.'

'No. No, I don't think that. Arthur's not a fool. He wouldn't fall in love with somebody who was like that.'

'He said he was in love with me?'

'No. But I could see that he was.'

'You should know that I've always been honest with Arthur. I haven't led him on. He's always been a very dear friend. But I couldn't love him. Not in the way he wants. It's his choice that he continues to spend so much of his time with me.'

When Renton next looked at her, Meredith felt that he was beginning to see her more clearly. So it was a disappointment when, after a pause, he said, 'Please tell me what you want.'

'Don't you know yet?'

'No.'

'The truth?'

'Yes.'

'Are you sure?'

'Yes.'

'I've fallen in love with you. Which is something I very rarely do. But when I do it's sudden and it hurts . . . Now you be a gentleman and say something to spare my embarrassment. And when you do, let's pretend we've said all we need to say about Arthur . . . and let's pretend that Bowden doesn't matter. And that Royle isn't standing outside in the rain waiting for me.' She watched Renton go to the window and pull the curtain aside. 'Is he there?'

'Yes.'

'I'm sorry. I didn't want to compromise you.'

'What is he doing there?' Renton saw a match flare in Royle's palm, then another, then his cigarette was lit and the smoke fanned out from beneath the striped canvas canopy of the hotel's entrance.

'It's Bowden. He wants to know where I go. Who I see. All of it.'

'Why?'

'It makes him less frightened that he's going to lose me. And he could be right.'

'What about Arthur?'

'I told you. Arthur doesn't matter. No, that's not quite right. It's not that Arthur doesn't matter. Arthur does matter, but Bowden has decided he poses no threat so he allows me Arthur just as he allows me Royle.'

Renton let the curtain fall and moved to the bed.

Meredith said, 'You know what I want. I'm sure I know what you want. It's ridiculous denying it. That's what I told myself tonight. I was drinking another, yet another gin, with three men, all of whom wanted something from me that I didn't feel I could . . .' Renton sat beside her, forcing her to relinquish some of the narrow space. Nervousness propelled her thoughts on. '. . . The band was playing. People were dancing . . . and I saw your face. Your smile. It's barely been out of my mind since I first saw you . . . And I said to myself he feels the same. I just know he does. I saw it in his face. In that brief moment our eyes met. I saw it. So here I am.'

Renton made a closed book of his hands. He opened it, hinged at the spine, and covered his mouth with his palms. As he reflected on what Meredith had told him he slowly expelled the air from his lungs, warming his hands. 'I don't know what to say to you . . . Please don't imagine I'm not flattered . . .'

'Oh dear. How cruel those words are.'

'You know I'm leaving for Spain tomorrow?'

'I knew you were leaving. I didn't know when.'

'Doesn't that change things?'

'Why should it?'

'I thought . . .'

'What? You think I've come here to try and stop you leaving? You really don't know me at all, do you?'

'I can't possibly give you what you deserve.'

'Yes, you can. Anyway, that's no answer. That's a coward's way out.'

'I'm sorry,' Renton said.

Meredith swung her legs from the bed and pushed her feet into her shoes. The movement crowded Renton from the edge of the bed. He moved away from her to the door.

She was angry. Not at the rejection, but because she knew now that her first instincts about Renton had been right. She was offering him everything. Unconditionally. For the moment, until they had drawn up an emotional contract between themselves, all he had to do was to take it.

Meredith said, 'Perhaps you're too pure, perhaps believing in a cause makes the ordinary things of life seem too dull.' She reached sharply across the rumpled sheets to gather her coat.

'No. It's not that.'

'Isn't it?' she said, pulling on her coat, palming it straight, pushing her hands into the pockets, trying to calm herself. 'Look, Kit . . .' At last she had used his name again, and she loved hearing it. 'I know you're going to Spain. I'm sorry, I didn't mean to get angry with you . . . And I'm really not here to try and stop you leaving. How could I?'

'I don't quite know what to say.' Renton crossed to the window and drew back the curtain. Royle at that moment was looking up towards the apartment.

'Then why don't you just kiss me.'

Renton hesitated, then he approached the stranger in his room. She stepped out of her heels and they kissed. When they pulled apart it was because Meredith drew back.

'I thought so,' she said.

'What?'

'A kiss never lies.'

Renton smiled and said, 'You've been reading too many penny novelettes.'

'Is that wrong of me? . . . You're blushing.'

'Am I?'

'I can wait for you. Don't go and get yourself killed.' Meredith moved quickly to the door, but the drama of her exit turned to farce when the door stuck. As Meredith finally pulled it open she laughed at the absurdity and it was because of this more than anything else that Renton regretted having let her go.

Kit Renton was still trying to make sense of Meredith's visit six days later when he got off the train at Perpignan and set his bag down on the platform beside a neat pile of empty hessian sacks. He knew, however, that whatever he felt for her would have to wait. He needed all of his wits about him now to deal with the obstacle of crossing the border into Spain. Renton knelt to tie a shoelace to buy himself some time; as he leaned down, he twisted the noose of his neckerchief so that the sweat from the nape of his neck lay against his Adam's apple. Two baskets of chickens which had been stacked beyond the shade of the platform canopy complained at the heat and took turns to poke their beaks through the knit of the wicker. A door slammed shut in a distant carriage, a whistle blew and with a flush of steam and a sudden percussive flailing the train drew away, slowly unveiling the stage of the far platform. Two men were revealed sitting together on a bench. A board above them advertised a train for Salses but the men exhibited none of the curiosity and impatience of travellers. One was deftly dealing playing cards on to a tan leather briefcase which lay flat across his knee. The other, in a loose grey suit, drew on a cigar as he watched the cards go down. A plane of smoke drifted towards the face of a huge clock which ticked the seconds slowly away.

Renton took an envelope from his pocket and checked the address of his next destination. A name and a map had been scrawled in pencil next to it. As he walked away, beyond the reach of the station shadows, the sun on his back began to penetrate the knotted muscles of his shoulders. Renton shielded his travel-tired eyes and looked eastwards towards a citadel which crowned a small hill. Beyond it, distant in the clear air, the Pyrenees.

The hollow clack of the station clock was still audible when Renton reached the canal and leaned over the cold stone wall to gaze down at the dull lustre of the water. He followed the direction of the flow until he found himself in the Place Arago. Huge palms bordered the square, their ragged leaves stirring gently in the thin breeze. An old grey dog pissed a treacly stream against a magnolia tree and slunk away. None of the shirt-sleeved men playing cards or dominoes at the open tables outside the cafés awarded any interest to the visitor. Renton heard a car approaching him from behind. He turned and saw a young blonde woman at the wheel of a dusty black Fiat. After a moment's fierce curiosity she looked away from him. When she had pulled up a few yards ahead the woman leaned across to the passenger seat. She then emerged into the sun holding a thin leather bag. Renton watched her as she hurried into the Café Métropole, her tight black skirt constricting her movements. He checked the address on the envelope once more and followed her in through the beaded curtains.

The interior was dark but not cool. The air was thick with cigarette smoke and freighted with the heavy smell of stewed meat. As his eyes adjusted to the light Renton saw a bartender watching him with hostility. An old man drinking brandy at a table beside the bar looked up briefly, then returned his disdain to his newspaper.

'I'm looking for Monsieur Delouche,' Renton told the bartender who in return offered a begrudging shrug of his shoulders. He tried again, 'I was told in Paris I would find Monsieur Delouche here.'

The bartender called the name across the room, 'Delouche?' The waiter shrugged. He was standing in a pool of light beside the window and watching a woman across the square who was sunning herself in a shop doorway. Beneath his apron his right hand cradled his genitals.

'What do you want with Delouche?' the old man at the table asked. His thin face was ridged like a sultana, desiccated by years of exposure to the sun. A halo of flies circled his shallow dish of grey meat.

'I'd rather discuss it with him.'

'You're American?'

'English.'

'We have had a few English here.'

'Yes?'

'Though I can understand the motives of the English more easily than the Americans. I find them a different kind of . . . adventurer?' The old man continued to stare at him.

'Perhaps,' Renton said, 'there are as many motives as there are volunteers.'

The man laughed and his expression softened. 'I doubt that, young man. By and large I find myself encountering naïvety, but my wife is convinced that I see naïvety in everyone I meet nowadays. She suggests it's because of my age. But then, she didn't know me when I was young. Sit down.'

Renton took a seat, resigned to courting the old man if that was what it took for him to find Delouche. The woman he had followed into the café emerged from the kitchen tying on an apron. She walked directly across the room and set a wine glass down in front of him.

'Another adventurer,' the old man said to her and she nodded. 'My wife,' he explained and watched for a reaction. Renton was careful not to respond, judging the woman to be thirty years younger than the old man.

'You must be careful,' the woman said to Renton, her attention fixed on her husband's face. 'For your own sake, but also for ours.' She poured wine into Renton's glass as though it was one of a number of tasks in the day she had too little time to complete.

'My wife is less trusting than me,' the man told him. 'Each day I try to impress on her that the numbers of men who pass through Perpignan are of little consequence to the authorities.

Two, perhaps three or four, a day. They won't waste their time planting spies here.' He held out his right hand, palm-up. 'Let me see your letter of introduction.'

'You're Delouche?'

'Yes. Of course.' And because Renton didn't react he asked brusquely, 'Do you want identification?'

'I'm sorry. I've been travelling for five days,' Renton said and passed over the letter. The woman stood watching him as Delouche read it quickly.

'They speak highly of you,' the Frenchman said. 'Have you eaten?'

'Not today.'

Delouche's glance at the waiter prompted him towards the kitchen. The bartender moved out of earshot.

'So you're an Anarchist?' Delouche asked.

'Yes.'

'Don't look so worried, Renton. I'm not going to ask you to defend your beliefs. It's all the same to me.' The old man forked a piece of rabbit into his mouth and chewed until his teeth ground against bone. He chewed a little more, then spat the residue into his cupped palm. After examining the tiny leg joint, he laid it on the rim of his plate. 'You Anarchists want revolution, yes? I have read a little Proudhon, and Thoreau. *Civil Disobedience*. This is something we French are well versed in. So – here; now; revolution. And you are not afraid of destroying the world in the process?'

'I'm sorry, was that a question or a statement?'

'You choose.'

'We anticipated the bourgeoisie would destroy as much of the world as they could as they retreated.' In his mind Renton saw a small dusty room. A man framed in the window. A wall of books prescribing the life of the man, the woman and the five children. Six for the duration of his stay with the family. He shared a bed with two other boys. They stank in an earthy way the boys at the college did not. Because of their proximity he slept deeply. He felt safe. When occasionally he woke he could hear the shouts of the men from the station; the shunters marshalling the trucks in the night.

'And this . . . trail of destruction is how you view the situation in Spain?' Delouche said.

'Yes. But not just in Spain.'

'The United States of America?'

'Yes, of course. In other ways.'

'And you're not afraid of inheriting ruins?'

'The world is ruined. No, we carry a new world in our hearts.'

'Which I imagine leaves little room for love. Or do you not recognise the condition?'

'No, of course I recognise it.'

'I'm so glad. But I'm afraid that if you continue to pursue your quest you'll find it necessary to take on everybody. When you've defeated the Fascists you'll then have to fight the Communists.'

'We're anticipating that.'

'You can't honestly believe you'll succeed?'

'All I know is that if we are to succeed then Spain is the place we'll do it.'

In the pause that followed the woman said, 'Perhaps you'd like to wash?' and Renton gladly followed her behind the bar. In the small, sweltering kitchen the waiter was standing close against the back of a squat troll of a woman dressed in black. She was stirring a dull metal pot on the top of the stove. The waiter was pressing his hips rhythmically against her buttocks but pulled away as they walked in. He blushed. The cook giggled.

'Fool,' Madame Delouche said. Renton followed her through and out into the fierce light of the small yard which she crossed before pushing open the door of a small whitewashed building. Renton went in and saw immediately that the single window was barred. The recesses of the narrow room were dim. There was a washbasin against the wall, a stinking *chiotte*, and a galvanised bathtub with three inches of brackish water and a number of empty wine bottles in it. Lying over them, a mist of thick cobwebs.

'. . . Thank you,' Renton said towards the door as the woman pulled it closed. He heard the sound of a bolt and tried the door but it was locked. He had done what the loyalist in Paris had told him never to do, he had trusted too soon. He knocked without hope and waited. He heard the woman issuing urgent instructions in the kitchen and knocked again. The voices in the kitchen fell silent. He heard a cleaver against a chopping block. He pushed his face between the bars of the window but the angle was too narrow to enable him to see anything beyond a stack of damp wooden crates full of empty wine bottles. He felt the grit-dust of rust on his cheeks. He tried to digest the taste of panic by forcing himself to breathe slowly, offering his fear the only explanation that would tame it: they had locked him up because there had been something in the introductory letter that hadn't satisfied them. Even now they were telephoning the Paris contact for confirmation. Soon he would be released. He would sit down with Delouche and they would eat together and he would win the old man over. They would become drunk. The woman would join them. All of this when the Paris call had been made. But the fear overwhelmed him when he remembered the rumours of volunteers being found floating in the Mediterranean with their throats cut.

'Open the door,' Renton called and beat his fist against it. His ears strained for a response. The kitchen was silent, a voice was raised in the square, a lorry passed, a man laughed, a dog barked, birds sang, ivory dominoes slapped against soft wooden table tops. He returned without hope to the barred window and found Madame Delouche staring back at him through the bars. Shocked, Renton backed off a step.

'Have you finished washing?' the woman asked him.

'Yes,' Renton said. 'I've finished. You can open the door now.'

The face slid away from the frame of the window. One, two,

three steps to the door. A pause in which he was convinced she had returned to the kitchen. When he heard the bolt being drawn back he put his weight behind the door. As it hammered open against the wall he fell out into the yard, gulping in the air.

Madame Delouche looked at him disdainfully before turning on her heel towards the kitchen. Renton caught her arm and said, 'Why did you bolt the door?'

'I didn't. Please let go of my arm.'

'But the door was bolted!'

'The door was not bolted.'

'I was locked in!'

'There is no bolt.' She returned to the door and demonstrated the heavy, rusty catch.

'Why didn't you come when I called?'

'I didn't hear your call.'

'Of course you did. How could you not have heard me?'

'Please . . . come and eat.' Madame Delouche took his hand like a child and led him once more through the kitchen. At the beaded curtain into the bar she hesitated and then asked, 'Are you sure you're prepared for war?'

'Of course. Are you suggesting that I'm afraid?'

'No. Why should I suggest that?'

'Yes. Of course I'm prepared to go to war.'

'That is not quite the same thing. You must always remember that in those conditions your life is worthless to everyone but yourself. Everything is sacrificed to the greater good of the cause.'

'Worthless?'

'I have seen too many young men pass through here who won't be returning home. Guard yourself. You're not a soldier?'

'No.'

'Then listen and learn. There will be those who can teach you. Don't waste your time masquerading as a strong man.'

'No. That's good advice. Thank you.'

'Humility before bravado.'

'Yes,' Renton said.

Madame Delouche's eyes searched his face. She reached up to feel his forehead and said, 'You have a fever.'

'I'm not used to the heat.'

'You should rest.'

'There's no time.'

'Don't worry, young man, the war will safely proceed without you for a few more days.' For the first time she allowed herself a smile.

'Then perhaps for an hour.'

Madame Delouche called an explanation towards the restaurant, then led Renton up a flight of stairs. At the top she opened a small door and they ducked through it and walked up a steeper flight into a garret room.

When Renton woke some hours later he sensed the night just beyond the thin slates of the roof. He felt a hand on his brow and heard a soothing voice which lulled him back to sleep. He woke again, tasting the sweet metal of fever, and was aware of a body next to his. When he had fallen headlong into another dream he felt himself being carried down a flight of stairs and handed roughly to somebody who was waiting at the foot to receive him. A moment later he was beneath a huge black sky. He could feel the cold on his face and he could smell the sweat and perfume of the woman who was cradling him. When he woke again he was in a cot which was not familiar to him. The wooden-barred prison was beneath a window. All he could see out of it was the winter sky. Over the weeks he learned to differentiate the grades of white. Sometimes the black rag of a crow was blown across the frame. Birds terrified him. Rain relieved the boredom and comforted him. At night he watched the snow of the stars. He learned not to cry because if he did the woman treated him roughly. Finally he was lifted out and not returned to his prison. The man who held him to his chest smelled familiar, as did the cot to which he was returned. And from that moment on he no longer reached to suckle the milky nub of the tit of the woman whose smell was so comforting to him. She was gone and although time had stitched the gap in his life back together the seam always tore open when he was ill or lonely or afraid.

Four days later the fever had died down sufficiently for Renton to continue his journey. On the evening train to Cerbère he stared out at the silver moonlit fields and found himself considering the vainglorious Delouche and his troubled wife. Her motives remained unclear to him. He considered that only when age had made Delouche bedridden, or impaired his mobility severely enough to warrant a chair, would she begin to emerge. Until then he knew she would live in his shadow, just as the border town the train was now approaching sheltered beneath the towering Pyrenees.

When Renton left the train at Cerbère he immediately saw two border guards casually approaching a young couple who were walking along the platform. When they drew level the guards moved swiftly, shoving the man and woman roughly against the waiting-room wall and demanding to see their papers. One of them began interrogating the woman while the other barred the young man's path to her with the stock of his rifle. Two of their colleagues patrolled the carriages at the front of the train, pausing to peer into each compartment they passed. The driver was leaning out from his footplate watching them swaggering towards him. Renton strode past the intimate drama of the interrogation as if it was an inconvenience he encountered every day. He heard the note of panic in the woman's voice and the young man's fragile bravado as he called reassuringly to her that she had nothing to be afraid of. His brave voice was silenced by a blow from the guard. Renton hurried away down the stone steps into the echoing piss-smelling chamber beneath the tracks.

Outside the station, following Delouche's instructions, he turned right and walked until he reached the mouth of a foot tunnel. A man was emerging from it. He was carrying a bunch of flowers. A youth with timid eyes loitered at the entrance. Renton went past him into the tunnel and finally came out into a square. He saw the skeleton of a leafless tree, its trunk painted white and the branches dressed with a garland of coloured electric bulbs. The lights were also lit in two small restaurants. The proprietor of the nearest stood in the glow at the doorway, shirtsleeves rolled to his elbows, arms folded, watching the scant human traffic pass. Outside, a table of troops was drinking noisily. Renton continued towards the canal ignoring the half-hearted challenge of one of the soldiers. Once he was out of sight of the square he lit his petrol lighter and consulted Delouche's pencil map. The Frenchman had offered him a number of options to cross the frontier. He could go on foot through one of the steep mountain passes, he could hitch a lift on a lorry, he could try and convince a fisherman to take him round or he could risk the railway tunnel. Delouche had, however, warned him that even if he could get past the tunnel sentries it was unlikely he'd survive the trains that came through at irregular intervals. Kit Renton chose the tunnel route solely on the grounds that it was Delouche's least-recommended option.

When he emerged from a side street and saw the mouth of the railway tunnel to Port Bou the fear he had felt in the wash house returned. It looked like a passageway to hell.

Two soldiers were posted at the tunnel mouth. One of them, a solidly built man, cradled a machine-gun across the crook of his arms. The other, slighter, pale-skinned, was smoking a cigarette. In the silence of the night the machine-gunner was carefully explaining to the smoker the intricacies of a carriage clock he was dismantling at his lodgings. The smoker, whom Renton assumed must at one point have expressed some curiosity in his friend's hobby, was tonight uninterested in the intricacies of the flywheel mechanism. Each time the moon showed between the clouds he looked up eagerly like a sunbather, watching the lit clouds until their bright edges tarnished and the brilliant globe rolled away behind them. Renton sheltered in the shadows. He knew that once he broke cover he would be immediately visible to the sentries. The entrance to the tunnel was less than forty feet across. As he waited he calculated his options: he could choose his moment and work his way through the shadows to the sentries, then make a dash for the second machine-gun lying against a railway sleeper. Alternatively, he could look for some way of distracting the attention of the two men long enough to enable him to get into the tunnel. Having come to the conclusion that neither of these strategies was without significant risk, Renton heard a rumble in the tunnel. The sound provoked the smoker to amble to his machine-gun, heft the leather strap over his shoulder and cross the grey metal tracks to stand beside the clock-mender. A moment later a coal train hurtled out of the tunnel mouth, the line of trucks cutting the sentries off on the far side of the track. Renton looked at his watch and timed the passing of the train. It was a little over a minute before the rhythmic clatter of the trucks subsided and his ears adjusted once more to the men's lethargic exchanges. All he could do then was bide his time and hope that the next time a train came through, the men took up the same positions.

For half an hour he waited, edging as close as he dared to the open ground at the tunnel mouth. At one point the moonbather sidled out of sight and Renton considered running to the weapon which had again been abandoned by the track. But the other guard, left in sole charge, became more alert. He slowly turned a full circle. Something he saw to Renton's left prompted him to lift his machine-gun to his shoulder and squint through the sights. The shoulder strap hung loose like a trapeze. An owl hooted. Smiling, he let the weapon down again without firing. Five minutes later the moonbather returned holding up a bottle of wine. They took turns to drink from the bottle, staying at all times on the far side of the track.

Renton heard another din build in the heart of the tunnel. As he picked up his suitcase the moon slid out to light the dangers ahead of him. He tensed. When the front end of the locomotive appeared he took off, stumbling and running through the landscape of stones, half-bricks, stacked sleepers, piles of ballast, a broken shovel. He saw one of the sentries in the snapshot between each truck but the man was facing away. While he ran he immediately felt the fever rekindling and found himself tiring quickly. The distance was further than he had anticipated, his case was heavy, but he reached the tunnel mouth a moment before the cover of the train ran out. He slowed as he approached the trucks. The din was extreme. A loose chain from one of the couplings flailed and sparked, barely missing his chest. He flattened his back against the stone of the tunnel side and edged in. The final trucks flashed past. The echo of the roar chased after the train as it headed into France. Then there was a brief silence before the prosaic deliberations of the clock-mender began again.

Renton reached out blindly to feel the cold damp of the tunnel wall before taking his first careful steps into the dark passage that would lead him to Spain.

There was a knock on the door of Meredith's flat. A pause, then another. Arthur Lawler waited in the living-room, wishing the visitor away. Meredith was dressing in the bedroom and they were expecting Bowden and Royle to arrive for an outing to Brooklands where Royle was to race. The prospect of a few hours away from the routine appealed little to Arthur. For as long as he could remember, new experiences had always held more horror than hope for him. He was looking through the net curtain and up towards the grey London sky when there was a third impatient knock at the door.

'Arthur!' he heard from the bedroom.

'Yes.'

'Answer the door, will you.'

'Yes. I'm sorry, darling. I was just . . . thinking.'

Lawler dawdled to the front door and made a fuss of opening it. 'I'm sorry,' he called to the visitor. 'The lock seems to be stuck.'

'Get a move on,' Bowden called back.

'Ah. There we are,' Lawler said, swinging the door open and greeting Bowden with an opportunistic smile.

'I don't remember inviting you.' Bowden was dressed in a lush three-quarter-length black coat and a scarlet scarf. He also wore a mustard-coloured motoring cap which was fastened beneath his chin.

'I thought I might just tag along.' Lawler led the way back through to the living-room.

'Who is it?' Meredith called.

'It's Harry,' Lawler called back.

'Hello Harry,' the men heard. 'Get him a drink, will you, Arthur. I'll be out in a moment.'

'Better make it a large one then,' Bowden said. 'If she's not dressed yet.' He sat heavily, raising dust from the sofa, and loosened his scarf.

'Help yourself,' Lawler said, gesturing towards the drinks trolley and going out into the kitchen. He had no intention of waiting on Bowden but nevertheless felt compelled to watch him through the crack in the door as he sighed and raised himself from the sofa and went to the trolley where he lifted a bottle of gin and held it up to the light.

'Any more gin?' he called towards the bedroom door.

'I won't be long,' Meredith said, mishearing him.

'Is this all we've got?' Bowden came into the kitchen holding the bottle in his hand like a cudgel.

'I expect so.' Lawler turned towards the sink and made a play of washing up an ashtray.

'Lucky I organised some supplies then.'

In the silence that followed, Lawler felt Bowden's presence behind him. He heard the first flint scrape of a cigarette lighter and smelt the flood of smoke from the first draw.

'They say Renton left for Spain,' Bowden said.

'Yes. So I heard.'

'The more fool him.'

Bowden went back into the living-room. When he was alone again, Lawler found that he was shaking; it was anger or fear, he couldn't quite tell which. He leaned the ashtray to drain against an upturned beer glass, dried his hands on a filthy tea towel and joined Bowden.

'No word from him?' Bowden asked.

'Who?'

'Who do you think?'

'No. No word.'

'I hear the French have closed the border. He may not even get in.'

'He'll get in.'

'And all for what?'

'I think we've been through this before, haven't we?'

'Who will get in?' Meredith said brightly as she came across the room and kissed Bowden on the cheek.

'Renton,' Bowden said. 'To Spain.'

'Oh, that.' Meredith looked towards Lawler, her good humour extinguished, and he took his cue to pour her a gin and hand it to her. She sipped it as the two men watched her. 'Where's Billy?' she asked Bowden as if his answer would set the mood for the day.

'He's gone to fetch the booze.'

'You mustn't let him drink until he's raced.'

'That's up to him,' Bowden said.

'You know what he's like.'

'You tell him then.'

'Yes. I will. Though he's your driver, so I would have thought the responsibility would have fallen to you.'

Lawler waited for the argument to erupt. Although it was between Meredith and Bowden, he knew he was just as likely to get drawn into it. The late morning was a bad time for all of them, the final sober hour of the day when they were still sufficiently clear-headed to see their lives for what they were.

'I just don't see any point in racing around a track in fast cars,' Meredith said.

'There are plenty who do.'

'Fools, all of them, I expect.'

'Then don't come,' Bowden said.

'All right, I won't.' Meredith went back into the bedroom, slamming the door behind her. A horn hooted in the street outside.

'Go and talk to her,' Bowden said, finishing his drink. 'I'll be out in the motor.'

'Me?'

'If she's not out in ten minutes we're leaving without her.'

With Bowden gone, the discontent was left behind him, sealed in the vault of the flat. Lawler waited by the window until he saw him emerge into the street, open the car door, gather his coat round him and climb in. He heard Meredith blow her nose and then a number of sniffles pitched loud enough to be a call for attention. Taking his drink and fetching hers from the mantelpiece he went to the bedroom door and called her name.

'Go away,' she called back.

'It's all right. He's gone out to the car.'

'Good riddance to him. Bloody man.'

'. . . What do you want to do?' Lawler asked, but Meredith didn't reply. He tried again, 'Meredith, can I come in?' There was still no reply so Lawler opened the door. The room was dim, the thin drapes drawn. The clothes Meredith had discarded while dressing were scattered over the floor. Two wet towels were among them. The air of the room was sweetened by the smell of powder. Meredith was sitting on the bed smoking a cigarette. She was holding a handkerchief, tightly bunched like a pincushion, in her right hand and she was slumped slightly forwards, staring hard at the rug on the floor.

'Are you all right?' Lawler said.

'Why does he have to bring Kit up all the time?'

'I think he . . .'

'Every bloody minute of the day. He can barely say anything nowadays without bringing his name into it.'

'I'm sorry, I didn't realise.'

'Every minute.'

'Yes.'

'I can't tell you what it does to my nerves. And he knows exactly what he's doing. Stupid, stupid man.'

'Why don't you say something to him?' Lawler moved towards the bed, cornering her like a frightened cat.

'Don't be ridiculous. You know Bowden. What could I say?'

'Well . . .' He sat down beside her.

'I mean the whole point is that nothing can be said . . .'

'Yes, but . . .'

'. . . Which is exactly why he knows he can always hurt me.'

'I . . .'

'It's his . . . acknowledgment of Kit's importance to me. It's his . . . fear of losing me to him. That's why he does it.'

'But why should . . . ? I mean it's hardly a real prospect, is it?'

'Oh, Arthur . . .'

When Meredith looked at him and their eyes met, Lawler knew that he had lost her for ever.

'I see,' he said. '. . . I didn't realise at all.'

'Didn't you?'

'. . . Well, perhaps I chose not to.' He smiled sadly.

'I'm sorry. I should have said something to you. I would have done when the time was right.'

'Yes . . . well . . . Well, there we are then.'

'I love him. That's all.'

'But you barely know him.'

'I feel as though I've known him all my life.'

'. . . And so you imagine it's because Bowden feels threatened that he wants to hurt you?'

'Yes. I suppose it's quite pathetically touching in some ways.' Meredith took the drink from him, raised it to her lips, then sent the glass crashing against the wall. 'No!' she shouted. 'No, I won't.' She sprang to her feet, crushed her cigarette out in the ashtray and went to the window.

'You won't what?'

'I won't let him do it. I'll . . . I'll hurt him in the way he hurts me. My God I will.'

'I don't think Bowden can be hurt, can he?'

'Don't you believe it. Men can always be hurt, but you sometimes have to get them alone to do it.'

'Yes, I suppose you do.' Again, as had happened so often in the past, Lawler was on the receiving end of Meredith's casual cruelty.

'Well, do we go, or do we stay?' Meredith said, although she was asking the question of herself.

'What would you like to do?'

'I'd like to go. I'd like to see Billy race . . . But I'm not going to. I'm going to wait here until he leaves and then . . . and then you're going to take me to Brighton for the day.'

'Brighton?'

'Yes.' Meredith turned and smiled as the plan formed in her mind. 'And we're going to have a wonderful time and when we come back I'm going to tell Harry all about it: everything; from the tram ride to the front, to the walk on the pier, the lunch at . . . where?'

'Wheelers?' Lawler suggested, rising from the bed and taking Meredith's hand.

'Yes. Wheelers.' She drew Lawler to the window and together they looked down on the roof of the car.

'And then we could take tea in the Metropole Hotel.'

'Yes, Arthur. We could do that too. Anything you want. Just us. It will be our day.'

'Well, that sounds wonderful. Absolutely wonderful.'

They stood in silence, Arthur contemplating the day ahead, Meredith weighing up the plan in her mind, judging the consequences for her relationship with Bowden. They heard the sound of a horn from the street. Looking down at the car, they saw the driver's door open and Billy Royle getting out. Bowden called him back. Royle leaned down and took his instructions. He closed the door and sprinted into the building.

'He's sent Billy in to fetch me,' Meredith said.

'I'll talk to him for you if you like. Send him packing,' Lawler said, energised by the plans for the day.

'Yes, you could.' But as she looked beyond the day to the weeks ahead, Meredith's resolve began to weaken. She knew that Bowden wouldn't call her for days and she would have to contact him and apologise and he would have the upper hand again. The truth was that until she found her way back to Kit Renton she needed a benefactor to finance her life. Especially now. For two weeks she had begun to suspect she was carrying a child. Bowden's – or perhaps it was Royle's. It hardly mattered.

'Why don't you go into the bedroom and I'll tell him you're not feeling well?'

Meredith released Lawler's hand and went to pick up the shards of glass from the floor.

'Leave that. I'll do it.' Lawler knelt beside her, oblivious to the dusting of glass beneath his knees. 'You go into the bedroom. Go on. Then you won't have to talk to him and I'll . . .'

'No. You go and let Billy in.'

'And tell him what?'

'Tell him . . .'

'Yes.'

'Well, what do you think I should do?'

'What I think you should do is stick to your plan and come down to Brighton with me.'

'Yes, darling. I know that's what I *should* do.' Meredith stood and carried the handful of glass towards the kitchen. That way she didn't have to meet Lawler's eye. '. . . But we will do it soon. I promise.'

'Promise?'

'Yes. I promise.'

Slowly, Lawler went to the door and let Billy Royle into the flat. Five minutes later they were on their way out of London towards Weybridge and a day at the races.

To Barcelona: Two Days Later

Kit Renton heard the Englishman before he saw him. He was passing through the swaying dining-car on his way to the train's only unlocked lavatory. In the five hours since they had left Port Bou he had acquainted himself with the two bolted cubicles in third-class and one in second-class. The lavatory beyond the dining-car, he had been informed by the prim woman sitting beside him who regularly made the journey along the coast to visit her daughter, was used by the train staff and was serviced accordingly. It appeared that the revolutionary zeal had yet to extend to improving the sanitary conditions of the Spanish railway system. The Englishman was talking loudly to the waiter, enthusiastically praising the efforts of him and his Republican kin to preserve the country from the 'deplorable Franco'. The waiter, balancing on the balls of his feet and rocking to the rhythm of the train, was smiling benevolently. It was clear to Renton that the Spaniard didn't understand a word of what the Englishman was saying to him but something in the man's passion transcended the language barrier and the Spaniard nodded, encouraging him to go on.

Renton was beyond the man's table and grateful he hadn't been identified as a fellow countryman when he heard, 'They're still taking in the harvest, have you noticed?' He made the mistake of hesitating for a moment, his hand on the catch of the carriage door.

'I'm right, aren't I? You are English?'

Renton turned slowly and found the man's fleshy hand extended towards him.

'The name's Page,' he announced and Renton admitted, 'Yes. I am English. I'm Renton.'

'Thank God. I'm bored stiff. Come and join me.'

'Give me a moment.'

After he had used the lavatory Renton stood for a few minutes on the open platform between the carriages. Having stored away in London those parts of himself he employed when dealing with people he had no interest in, he felt ill-equipped for Page. Meredith Kerr came into his mind. She appeared to him as he had never known her; a sober, funeral-suited woman in a shadowed drawing-room. The curtains were drawn across the tall windows of the room but the sun had forced a beam through the narrow gap between them and that was what illuminated her: Meredith Kerr sat, smoking a cigarette in a holder, dust motes around her head caught in the sun. She was white-faced, with an expression he took to be grief, and staring towards him as if he was standing right in front of her.

When Renton returned to the dining-car, Page was fussily pouring wine into a second glass on the small table. The dishes from his lunch had been cleared. 'Oh, there you are,' he said. 'I was going to send out a search party. Sit down.' He swept the crumbs from the table with the edge of his hand.

Renton sat heavily as the train bounced over a set of uneven points. Page immediately leaned conspiratorially across the table towards him and said, 'I suppose you heard all that baloney about Franco?'

'Some of it.'

'Don't believe a word of it. All of these railwaymen are on the side of the Reds, did you know?'

'Are they?'

'Of course.'

'Look,' Renton said. 'I think it might be better if I went back to my compartment.'

'Why? I haven't offended you, have I?'

'Not me, no.'

'Oh, I see.' Page's smile curdled into a sneer.

'What?'

'You're a sympathiser – perhaps one of these volunteers I've been reading about in the *Express*, are you?'

'Yes.'

'Well, I shan't apologise. You can stay if you want. Doubtless you're curious to know what brings me here. Or perhaps it's of no interest to you whatsoever. Though perhaps it should be.'

Renton's attention fixed on the rich shining blue of the sea. Out beyond the feathered breakers a grey warship was steaming north. The white smoke from the funnel made an open-ended triangle with the horizon, presenting the illusion that the sea and the sky were being unzipped from one another.

'She's Italian.' Page announced in a quieter tone, closing his eyes with tiredness. 'Doubtless on her way home.'

'How can you tell?'

'I can tell,' Page said and sighed, opening his eyes and rubbing them with his knuckles.

Renton felt a stab of sympathy and a sudden affinity with his countryman. He was drawn by the fact that however much their motives differed, they faced similar obstacles. 'How did you cross the frontier?' Renton asked and took a sip of the wine. It was tart and provoked more thirst than it satisfied but he drank more.

'By train from Toulouse. Through from Cerbère to Port Bou where I changed. Same as you, I imagine.'

'Did you have any trouble?'

'What kind of trouble?'

Renton shrugged.

Page said, 'I showed my passport to a customs fellow but he didn't seem in the least bit interested. There was some delay at Port Bou where I was obliged to stand up in front of a committee of surly peasants in a building some distance from the station and explain my visit. It seemed to go down well with the man in charge because he issued me with a permit and made a point of shaking my hand. I then returned to the station where the police stamped my passport. Of course after that I waited for a train for four hours, but you have to expect that abroad. Why, did you have trouble?'

'Some,' Renton said, recalling the terrifying trek through the tunnel which seemed never to end, the drips of cold water on his neck, the nameless creatures scurrying round his feet and the awful roar and suction of the trains bolting past him as he cowered, holding his ears, pressing his face into the cold salt-tasting stone. Either Delouche or Page had lied to him. He had little doubt that it was the Frenchman, overstating the dangers of the frontier crossing either to test his resolve or put him off altogether.

After a pause, Page said, 'I remember a lot of rubbish being spoken about the border problems back at home. But you shouldn't believe rumours. I mean I'm not a seasoned traveller by any means but if you're expecting trouble sometimes I think you find it where it doesn't exist. Eh?'

'So tell me what you are doing here.'

Having shed his false bonhomie, Page was revealed as a sour, grey-faced man. He was sweating profusely. His podgy forearms, emerging from his rolled shirtsleeves, were pocked with red blotches. He smelt stale, like mutton fat. Renton estimated them to be a similar age, but Page looked ten years older.

'Doing here?' Page echoed. 'Bloody good question. As I said, I'm not a traveller, as you may have surmised.'

'I hadn't surmised that, no.'

'I'm a businessman – machine tools – that sort of thing.' He looked over Renton's shoulder towards the waiter who was now in easy conversation with two leather-hatted Civil Guards.

'Machine tools?'

'I hear the Republic needs all the "equipment" it can lay its hands on.'

'Weapons?'

'Keep your voice down!'

'Despite the non-intervention pact?'

'Eden counsels prudence in these matters. Prudence has always been my watchword.' Page scratched at his razor-burned neck. '. . . Do you imagine the temperature falls much at night here?'

'I expect so.'

'Of course,' Page said, 'Mexico was worse.'

'When were you there?'

'I went there as a boy with my father – twenty years ago.'

'Your father . . . ?'

'Had it on good authority – I never discovered quite what authority – that some rogue called Villa was interested in purchasing some rifles. Despite everything that was going on in France, off we sailed from Southampton on this fool's errand. That was my father for you.'

'And did he do any business out there?'

'Yes. I remember being sent to my room in a hotel when the discussion became heated. There were women involved. Astonishing women – immensely tall. I remember being struck by their beauty even at my tender age. Where was I?'

'Doing business.'

'Yes. A translator we took along with us said that Villa was ranting about a man called "Nigger Jack" – Pershing, you see – Pershing was after Villa and Villa's arms had dried up and so on and so forth . . . and here we are again: arms-starved rogues.'

'The Fascists?'

'You know which side I'm talking about.'

'Another revolution?'

Page seemed disinclined to pursue the line of argument. He said, 'My father is too old to travel now and you need to be a diplomat in my line and diplomats are hard to come by in Solihull. So here I am.'

'Your business is in the Midlands?'

'Yes. That's what I said, didn't I?'

'I don't think you did.'

Page craned his neck as the shadow of a station flew down the carriage. 'Did you see what that place was called?'

'No. It began with an "M", I think.'

'"M"?' Page said and unfolded a few squares of a Michelin map. '"M"?'

'Yes.'

'Mataró? Ah – no – no, it wouldn't be . . . because we'd stop there, wouldn't we?'

'I don't know.'

'It strikes me that you don't know very much.'

Renton was watching the sea again; he caught sight of a small fishing boat under a single russet sail being punched along by the wind.

'Yes or no?' Page challenged.

'What?'

'I made an observation that you don't seem to know a great deal about what's going on here.'

'Did you?'

'Oh, come on, Renton. Sing for your bloody wine, will you.'

'I didn't realise there was a condition attached.' Whether it was the heat or the remains of the fever, Renton realised with some relief that he no longer cared where he stood in Page's estimation.

'Oh dear. I've annoyed you, haven't I?' Page said, but for the first time since Renton joined him he looked genuinely interested.

'No . . . I'm sorry.'

'No. Let me apologise. I've obviously offended you in some way – perhaps the wine wasn't to your taste?'

'No. It wasn't the wine.'

'I must say,' Page sneered, 'I do find your type particularly hard to take.'

'Really? My *type*?'

Page shook his head as if he was trying to clear it. 'I mean, what in God's name are you doing here? After all, it's not your fight.'

'But I've chosen to make it my fight.'

'Why?'

'Because I . . . look, I'd rather not go into all this.'

'Of course. Besides, I don't think I could bear a lecture . . .'
Page was searching the carriage for something else to divert him.
A woman and a man were dining silently. A young man was eating
alone as if it was the last meal he was going to have. The two Civil
Guards were now passing through the far door. The waiter was
sitting down to a small meal, crumbling bread into a bowl of thin
soup. Page's attention returned to the man across the table. 'You
know, and forgive me for saying so, but you strike me as a man
who doesn't have much fun.'

'Really?'

'Yes. Is this what you do for fun? Because I've encountered
your type before.'

'No. I don't think I'd call it fun.'

'Then what do you do for fun?'

'What business is it of yours?'

'I'm curious about you. I've always found that serious-looking
men are usually the ones most desperate to laugh. It's certainly
true of the characters in my circle. I'm happy to jolly any
man out of his misery. In fact I have something of a reputation for it.'

'And why do you see it as your job to . . . ?'

'Answer me a question – two questions,' Page said.

'I might.'

'How old are you?'

'Twenty-eight.'

'Have you ever slept with a woman?'

Renton laughed and said, 'You tell *me* something.'

'But you haven't answered my question yet.'

'I have no intention of answering your question.'

'Well then, I'll have to conclude that the answer is no.'

'Conclude what you like.'

'Does anybody ever meet your expectations, Renton? Because
I imagine you have few friends.'

In the silence that followed Kit Renton stood up and walked away.

The next time he saw the man from the Midlands was outside the railway station at Barcelona. Just as Renton joined the end of the queue for a row of horse-cabs, Page, carrying a large suitcase, walked past the line, stopped and drew a city map from the inside pocket of his ankle-length coat. He consulted it, glanced left and right, then marched away towards Via Layetana. When, ten minutes later, Renton had finally secured a cab and set off for the Hotel Continental, he passed Page sitting on his upended suitcase on the port quay just a few hundred yards down the street. He was facing a boarded-up hotel and staring at it in a way that suggested it had no right being closed to him.

Then Page was behind them and the spry grey horse was tugging the cab along a quiet street, the shrill echoes of the horseshoes bouncing back from the dark canyon of shops and apartments. The sun had just dropped away and the buildings had unrolled their evening shadows across the hot, empty pavements. A curfew and a lights-out seemed to prevail. Some of the buildings were daubed in white with the huge uneven capital initials of the militias. The studded bank doors bore neatly framed letters explaining their expropriation. The cab clip-clopped past a church and the cabman turned to smile ruefully at his passenger. The walls were standing but the roof was gone and the shell of the building was still smoking. Renton glimpsed a long bread queue, as silent and still as statues.

It was in assimilating these disconcerting details, tasting them with his mind, testing them against what he had been told to expect, that he slowly built a sense of the besieged city: a place of barricaded streets, few people out, neither life nor light showing in the apartment windows. Renton breathed in the warm evening air, filling his lungs with the sweet unfamiliar scents and the sulphurous stench of broken sewers. He felt an affinity for the city that he had never felt for London and, in recognising it, it struck him that for much of his life he had been looking for somewhere to belong.

They passed a bare-headed youth, a rifle across his right shoulder, a girl on his left arm, his pride lying equally in both. A blue Cadillac cut fast round a corner towards them. Its headlights were taped across, which narrowed its beam into an angry stare. The Andalusian mare tugging the cab didn't rear at the advance of the car or the hoot of its horn, she merely stopped dead and her flanks quivered, absorbing the energy of her final step. The three passengers in the car waved from the open windows while the driver, maintaining control of the steering-wheel with one hand, draped the other through the window and banged out a rhythm on the door with his palm. The cab driver looked on patiently as the car skidded away. He flicked a loop in the long reins. It ran like a tiny wave along the leather and stung the horse into moving off again. The next obstacle they encountered was an unmanned barricade of neatly stacked sandbags. Beyond that, they negotiated a transport gang working in a small circle of oil lanterns. Bare-chested, the four men were repairing a sheared overhead tram cable. A tram on the approaching track waited for them to complete the job. The bald-headed driver was standing and reading a newspaper. Another road gang, a short distance behind them, was shovelling rubble into a shell crater.

Only when the cab turned into Las Ramblas was Renton confronted with the full scale of the revolution. This, he saw immediately, was where the colourful stage had been set; where the masses were to be found. Many of the hotels were draped in huge red or red-and-black flags. Magnificent three-storey posters of the revolutionary icons – Stalin, Lenin, Caballero – looked sternly down on their people walking the avenue. Enormous banners and large bright pictures called on the masses to fight Fascism and help build a better society. Loudspeakers blared out revolutionary songs. Hammers and sickles had been scrawled on walls. Men and women from the militias paraded up and down in civilian workclothes or blue overalls, many of them shouldering their rifles. Some stood sentry outside the commandeered hotels and stores. Like the blue Cadillac, all of the cars and many of the buildings had been anointed with the initials of the organisation that had appropriated them: PSUC, POUM, CNT-FAI. Renton found his pulse racing, his spirits lifting. For the first time in his life he felt that he could step out of the cab, walk up to the first man or woman he encountered and embrace them and they would understand and share his hopes and he wouldn't need to explain or self-deprecatingly acknowledge his beliefs. He was in no doubt that there was nowhere in the world that he would rather be at that moment.

Too shy yet to try out his grasp of the language, he had, by a series of gestures and only a few words, made it clear to the cabman that he was looking for the Anarchist headquarters, and the driver had in return made it understood that the Hotel Continental was the place he needed. When they came to a halt outside the building the civilian sentry lifted the barrel of his rifle. Renton paid off the cabman, his offer of a tip waved away, took out his letter of introduction and showed it to the sentry. The man glanced at it and waved him in. At the packed reception desk he showed it again. The clerk nodded and called another man over who led him through the busy entrance-hall. Because the lift was out of order they climbed the stairs out of the genial din to the third floor where the man knocked on a door, opened it without waiting for a reply, and ushered Renton in. A broad, shaven-headed man was standing, his hands anchored behind his back, looking out of the window. He was wearing neat blue overalls and a red-and-black neckerchief. Another man, untidy in a ragged straw-coloured suit, was sitting behind a typewriter, smoking a cigarette and taking dictated pencil notes on a small pad of paper lodged on the typewriter keyboard. His thick, lank, greasy hair fell over his eyes. Neither of the men acknowledged Renton. He listened as the man at the window continued to declaim, impassioned, in rapid words, occasionally pausing, trying out the weight of a phrase, then re-voicing it with more vigour. When he had finished, the man at the typewriter completed his notes, blew the ash from them, scanned them, then asked for an elucidation which was impatiently provided. After that, the note-taker stacked and sheaved his papers, pocketed his cigarettes and walked to the door. He offered Renton a brief nod as he passed him and slammed the door behind him. The draught ruffled the papers on the desk. Only then did the man at the window turn. He looked at Renton for a moment, then held out his hand and Renton, knowing now what was expected of him, offered his letter of introduction. After reading it the man handed it back with the curt observation, 'Another Englishman who no doubt speaks no Spanish.'

'Some.'

'We don't need any more volunteers. What we need is money – and arms, and medical supplies. And of course food. We can barter for many things, but arms are proving the hardest to find.'

'. . . I see.'

'I'm sorry. You will understand that we are all operating with very little sleep. For me, I have a mattress in this room which I use irregularly. We are sleepwalkers. So forgive me if what I say sounds harsh.'

'Not at all.'

'I understand that you have all made sacrifices to come here, but we don't have rifles for you – nor can we feed you.'

'Well, what would you recommend I do?'

'If the situation changes, then of course, should you choose to stay in Barcelona, you will be informed. Until then, I suggest you look for accommodation. You may be able to secure a room here. That's all.' He had nothing more to say but he seemed disinclined to move until Renton had left the room. When he had done so and closed the door behind him, he heard the man's footsteps cross the floor and the scrape of his chair as he sat down behind his typewriter.

Renton walked slowly back through the hotel. Once outside, his eye was caught by the white column of a searchlight sweeping the sky. The operators were moving it back and forth to a strict rhythm. As Renton stood on the hotel steps and watched it swing hypnotically away and then back again, he found he needed nothing more to fill his numbed mind than the impulse to follow the movement of the beam. A figure emerged from the doorway and stood beside him, similarly transfixed by the light. Cars passed up and down the street, choking the air with exhaust fumes.

'There are three barracks,' the man said.

'. . . I'm sorry, are you talking to me?' Renton saw it was the note-taker, standing beside him on the steps.

'You'll find yourself welcomed at these barracks – Bakunin, Espartacus and Salvochea. Here, I've written down where you should go.'

'Thank you,' Renton said and took the paper from him.

'The first of our men will be returning from the front in a few days. Members of the Durruti Column are expected imminently. They will need to be replaced while they rest here.'

'I was told that no more volunteers were needed.'

'I'm sure you were. But they are. They will be.'

'Well, that's . . . that's changed everything. Thank you.'

The man smiled and said, 'You'll soon come to understand that in Barcelona there are currently disputes over many issues: who we are fighting, why we are fighting, how we should fight, whether we should join the *Generalitat* or form our own. Whether we should be involved with the new Comite Central de Milicias, indeed whether, perhaps, we should even go so far as to engage in open combat with the *Generalitat*. The question of how many volunteers we should accept is a relatively recent issue we have begun to debate – and I'm glad to say there is still a great deal of life left in this discussion. Of course I try to represent as many of these arguments as I can.'

'You're a journalist?'

'There's a daily newspaper I have some responsibility for – the *Solidaridad Obrera*. Though this, of course, being Barcelona, is another matter of dispute. The other parties also have their own newspapers and report similar issues often in a conflicting way. The truth – the absolute truth, if such a commodity exists – has temporarily been exiled from our country. No doubt it will receive a hero's welcome on its return when the war is won.' The man lit a cigarette, then, belatedly, offered the packet to Renton who declined it.

'Would you let me buy you a drink?' Renton offered.

The man looked at his watch, then towards the searchlight again as if the answer lay in the patterns it had drawn in the sky and said, 'Yes. Why not. I'll share a drink with you.'

Renton followed the journalist as he moved quickly through the crowds. The man was greeted and questioned and congratulated by a number of the people they passed. He parried all of the demands on his attention with an equal firmness; if Renton had not known their destination he too would have been taken in by the man's impatience. It was clear that he had important matters to attend to and he set his face sternly to ward off anybody who threatened to take too much of his time. None of the interruptions warranted anything more than a slight reduction in their speed; their progress was never entirely halted.

In the small bar, the journalist drank with haste, each sip of wine a punctuation in another statement of intent, each statement parenthesised by a deep draw on his cigarette. Renton listened as the man said, 'You must first recognise that the PSUC and the POUM are fighting a war, whereas our ultimate goal is social revolution and we must organise accordingly. For the revolution to become fact we must demolish the three pillars of reaction: the church, the army and capitalism. The church has already been brought to account. Our revolutionary aspirations, by necessity, must wait until the war is won. We can't compete on every front.'

'And in practical terms?'

'Some collectivisation, though we proceed slowly here in that respect. We barter where we can. But, for those who are fighting, we have adopted libertarian principles in our militias. We cannot ask our men to swear allegiance to an officer they have had no say in appointing.'

'I understand that the militias are made up of volunteers from the unions?'

'Yes. Columns of volunteers and sympathisers which operate under the political control of CNT-FAI. These are funded by the factories and unions which we – as an organisation – control. In practical terms the militias are formed of small units, each of which elects a delegate to the war committee. The columns are commanded by political commissaries who appoint their own advisers – these are men, generally men, who have had some military training.'

'And the others?'

'The Communists are hand in glove with the *Generalitat*. They formulate their plans in the Hotel Colon. But the CNT-FAI control Barcelona – not the POUM or the PSUC.'

'I'd very much like to join you,' Renton said, but the journalist was now looking through the bar window at a woman who was staring in.

'This happens,' the journalist said. 'Women come to Barcelona for their own reasons, they sometimes bring weapons, and occasionally they bring food, and they join us and they are all welcomed as we welcome men. The revolution does not differentiate. It is blind to the sex of its participants.' He laughed. 'Which, as a good Anarchist, I feel I should applaud. But part of me . . .' He cupped his balls in his right hand and gave them a tug. 'Part of me will not comply with these noble intentions.'

'She looks lost,' Renton said.

'"Trail her, *muchacho* . . ."'

'I'm sorry?'

'Lorca. Quote Lorca to a woman and she will believe his words are yours. Poets should be cherished if only for this reason: "Trail her, *muchacho*, down every byway, and if you once catch her crying, or thinking it over, paint this on to her heart and spray it with glitter and tell her not to cry if she should stay single."'

The journalist put down his glass. Renton watched him walk out of the bar, approach the woman and bow and gesture towards the place in the room where he was standing. The woman nodded but refused his help in carrying her bags. Soon she was laying her belongings at Renton's feet as the journalist continued to question her and she continued to answer him. Renton was not introduced, but he was content to stand and listen to the two of them talk; the urgent questions of the man meeting considered responses. She would not be rushed. Renton found himself trying to read her mood through her tone of voice, her open-handed gestures which left her body unprotected, the sudden sparks of anger in her dark eyes which slowly softened to comprehension or forgiveness. She was, it seemed – as everybody was – just another source of information for the man from the *Solidaridad Obrera* which lent his curiosity legitimacy.

It was her lips Renton remembered when they parted later that evening. Her lips, he found himself thinking as he lay alone in a room of the Hotel Continental, were the shape of a heart, gently squashed flat.

London: September

Three days of rain had saturated Arthur Lawler's clothes. Since he had given up his room at the hotel he had had nowhere to dry his coat or his jacket; the gas supply had been disconnected from the vacant flat he had taken refuge in next door to Meredith's. Each time he returned there he expected to find his suitcase waiting for him outside the door, but so far he had remained undetected. He had been sleeping on a single mattress beneath the front window. He felt secure lying against the hem of the long curtains, but he dreamed recurrently that he was kissing the perfumed feet of a woman in a velvet dress.

Though he had occasionally been aware of men's voices on the other side of the wall, Lawler had not seen any of the crowd since the day at Brooklands two weeks before. He was surprised not to have heard Meredith or her dance-band music; she was a creature of regular habits and one of them was to rouse herself in the early afternoon by switching the radiogram on loud to accompany her first drink of the day. Each fed the other in lightening her mood and ridding her mind of the last foggy traces of the Evipan which she seemed always to need for sleep.

It was Lawler's hunger rather than the discomfort of his clothes, the lumpy mattress he was lying on, or his need for a shave that led to his decision to knock on Meredith's door and put himself at her mercy. He resolved to do it later when, courtesy of one of his bar tabs, he was no longer sober. Unlike Royle, he had never run up a tab before, but once he had set up the first and discovered how easy it was (a smile, a casual mention of delayed funds) he did the same in three other pubs, though he kept them all two or three miles apart to minimise the chances of the landlords running into each other and discovering his game.

Rolling over on to his back, Arthur Lawler stared up at the cobwebs woven in the cornices and Quinn's sage financial advice came to mind. Since he had become insolvent, each course of action was now determined solely by how effectively it served a means to an end – to drink, or food, or cigarettes. He had even allowed the barmaid of the Posts to buy him his lunch at the Lyons on the corner of Coventry Street. But he could barely taste the pilchards with the dry-mouthed shame he felt as he sat across the small basement table from the girl, listening to her bright, banal chatter, her plans for her afternoon off (a film called *Fury*), her guilt over not seeing her mother often enough. On and on and on she went, her voice chirruping in the huge room as the waitresses artlessly collected the plates and women with shopping bags came in to chat around them. Sometimes a man would arrive with a newspaper and drink tea and eat bread and margarine and then demand the bill with an impatience and pomposity the women never seemed to show.

Lawler had resisted the girl's shy insistence that the meagre meal they were sharing constituted a 'date'. It was a loan, nothing more, and one he would repay when his money came through. When she left him after lunch she gave him a quick peck on his cheek and he smelled the staleness of her breath. As she walked away to a late-afternoon showing at the Plaza, Arthur Lawler wondered whether he would ever be free of Meredith Kerr. He knew that his life had the potential of being so much simpler and a great deal happier. If he could break the tie perhaps the opportunity would even arise for him to plan for a day beyond the next, to make arrangements that entailed something more than the decision over which public house they were going to start the evening in. Despite Meredith's professed feelings for Kit Renton, life without her was unconscionable. She was his past and his present, so it was foolhardy of him to contemplate an existence with a simple, loving woman who would sometimes reach for his hand, occasionally show something in her eyes for him beyond indifference or irritation, and who would, at least for a year or so, love him.

Lawler sat up on the mattress, his head thick from the drink of the previous night. His intention of spending an evening sober had lasted until six-thirty when the dry sponge in his stomach had become an ache that he knew only alcohol would ease. He enjoyed the first Scotch of the evening more than he remembered enjoying a drink for years. He enjoyed it because he was drinking it sober, but he didn't remain sober for long, and since he woke he had been paying for it. With effort he found the will to get up and go to the damp-walled kitchen where he filled a cracked teacup with water, drained it, filled it again and dipped in his finger, which he then used to rub against his furry teeth. In the small cracked mirror glued to the geyser above the sink he saw that his unshavenness could now pass for a close-cropped beard. He walked trouserless to the bathroom and urinated, pulled the chain, covered his ears to protect his head from the din of the water crashing down from the cistern, then he returned to the living-room and removed his trousers from beneath the mattress where they were being pressed. They smelled damp, as did his jacket. He took his one remaining clean shirt from his suitcase, slid it out from the thin parcel of laundry paper, shook it out and put it on. He pinned on a collar, linked his cuffs and tied his tie. Returning to the mirror he saw that his parting remained respectably straight and, with his tie now tied under his beard, he was confronted by the image of a retired sea captain or, he judged, perhaps somebody less grand, like a Thames barge pilot. He had, after all, occasionally been accused by Meredith of spending too much of his life with his eyes locked on the horizon.

Lawler tidied away his hairbrush case into his suitcase, closed and locked it and put the case away in the cupboard. He returned to the front room and opened the curtains to be confronted not by the expected view but by a thick brown fog. The breeze was stirring it, causing it to eddy and rush in small pockets. He heard a fog alarm going off at the end of the street, then a police whistle. The nose of a tram pushed through the mist, and as it sailed past his window he saw a boy in the stark light of the top deck staring at him, their faces almost level. When the tram went on, the curtains of fog dropped down around its flanks.

Lawler went to the door and opened it carefully, locking the catch back and pulling the door shut behind him, wedging it closed with a pad of newspaper. He walked slowly down the first flight of twenty-seven stairs, more quickly down the next flight and at the bottom he skipped briskly across the chequer-tiled hallway, past the tall vault of letterboxes and out on to the Euston Road. He turned left and saw the headlights of a lorry, mustard-coloured in the fog. A car followed it slowly, tailed by a man on a cycle in a yellow waxed cape who was blowing a whistle to alert the motorists to his presence. The tall thin silhouettes of the streetlights petered away into the near distance. Like pairs of weak moons, the hanging globes of light made little impression on the dark. As Lawler picked his way along the street, shapes of objects loomed towards him, were revealed, understood and momentarily possessed by him, then recloaked by the fog, discarded. He carried the space around him like a swollen consciousness. As he walked on he came upon trees which were only trees for the few moments he could reach out and touch them. When they were behind him they were as insubstantial as dreams. Birds had lost their fear of him: he was a ghost, but without menace.

Two dark smudges, swift charcoal sketches of men in black coats, approached him. It was only when they were in his world and fully rendered that he saw it was Royle with a shorter, elderly man who seemed annoyed to have been discovered in Royle's company. The man was holding a large white handkerchief over the lower part of his face. A moon of yellow filth marked the position of his mouth.

'Arthur,' Royle greeted him. 'I wondered when you were going to show up.' He smiled, and as an afterthought took his right hand from the pocket of his mac and patted him on the shoulder. The man with him continued on, saying, 'I'll go in. I presume there's still somebody with her?'

'Yes. Quinn's there,' Royle assured him, and the man disappeared.

Lawler stood with his old friend and watched him lean his back against a brick wall, sigh heavily and bang his head back softly three times against it.

'God,' Royle said. 'God.'

'What's happened?' Lawler asked him and Royle laughed. 'What?' Lawler pressed.

'You know it's almost a relief. Quite a relief. To see you, I mean. I was wondering how I was going to tell you.' Royle had the garrulousness that came with the first drinks of the day. A woman pushed a pram past them and Lawler wondered if this was what was meant when people talked of the moments before death: the first of a rapid parade of images provoking a regret for what was being left behind.

'Tell me what?' Lawler said.

'I suppose we shouldn't do it here. Let's go and have a . . .'

'Tell me what?' Lawler asked again.

'Meredith. She's . . . she's quite ill. Quite not well.' Neither phrase to Royle adequately conveyed the feel of the fevered few days; the fear he felt as the doctor was called. But there was no need to burden Arthur with any of the details. It wasn't his fault.

'The old man's Bowden's doctor. It's quite all right. Bowden's paying for it all. He's not a quack.'

The fear of losing his love crowded into Lawler's mind, but it was almost a relief. At least now he could begin to face up to it. Fighting it, turning away from it, had driven him nearly mad. Perhaps he was a little mad. Lawler found himself thinking of the barmaid in the Posts and her lipstick, her cheap perfume and her awful plum-coloured coat, her gullibility and her hope; and he considered how incredible it was that the two women belonged to the same sex. Beauty, he had come to believe, was a species all of its own.

And then he was running and passing the woman in the pram who sensed danger and turned the pram towards the road. Lawler could hear Royle behind him, shouting, 'Don't go up. Wait for Pugh to finish. Arthur . . . Arthur . . .'

But Lawler ignored him and ran in through the hallway while Royle chased after him, still calling him back. Lawler was soon at Meredith's front door, shoving it open, striding along the short corridor and pushing into the stale, stifling sweetness of the unventilated living-room. There was a faint formal odour of a hospital chemical and a foul smell of decay that the filthy plates on the floor contributed to but were not solely responsible for. Quinn was lounging back on the sofa in his waistcoat and shirtsleeves, smoking a cigar. He had a glass of beer balanced on the arm of the sofa; the tall brown bottle of Watneys was on the floor. He was reading a racing paper while warming his stinking, stockinged feet in front of the gas fire. Having looked up and established who had arrived, Quinn looked away again as if the door had been blown open by the wind.

Meredith's bedroom door was closed. Lawler turned the handle but hesitated when he heard somebody call, 'Not now!' from the inside. Nevertheless, he couldn't stop himself going in, although the moment he was inside the room he wished that he had. Pugh hadn't taken off his dark overcoat. He was wearing white surgical gloves. The lump of dressings in them was red. Not the bright fresh blood Lawler saw each time he cut himself shaving, the pulsing new blood that augured health and vitality. To Lawler, this looked like the dull, stagnant blood that prefigured death.

'Not now, please,' the old man said again in a more measured voice. This time he stared like a mesmerist, pressing the meaning directly into Lawler's brain, forcing him back and out of the room. When he had closed the door he realised he hadn't seen Meredith, so transfixed had he been by the blood on the old man's hands.

Quinn licked his thumb, turned a page of his newspaper and said, 'Why don't you sod off out of here and leave the man to his work.'

'Arthur, he does know what he's doing,' Royle said from somewhere behind him.

'Yes,' Lawler said. Then, 'Does he?' and felt a hand on his back guiding him out of the flat, down the stairs and into the brown fog again.

They passed a policeman lighting a fog flare. The flame hissed and leaped in the barrel. Lawler felt the burn in his throat and tasted it. Even when they were standing against the bar at the Posts and Royle was holding the glass to his lips, helping him drink, he could still taste the acid fur of fog and flare on the roof of his mouth.

'Come on, old man, easy. Easy . . .' Royle cajoled, rubbing his back and at the same time explaining to the barmaid, 'Arthur's had a bit of a jolt. Better keep them coming, love.'

When Lawler caught the barmaid watching him he expected sympathy but he saw only anger. Perhaps it was his beard or his red eyes – or the dreadful pallor of his skin. Or perhaps it was his conversation. He seemed to have forgotten how to ask questions of people and offer opinions and smile at jokes and pretend to belong. All he could talk about was the blood on the doctor's hands.

'You see the point is,' Royle was saying. '. . . Arthur. Look at me.' Arthur complied. 'I think it would be better if you stayed away for a while. Do you understand? What I'm suggesting is that it would be best for all concerned if you kept out of it. That way, if anything occurs – and God forbid it does – but if Meredith does take a turn for the worse, the fewer of us around, the better. I mean Pugh and Bowden have presumably cooked up something between them but I hesitate to . . .'

'I need to use the lavatory,' Lawler said.

'Of course, old man. Of course.'

Lawler listened to the distant voices in the bar as he leaned into the porcelain stall and unbuttoned his fly. Nothing had ever occupied so much of his mind as the act of pulling out his penis and pointing it at the urinal. His head was burdened by something that was blocking the rest of his thoughts. As though a spanner had been dropped into the cogs of a machine, the wheels were straining to turn but the obstacle was preventing them from doing so, and the pressure was building and building, pushing at the weakest parts, looking for a release.

He pissed and sighed. Straightening up, he returned to the bar to find Royle leaning across it and pouring his charm over the barmaid. She was attempting to maintain both her dignity and her sovereignty over the lounge bar by adopting what she considered to be a haughty but alluring pose. She polished a pint mug with a corner of her apron and the white linen corkscrewed inside the glass like a mouse in a jar.

'Here he is!' Royle called with such enthusiasm that Lawler waited for him to follow it up by striking up a chorus of 'For He's a Jolly Good Fellow'. Instead, Royle anchored Arthur to the bar with an arm round his shoulders and asked, 'Feeling better, old chum?'

'Yes, better.'

'Good show.' Royle winked at the barmaid and said, 'I was telling Deirdre here that we were at school together. That right, Arthur?'

'Yes.'

'But Arthur was always the clever one. He was always working away while the rest of us were . . . I don't know what.'

'Up to no good, I shouldn't wonder,' Deirdre offered.

'Yes. Absolutely. Up to no good. No good indeed.' Royle stopped and scented something on the air. 'I don't expect you could frighten us up some food, could you?' The glass sandwich-dome at the end of the bar was empty.

'I don't know about that. We stop serving at half past one. The governor likes to let the girl in the kitchen go off then or he has to pay her for another hour.'

'We're not looking for anything elaborate, are we, Arthur? Just some cheese. A couple of slices of bread. Margarine? Some pickled onion. Eh?'

'I'm not sure about that.'

'But we're starving. Particularly Arthur. I mean anybody can see the man's not eaten a square meal for days.'

At this Deirdre weakened and offered, '. . . I think we've got some beetroot – pickled beetroot – I'm sure I could find some bread.'

'That'll do the job.' Royle rubbed his hands. 'Fetch us some pickled beetroot, a few slices of bread and some good strong cheese. That all right for you, Arthur? . . . We'd be very grateful, Deirdre.

We'd be more grateful than you could ever imagine.' Royle leaned towards her and whispered in her ear. Deirdre giggled and offered a small curtsy and said, 'I'll see what I can do. Why don't you two gentlemen take a seat and I'll fetch it over for you.'

'Good girl, and if we see the governor we'll make a point of letting him know what a good little worker he's got on his hands. Won't we, Arthur?'

Deirdre went off happily, charmed by Royle's valueless promises.

In the window seat, behind the circular copper-topped table, Lawler and Royle sat in silence. Royle seemed to have expended his reserves of energy and bonhomie in coercing the barmaid to find them some food. He stared gloomily towards the bar, breaking off only to peer into his diminishing measure of Scotch. He picked up a spent match from the stone ashtray and flicked the tiny black head from it with his thumbnail. It chinked on the glass lampshade of a bar light. 'I suppose you muddle along,' he said dully, picking at his teeth with the matchstick, 'and you don't pay much heed to the future, but you think everything will somehow . . . somehow fall right for you. Arthur?'

Hearing his name, Lawler nodded. He wasn't listening to the words Billy Royle was using but he found the gentle tone of his voice quite soothing.

'. . . because at heart you're not a . . . not a bad chap really. And then something goes off and you dismiss it as . . . fate, I suppose: *That's just fate*, you tell yourself, but you convince yourself that because you're not a bad chap at heart, fate will leave you alone for a while. But it doesn't. Once fate has found you, it tends to keep on . . . knocking.' Royle looked over his shoulder at the fog outside the window. 'Doesn't it? . . . I suppose we could go and see Wilson. I find tormenting old Wilson always puts me in better spirits. I suppose that's something you learn at school.' He smiled wearily and fondly and said, '. . . Before the booze, before you discover what that can do for you, you learn the . . .' Another fog alarm ignited on the street. A woman came into the bar chased by a ghost shadow of mist. When the automatic arm yanked the door shut behind her, the wisps of mist melted. '. . . I couldn't bear to go to prison, could you?'

'I don't know.'

'You're a strange fellow sometimes, Arthur. You say the strangest things.'

'But why *should* you go to prison?' It was a mark of his state of mind that all Lawler could deduce was that somehow Royle had taken responsibility for his bar tabs. No other misdemeanour seemed remotely likely to have any bearing on either of them.

'Look out,' Royle said, happy again. 'Here's Deirdre.'

The barmaid ducked under the bar and came to stand angrily at their table. Her face was flushed and she was breathing heavily.

'Where's the grub?' Royle asked.

'There's no *grub*,' she said, crossing her arms.

'Why not?'

'You've got me into trouble, you have. With the governor.'

'Surely not!' Royle's indignation suggested he could imagine nothing worse. 'Hear that, Arthur?'

Arthur didn't seem to be hearing anything so Royle said, 'Tell us what happened.'

'Well, I goes to the kitchen and I gets out the bread and I starts cutting the bread with the bread knife and he comes in, the governor does, and he asks me what I expect I'm doing and I tells him I expect I'm making some lunch for some gentlemen in the lounge bar and he shouldn't worry because I'm not asking the girl to do it . . .' Deirdre checked behind her for the governor and lowered her voice. '. . . and he ever so politely asks me if I can tell the time, and he's sarcastic like he can be sometimes when he's had a bad day . . .' The weight of emotion this provoked in the barmaid caused her to break off and fan her face with her hand.

Royle, misinterpreting her response as excitement rather than the terror of losing her job, prompted, 'And, in return, you said . . . ?'

Deirdre stiffened and said, 'You know, you aren't half as smart as you think you are. You aren't half . . .'

'Look, my dear, I was only trying to put myself in your place,' Royle offered. '. . . Arthur, tell her. I think Deirdre believes I'm amusing myself at her expense.'

'Deirdre!' Lawler announced, remembering at last. 'Of course: Deirdre.'

'See?' She said to Royle. 'He remembers now who it was bought him pilchards on toast for his lunch and then was left to fend for herself all afternoon.'

'You know her, Arthur?'

'Yes. I'm sorry. Deirdre. I owe you money.'

'No, you don't owe me anything. Besides, we weren't talking about a girl being let down, were we? We were talking about a girl set to lose her job on account of trying to be good to some customers.'

'Of course we were. And whether or not Arthur is in your debt, we can't have you in the governor's bad books, can we?' Royle drained his glass and slammed it with some force on to the metal of the table top. 'Call him. Tell him one of his customers would like a word with him.'

'He won't like that.'

'I'll take full responsibility. Where is he?'

'He's having his lunch upstairs. He always has his lunch with the girl who does the food. It's the last thing she does before she goes off. After she's washed her pots she has her lunch with the governor. But it's on her own time.'

'Upstairs, you say?'

'In the front. In the function room . . . he won't thank you for disturbing him.'

'Righty ho.' Royle found the energy to spring to his feet, cross the short space to the bar, throw up the flap and march through the door marked PRIVATE. Deirdre had long since learned not to argue with Royle, just as she had accepted that from one week to the next he would forget who she was. Pubs, after all, were one and the same to Billy Royle. Each warm, small, cigarette-brown snug bar merging into the next, every old man in the corner nursing his bottle of Blue Bass, the same man with the same story to tell: the death of a beloved dog, mate or missus. And every barmaid the same woman withholding the same gift: passing through the beaded curtain of the George to emerge into the light and shadows of the Crown and Sceptre.

Deirdre prided herself on remembering the face of every man and every woman she had served. She interpreted them as her mother read the leaves left in a teacup. But her readings were equally prosaic – does she or does she not have a future with this person in front of her? In Lawler's case (the man she knew only as 'Arthur', which she pronounced shrilly, like a command), she had hopes. She had always had a soft spot for him because, unlike the flash con man Billy Royle, or the beautiful, bad-tempered tart he was always with, or the big bully in the nice black suits who tried to touch her up when she fetched the glasses, she believed that Arthur had heart. He knew how to say please and thank you and when he looked at her he did it as though he meant it. He couldn't see it, but Deirdre could, and as far as she was concerned, they were killing him, stealing his goodness, taking his life away from him and using it up for themselves because without the booze they had nothing left inside to light them. What a sad and lonely man he looked now. Deirdre couldn't be angry with him any longer.

'You look like you need taking in hand,' she said and felt that she may have used the line before. Perhaps it was the one that had first led them to the Corner House and the pilchards and the film about the wrongly convicted man she had tried to watch through the tears when the awfulness of her circumstances overwhelmed her, as she occasionally allowed it to do.

Arthur Lawler looked up into the face that was no longer the face of a stranger. He was crying for the simple reason that he often cried when he was very drunk and a woman was kind to him. Deirdre took his hands and soothed him, saying, 'Now that's quite enough of that . . . there, there . . .' She offered more words of sympathy and understanding and gradually Lawler succumbed, relinquishing his misery into her care. For the first time he heard a canary chirrup from the snug bar and it took him to a world of trees with summer-dry leaves and branch shadows cast on the ground and a warm tartan rug, all of which somehow spelled happiness.

A bell rang at the bar. Deirdre reluctantly pulled away from Lawler and caught a whiff of his damp clothes as he shifted on the seat. 'I've got to go back and mind the bar. Why don't you come and talk to me up there,' she said, offering her hand. Lawler took it, and she led him to a stool at the end of the bar. He watched her smile as she served the young man who had been waiting, diffusing his impatience with coy remarks about his 'missing her' and him 'being jealous of her sitting with another man'. In short, building a temporary and convincing world in which she and the customer happily cohabited – a place to which she had now returned. Nobody could have resisted her. When the young man left the bar, smiling and charmed, Deirdre checked to see that the governor had not sneaked down into the snug. She then looked along into the public and, having established she was alone behind the bar, snatched a glass from the shelf and pumped three Scotches in rapid succession into it. Lawler watched the chamber in the optic empty and flood, empty and flood, empty and flood, and found the golden Scotch sailing through the air towards him.

'Here,' Deirdre said, pressing the glass into his hand. 'And make it last. And if anybody asks, you paid for it before.'

'Thank you.'

'I'm not going to make a habit of this, Arthur. Because I don't believe that drink holds the answer to any question I've ever heard asked, but there's times when you need to save the questions and the answers until later. So make it last . . . love.'

Lawler heard the endearment ringing like a bell. It called him back from the blissful nothing into the something world where an indulgent woman with a woman's good sense was making a claim on him. He was saved by Royle emerging from the door marked PRIVATE with the short, pig-faced, stout governor in tow, followed by a consumptive-looking girl in a meat-juice-stained white apron carrying two large plates of sandwiches. What Lawler had taken to be a brass metal disc in the crook of the governor's arm was revealed as the lid of a jar of pickled onions as he put it down on the bar. The landlord brushed his hands together and offered a handshake to Lawler along with his sympathies. Quite what for wasn't clear but Royle was quick to use the momentum of the man's arrival to steer him along and away into the snug. The girl followed in his wake, which meant that, shortly after the frenzied arrival, Lawler and Royle were alone again and silent at the bar. Two plates of sandwiches were before them, a large jar of pickled onions and the governor's own device for withdrawing the onions from the brine: a long silver fork with a spring mechanism triggered by the press of the thumb which ejected the onions from the sharp, barbed tines.

Deirdre watched them as they ate the sandwiches in silence, Royle gently prompting Lawler to take another mouthful each time he had finished the last. She was surprised to see that the good-looking man seemed genuinely to care for him. Lawler occasionally glimpsed the barmaid wagging a finger in his direction and this image soon became a part of the eternal afternoon: a barmaid telling him to 'make it last', the stately figure of a straight-backed cyclist, a woman pushing a pram shrouded by the yellow-brown fog, alarms going off, and a man in an overcoat holding a handful of red bandages.

Or perhaps Lawler had misinterpreted it. Late in the afternoon, as he lay in his damp coat, alone and cold and frightened on his mattress, he wondered if what the man was holding in his hands was all that remained of a tiny, mercifully short, life.

The Aragón Front

A seventeen-year-old boy, standing strong and thin like a sapling on the hill, was addressing the new militia unit to which Kit Renton now belonged. His name was Antonio and he had called the group together because a sharpshooter had just fired at them and none of them had known how to react. With a carefully judged irony, the youth was explaining to the new recruits that when they heard the sound of a shot they should take immediate evasive action. Soon enough, he assured them, keeping their heads down would become second nature, but until it did they should take the precaution of diving to the ground every time they heard the sound of a bullet. Gesturing towards the distant plumes of artillery smoke, Antonio reported that the fighting was intense, the lines were yet to be established, and, until they were, the snipers could be roaming anywhere. The eight men and one woman travelling with Renton accorded the boy the respect he had earned from them during the two weeks of basic training they had just completed at the Espartacus barracks in Barcelona.

Antonio had won them over by his open-faced honesty and his expertise in stripping down and reassembling the Lewis gun, liberated by him from the Sant Andreu depot and kept under lock and key in a metal cabinet at the barracks. During such demonstrations Antonio was characteristically to be seen hunched like a shepherd over the oiled shanks of the weapon, a cigarette between his bared teeth and his right eye squinting against the smoke. He concluded each performance with a flourish – slapping the cartridge pan on top of the weapon, jumping to his feet and flicking the cigarette over the heads of his audience.

Early in the training period Eduardo, a railwayman who had fallen out with his Communist colleagues and joined the Anarchists to spite them, established himself as the spokesman of the unit. Renton he chose as his lieutenant largely because the Englishman's diffidence meant that he posed little threat to his authority. The sole woman in the group, Justina, had been a young sales assistant at the El Siglo store. It was Justina whom Kit Renton had met in the bar on his first night in Barcelona. She had been given the same advice as he had by the journalist, and she and Renton found themselves reporting to the same barracks the following morning. She was curt with him. He was an outsider, his motives suspect. The oldest man in the unit, Jesus, intense, fastidious and hard of hearing, drew Renton aside on the first night and sombrely informed him of his occupation, a mason, which he clearly believed carried sufficient weight for Renton to award him immediate respect. His overriding concern during the training had been that he would miss hearing something important which meant that it was often his voice that was heard shouting Eduardo's down.

The others revealed themselves more cautiously. The huge, blond German, who was always late for training, said very little during the first three days except to himself. His name was Wertzel and he sealed his reputation for unreliability on the day the unit left for the front by arriving just as the train was drawing out of the station. He was dragging a large canvas bag behind him which, with great force of will, he somehow managed to heft into the moving carriage before grabbing the handrail, losing his footing and hopping in lengthening strides as the train gathered speed. Just as it seemed he would fall beneath the wheels, he found the strength to hoist himself into the carriage, where he slid to a stop at Justina's feet like a huge fish landed in a small boat. Gasping for breath, he stood grinning, and dusted himself down. He then opened the canvas bag and reverently drew out an ancient metal breastplate which he strapped against his chest before falling back, exhausted, into the seat that Jesus had vacated to help him into the carriage.

After an hour on the slow train they disembarked and were marshalled to the rear truck in a line of three that was waiting for them beside the railway. The convoy's progress to the front was regularly interrupted by roadblocks at which the driver was ordered to display his papers to the guards representing the elected committee of whichever village they were attempting to pass through. The committee men, often ludicrous and always pompous, pointing ancient shotguns and wearing bandoliers of rusty cartridges, tended barely to glance at the passes. But, keen to be seen taking their responsibilities seriously, they greeted the lorries with a hostility as unwarranted as the friendliness they later exhibited when they waved them through. The Durruti Column, Antonio explained as they continued their sweltering journey towards the front, had liberated each village they came to as they pushed west from Barcelona towards their ultimate goal, Saragossa. As they purged each village of Fascists and tested the loyalty of the occasional pocket of Civil Guards they encountered, the revolution advanced with them until their progress was halted by exhaustion just short of Saragossa. It was the task of the new militias coming out from Barcelona to reinforce and renew the attack, the aim still being to liberate Saragossa. 'Which we will achieve!' Wertzel announced, banging his breastplate with his fist before falling silent in embarrassment.

Renton had not forgotten Madame Delouche's advice to listen and learn, but he considered himself no more equipped as a soldier than he had been when he arrived in Barcelona. Although he had never questioned Antonio's abilities or character, Renton had been dismayed to find that his training sessions consisted of little more than the boy leading them in lunatic marches round the Barcelona Public Gardens (they moved in short shuffling steps with rapid turns round the flower beds and unexpected halts which caused them to cannon into one another). They had discussed neither tactics nor first aid. They had seen neither working rifles nor pistols, and the one time they attempted to debate the principles behind the war the discussion quickly degenerated into a litany of the crimes and cruelties perpetrated by the Fascists. Calls for Antonio to explain why none of the so-called allies, particularly the French, had done anything to help the Republican cause had been met by the boy explaining that they read the same newspapers as him and therefore knew as much as he did.

Now they stood, disorientated and silent, in twos and threes on the hillside at the edge of a meagre village chilled by its altitude, which comprised a handful of small stone dwellings huddled round an ugly stone church. The truncated bell-tower pointed like a crooked finger towards the weak sun. Despite its proximity to the fighting, the village remained unscathed and the villagers dawdling about their business rarely glanced towards the front. A group of filthy militiamen, hollow-eyed with fatigue, lolled against a wall smoking, waiting for transport back to Barcelona. The new recruits watched them with respect. A man whose age was impossible to judge due to his beard and the mud on his face, raised himself painfully from the ground, yanked down the wadded, filth-stiffened cloth of his trousers, squatted and shitted a caramel-coloured liquid stream on to the mud. Sickened, Renton turned to face the plain below them and saw the lines of supply vehicles and ambulances waiting to advance under the cover of darkness. They sheltered among a cluster of roofless, smoke-stained, whitewashed farms and huts. A mule train was being driven slowly between them laden with barrels of water. On the hills beyond the plain, the blank vegetation of the hills was broken by the brown gashes of trenches, pale outcrops of limestone and the dull yellow walls of hastily sandbagged positions. Above those positions, which had been established on the crowns of four of the hills, a red or red-and-black flag flew. A number of small fires were burning and the thin smoke clung to the hills. Occasionally a fire-fight broke out, and short, sheer columns of earth and richer plumes of white smoke flared up over the location. Even from the distance he stood from the action, Kit Renton was chilled by the din of rifle fire and the metallic clatter of machine guns. He squinted against the sun to see the enemy but all he could distinguish was the occasional flash of a figure making a sudden stooped dash from one piece of cover to the next.

Since their arrival at the staging-post, Antonio had been moving through the group, calming their excitement and assuaging their fear. When he reached Renton he told him, 'The positions are changing by the hour. It is imperative that we move forward and provide support.' He clasped the Englishman's shoulder. 'Tonight, when it is dark, we will follow the supply lorries across the plain. It is less hazardous. We will be facing enough danger when we get there. But the plain is booby-trapped with tripwires so we must be cautious.' Antonio consulted his watch. 'Soon it is siesta time.' The boy was blushing. Sometimes the burden he carried overwhelmed him.

'Even the soldiers sleep in the afternoon?'

'Of course.'

Renton, looking towards the militiamen, asked, 'And how long have they been fighting here?'

'Three weeks. We took Sietano, then lost it, then again we took it – but the fear is that we may again lose control.'

'And casualties?'

'High. Very high.' Antonio turned to face the convoys on the plain. 'Both the buses and the ambulances will transport the casualties back to Barcelona.'

'I see. I'd imagined they were bringing supplies.'

'Some of them, yes.'

'Is this your first visit to the front?' Renton asked him.

'No . . . no.' And remembering his experience, the boy added, 'Acknowledge your fear. It may be that which keeps you alive.'

'I don't feel prepared,' Renton admitted. 'I'm afraid that I won't know what to do.'

'You will.'

'How?'

'Look for cover and stay low until you are sure you are safe. There are many good men with experience fighting for us. Watch them. They will lead you. Within hours you will know what you need to know. And we are progressing. The deserters are crossing to our lines – not from us. Now find somewhere to rest. Save your strength for tonight.'

Antonio strode away from the village with a shouted promise that he would return before dark with supplies. As he vanished over the prow of the hill another shot rang out and this time, without exception, all the members of his unit threw themselves to the ground, provoking an immediate gale of laughter from the militiamen sitting against the wall. When Renton raised his head from the dirt he saw a tired man waving a *porrón*, beckoning him over to join them in their drinking. Eduardo was watching, monitoring his response. Renton declined the offer, choosing to join his comrades as they settled behind the cover of a low wall. Some were smoking, some had closed their eyes, trying for a few moments of sleep.

'We don't even have rifles,' Eduardo said, breaking into the embarrassed silence. He shrugged and asked, 'What do they expect us to do?' Rifles, he knew, would have made them no less impotent, but Eduardo's protest salvaged their pride after the humiliation. Even Jesus, the mason, nodded his agreement and, within moments, their mood had changed. Give them rifles, Wertzel announced, and they would launch their own offensive against the Fascists. 'God help them all! The bastards won't know what has hit them when this unit gets its rifles.'

'Antonio will provide,' Justina announced briskly. Having claimed the filthy mattress which lay behind the wall she was now unpacking her small knapsack. She first pulled out a hand-mirror and, after checking her tidy hair in it, she turned it, handle-up, and balanced it on a flat stone which protruded from the wall to form a shallow shelf. The others watched her with fascination as she established her home: taking out a squared white bedsheet, a water bottle, a candle, a flint lighter and a bulging, floral-patterned cotton toilet bag which she placed on the ledge beside the mirror. Finally she unrolled her thick grey blanket, stood up, shook it out, knelt down and rolled it up again. 'Well,' she said, embarrassed by the attention, 'what else should we do? I like to make myself comfortable. Don't you?'

Eduardo laughed at the absurdity, prompting Wertzel and the others to join in. Jesus, who had moved a short distance away from them and was now squatting on his heels facing them, watched with incredulity. With Antonio gone, he now had nobody to turn to to make sense of the growing hysteria.

'We should post a sentry,' Eduardo suddenly announced, looking round for volunteers, careful not to catch the eye of the militiamen by the wall. 'Or a lookout.'

'I'll do it,' Jesus said, scrambling to his feet. 'I'll be the sentry.' He launched himself towards Eduardo, stood too close to him, and waited, breathing heavily, for further instructions. Embarrassed, Eduardo smiled and gently suggested, 'Why don't you keep a watch above the wall?'

'Of course.'

'. . . But be careful of sharpshooters.'

'Sharpshooters. Yes. Of course, I'll be careful.'

'And . . .' Eduardo improvised, growing in confidence, 'alert us to any enemy activity.' He nodded, pleased with himself. 'We can then take it in turns. After an hour you will be relieved.'

'Yes. An hour,' Jesus said, and made a salute.

'Yes, we'll take it in turns, Eduardo,' Justina said loudly, combing her hair. 'And when we see a Fascist running towards us we'll throw some of this dry shit at him and he'll run away again.'

One of the militiamen laughed, digging his elbow into the ribs of the dozing man next to him to make him pay attention to the novices.

'Would you suggest we do something different?' Eduardo asked.

Justina shrugged and tugged the hairs from the bristles of her brush. When she released them the tiny black bale sailed away on the breeze towards the plain. Renton watched it until it was invisible to him.

'No,' Jesus said, 'Eduardo is right. We must organise ourselves. Instil some discipline. It is very easy under circumstances such as these to lose all sense of purpose and discipline.'

'As if you would know,' Justina said, this time more quietly.

'Thank you, Jesus. Now begin your watch,' Eduardo ordered. 'Justina will relieve you in an hour's time.'

Justina swore and Jesus took up his position by testing his weight against the low wall and leaning his shoulder against it. Every few seconds he raised himself to his full height and stole a look above it. 'All clear,' he reported shyly and Eduardo rewarded him with a thumbs-up.

Renton tugged his knapsack from the bottom of the pile, moved away from the group and found a space to stretch out. Using his sack as a pillow he lay down and settled his shoulders until he had achieved a relatively comfortable position on the cold earth. Then he closed his eyes and tried to sleep. But, despite his exhaustion, the din from the hills and the nervous bursts of laughter from Justina held sleep at bay. As had become a habit of his since he arrived in Barcelona, Renton took himself to his room in Berners Street and his cramped bed and his shelves of books. Slowly he added the details: the cooker, the rug, the gas mantle, the sound of rain. Always the sound of rain. The porter in the lavish maroon coat with gold epaulettes standing beneath the canopy of the hotel across the street, shuffling his feet against his boredom and the cold.

A shout woke him. He sat upright and looked at his watch. He had been asleep for an hour and a half. Orientating himself by the hour, he filled in the details of the location and the circumstances: Spain, war, the cause, the sacrifice, the fear. Simultaneously his deeper consciousness asserted itself; the limitations of his identity slipped into place and finally the physical manifestations – thirst, cold, hunger. He sat up and tugged the cork from his water-bottle with his teeth. The liquid was warm and stale and tasted of Barcelona. He felt it irrigate the dry leather of his mouth. As he drank he heard shouts from the village and the petulant barks of hungry dogs. A low chuckling thud of ordnance and the shrill cackle of machine-gun fire resonated from the hills. Thunder rambled around the sky. The temperature had fallen sharply, wisps of mist were tangled like white gauze in the bushes. Behind him the other members of the unit had gathered. Renton knew them well enough to discern the excitement in their voices. Justina laughed shrilly, Wertzel laughed too to keep her company, even Jesus chattered at a speed and lightness he hadn't heard before. He corked the water-bottle, pressed the stopper home with the heel of his palm and joined the semicircle hunched behind the wall. Justina looked up and offered him a smile. The sleep had charged Renton with optimism. He felt grateful for the new friendships he had forged. Antonio was at the centre of the group, squatting on his heels. In front of him was a pile of old dull-grey rifles.

'. . . Now, please take a rifle each,' Antonio was saying, picking up the nearest one and squinting down the barrel. He lifted the butt higher and a small pebble rolled out. In turn, each of them came forward and took possession of a rifle. Without exception, the weight of it was a surprise to them. Among the men this immediately translated the process into a contest of strength. Only Wertzel, who was the last to draw his rifle, retrieved it without suffering the indignity of using both hands.

Awkward with the adopted weapons at their sides, they waited for further instructions, not knowing whether they should touch them, stroke them, or, like one of the older men, treat them with immediate disdain. At the back of their minds was the inevitable question: are these rifles loaded, and, if so, are they safe?

'Good,' Antonio said, looking around the group. 'These rifles, as you will see, are not new. They originate, I understand, from Russia. But I am assured that these fine weapons will suit their purpose. They have all been repaired and made even better than new at Sabadell. And if their barrels seem a little short please do not assume they are in any way inferior. Now . . .'

'But why are the barrels short?' Justina asked.

'That is not important,' Jesus said.

'It is important to me. Antonio, why are the barrels short?'

'Please. Let Antonio explain to us how we use these weapons, we don't have time for such details.'

Justina rounded on him. 'I want to know why the barrel of my rifle is short! Now if you let Antonio answer, then he can continue the lesson – or would you prefer that we argue between ourselves until the night falls?'

'The barrels are short because they split when they were fired.' The explanation came from one of the militiamen who had crept up silently and was now standing behind them making no attempt to use the cover of the wall. Antonio nodded in deference to him.

'Thank you,' Justina said, glowering at Jesus and turning her back on him. She looked at her truncated weapon with distrust.

'Do not rely on these weapons. They will jam when you have most need of them.'

'So. Back to throwing shit, my friends,' Justina said.

'You talk too much. And you don't listen. This is not Barcelona. When you have seen a few of your friends die then you will listen.' The militiaman, having thus pronounced, walked stiffly away.

At nightfall Antonio called them together. Following his instructions, they gathered their kit, shouldered their rifles and set off in single file down the narrow, winding track towards the sierra. Renton found himself following Justina. As they negotiated the track none of them spoke, they were intent on proving themselves equal to this first act of war and carried with them the gloomy prediction of the militiaman. Each of them wondered who would be the first to fall. Renton felt numb with cold and fear. As he tensed his shoulders in anticipation of a bullet, a shiver racked his body. He sensed a threat from every approaching shape he could not immediately identify. Only when he had reached the convoy did he relax a little. The familiarity of the lorry daubed with the initials of the FAI reassured him that somewhere out there were others committed to the same cause. He had begun to feel that the fellow members of Antonio's unit were the only ones left fighting the Fascists. He watched Justina and the others looking around them at the huge arena of war. Renton tried to pick out the shape of the village they had left behind but even the tower of the church was swallowed by the broad black shadow of the hill. Ahead of them the fighting had ceased and more small fires had been lit against the chill of the night. Already some of the trucks were moving off behind thin beams of light. The headlights of another convoy were visible as it approached from the east.

Somebody shouted a command in the darkness. A diesel engine fired and idled noisily, then another and another. More shouts to the left and right of them, rapid shadow movement, and barked orders to them to climb on to the back of the nearest truck and hold tight. In the confusion Antonio was nowhere to be seen but Renton obeyed the call and found himself sitting next to Justina in a covered truck stacked high with wooden crates. Justina lit her lighter and Renton saw the anticipation in her face. When the flame was extinguished and the red coal of her cigarette glowed, Renton felt the gentle pressure of her thigh against his. Neither of them spoke as the truck bumped across the plain towards the battle.

Brighton: The Same Day

Immediately after they had passed through the turnstiles and on to the damp boards of the West Pier, Harry Bowden took Meredith's arm. For a moment, she was touched by the caring gesture, but seeing him staring down through the gaps at the grey sea below, she realised he was seeking comfort, not giving it. They had been in Brighton for three days. Bowden had organised the holiday so that Meredith could continue her convalescence by the sea. He had done it without any reference to her but Meredith didn't protest. Since the day at Brooklands she had become a model of subservience. It was just another role to her, and one which she enjoyed playing. Checking almost all of her natural impulses prevented her from feeling bored. She no longer hated herself quite so much. And at least she had a self, unlike Arthur Lawler, who she pitied because increasingly he seemed to exist only in the reflection of others.

When she had fallen ill after the botched abortion she had been grateful for Royle's and Bowden's discretion and care. It was through Bowden that Pugh had been found and Pugh had saved her life. Neither Bowden nor Royle had pressed her about the paternity; both seemed afraid that the responsibility may have lain with the other. Meredith didn't know and didn't much care. As soon as she had suspected she was pregnant she had acted. Bringing the child of either of them into the already dark world was unacceptable. This was the rationale she employed to harden her heart to the emotional consequences. She refused to allow the subsequent hormonal tide to soften her defences. When she had a child it would be with a man she loved. And that child would be born from a moment of mutual pleasure. He or she would be loved and the world would be a better place for that child being in it.

Meredith and Bowden walked in silence, sheltered from the westerly breeze by the wood-and-glass partition against which the deckchairs were lined. Bowden's grip was tight on Meredith's arm. A Punch and Judy man in a damp grey suit was unpacking his candy-striped tent; a bandsman carrying a tuba passed them on his way to the concert hall; the pier photographer sat sleeping on a wooden chair while a monkey in a tiny fez kept a fussy guard at his feet. On this wet September Friday there were few other visitors.

Bowden had never had any small-talk. His conversation was entirely functional, which suited Meredith. It gave her more time for Kit Renton. In her fever she had constructed in her mind a cheerful, colourful cocoon for them to meet. One which she could enter in a second; a warm place where the feeling of his every touch was channelled to her heart.

'This'll do,' Bowden said, stopping just short of the entrance to the pier's theatre.

Meredith looked around them. As far as she knew, they had come out for a walk before lunch, there had been no other purpose. Bowden leaned his wrists on the railing, laced his fingers and looked down at the plane of the sea which seesawed around the rusting pilings.

'Harry?' Meredith said, adopting his stance. It struck her that perhaps she was meant to be looking at something: at a small aeroplane from Shoreham tugging a banner across the sky which would proclaim Bowden's love for her; at a pleasure boat writing her name in the waves. But Bowden was working up to something. A long-digested thought was finding its way back out. He reached across and his huge right hand covered hers. The contact was heavy but Meredith realised it was a clumsy attempt at a gesture of affection.

'I know my shortcomings,' Bowden said. 'I know what people think of me . . .'

Oh God, Meredith thought. Not this. Not now.

'. . . What I mean is, you might think I don't care. But I do. I'm not a bloody fool, you know.'

'I don't think anybody would ever accuse you of being that, Harry.'

'And I know why you laugh in my face.'

'Please . . .'

'No. Hear me out. I'm trying to say something here. Hear me out.'

'I'm sorry,' Meredith said, knowing now what Bowden was leading up to. At that moment the brass band started tuning up and a series of flatulent calls came from the direction of the concert hall. It seemed fitting somehow, as Harry Bowden fumbled for the right words to ask Meredith to be his wife, that a band struck up a military march and every so often the music would stop and the conductor bawl something out. Meredith was torn between the competing demands on her attention. Bowden's proposal was little more than a cry for help. His long-winded plea, about wanting to share his life with somebody like her, wanting to leave something behind (surely, after all that's happened, he can't expect me to have his children, Meredith thought with horror), how he had more than enough money now and he wanted somebody to help him spend it. But nothing about her. No words of love or care. It was all about Bowden and what he needed, finishing with the inevitable, 'You don't have to give me your answer now.'

But why not? Meredith thought. Who could possibly need more than a second to answer a proposal of marriage?

'Harry . . . Harry, darling. I just don't know what to say.'

'Think on it,' he said. 'Just think on it.'

'I will, darling. How could I possibly think of anything else?'

'You're a . . . marvellous woman, you know.'

'Please, you're embarrassing me.'

'Only, these things go unsaid.'

'As they should, Harry. As they should.'

There was a brief moment in which the music from the concert hall stopped and they could hear the sea heaving up against the pebbles and falling back to what sounded like applause. In that moment Meredith felt a jolt of loneliness and when she tried to rid herself of it the picture of Kit came into her mind again. There was an urgency in her now. Why should she wait for him to come back? Why should she tolerate another week with Bowden? For much of her life she had been waiting for others to act so that she could move on. There was only one thing to do. She would go to Spain and join Kit and everything would be right.

'Happy?' Bowden said, seeing the smile show on her face.

'I am now.'

'So am I,' Bowden said.

London

Fifty-five miles to the north of the couple on the pier, Arthur Lawler found himself on the upper deck of a tram. He was in the company of Deirdre the barmaid who was wearing her plum-coloured Sunday-best coat (though it wasn't Sunday) and had draped her white gloves (which he had never seen her wear) across the handbag on her knee. They were on the way to lunch with her mother and Deirdre was in one of her 'moods', which were comprised of long periods of bitter silence punctuated by heavy sighs. Arthur had given up trying to cheer her out of it and was now peering out of the rain-teared window at the patchy grass on the common. He had seen neither Royle nor Bowden for two weeks. The doorbell went unanswered at Meredith's flat, and Quinn, on his occasional visits to the Posts, ignored him entirely.

Deirdre sighed and, as she refolded her gloves, said, 'I expect she'll be all nice to you.' The tram stopped with a lurch and the accusation carried all the way to the rear of the top deck.

'Who?'

'Who do you think?' Deirdre whispered fiercely. 'My mother. That's who. She's always nice as pie to visitors.'

'Would you rather . . . ?'

'You should hear her when I goes there on my own.'

'Don't you get on?'

'Oh, we get on. We get on well enough. But I can never do the right thing by her. Nothing I do is ever right. Nothing.'

'Oh.'

'Oh,' she mocked.

'What do you want me to say to you, Deirdre?'

'There's no need to get sharp with me, Arthur.'

'I'm not getting . . . sharp. I just don't know what you want me to say, that's all.'

Deirdre looked darkly towards him. 'What's the matter? Need a drinky, do we? Is little Arthur getting thirsty?'

How had it happened? Arthur wondered as he watched a poor-looking boy tugging a reluctant mongrel across the common. How, in two weeks, had he relinquished control over his life to this woman? Even the eternal evenings with Royle and Bowden were beginning to feel preferable to a life chained to Deirdre. At least they were leavened by Meredith. If only he hadn't wasted his contingency fund on Meredith's sable he'd still have his tiny room in the commercial hotel and he wouldn't now need to be begging money from a barmaid who barely seemed to have sufficient to support herself. But Deirdre had unlimited access to booze and that was what kept him from running away from her. He could tolerate her bitterness so long as she didn't curtail his supply. In celebration of this short-term consolation he pulled the tiny cork from his pewter hip flask and took a quick, chest-warming sip of Scotch. His mood immediately lightened and he reached for Deirdre's hot hand. He had often seen such displays of affection paying dividends, though Meredith had always proved immune to them.

'You're just nervous, that's all,' Arthur said, squeezing her bunched knuckles. 'That's entirely understandable.'

'Nervous? No, Arthur, I'm not refined like you. I don't get nervous. I get scared.'

When she came close to the truth, Arthur found Deirdre more appealing. He could deal with her authentic despair; what he couldn't bear was her play-acted bravery.

'Scared of what?' he asked her.

'I don't know. Scared she might . . . Oh, I don't know.'

'Scared she might frighten me off?'

'God, no. Not that.'

'What then?'

'You wouldn't get it.'

'No?'

'No.'

Deirdre smiled for the first time since the journey began and Arthur remembered that there were moments with her when life wasn't so desperate after all.

She said, 'But don't you listen to her if she starts going on about my father. It wasn't ever all his fault.'

'All right.'

'Oh, give me a drink, Arthur, and stop dreaming about that tart.'

Arthur handed over his hip flask and Deirdre, grimacing, took a short sip, coughed and fanned her face with her gloves.

'I don't know how you can drink at this time of the day, I really don't,' she said.

Arthur's response, had he offered it, would have been to ask Deirdre how she could deal with the morning without drink. Like facing an unshaded light bulb, the world was far too bright without the booze to dull it.

'Tell me you're not thinking about her.'

'But I was,' Arthur said. He hadn't yet learned to censor his replies to her. 'I'm sorry.'

'She's gone. Forget her.'

'Yes, I suppose she has.'

'Besides, she was never good enough for you.'

'On the contrary . . .'

'Listen, Arthur. I don't want you ever going round there again. I don't want you seeing her and I don't want you ever talking to her.'

Arthur waited, and this time judged his reply. 'I won't. I won't ever see her or Royle or Bowden again.'

'Do you mean that?'

'Yes, I mean every word of it.' And, for good measure, he added, 'Darling.'

Deirdre looked at him with awe. 'I could love you, Arthur. I mean properly love you.' Shyly, she turned her face away.

'Really?'

'Yes. Honest. Cross my heart and hope to die. I could give you all kinds of things you've never had before from a woman.'

'Yes? Like what?'

'Oh, I don't know. I could . . . I could kiss you so hard it would make your toes curl up.'

'And?'

'And . . . I could cook you lovely meals when you came home at night after work. Pies and chops and things with gravy.' She pinched a fleck of dandruff from his shoulder.

'Work?'

'Yes, work. I know you'll find a position to suit you soon enough.'

'Yes. Of course. Of course I will, once I get straight in my head . . .' Lawler pondered what such a position might be but drew a blank. 'Tell me something else you'll do.'

'Oh, I don't know. I think . . . I think just loving you. Loving you properly would be enough. Don't you?'

'. . . Yes. I expect it would.'

'And could you love me?'

'Could I? Of course I could! Perhaps I already do.'

Deirdre rested her cheek against Arthur's shoulder and confided, 'I do hate it at that pub.'

'Do you?'

'I hate the governor. Especially in the mornings. He's horrible before we open up. Bossing everybody around. "This brass's got fingermarks on it, this slops tray wants pouring into the mild barrel, this lino hasn't been cleaned right, the fire in the lounge bar needs making up . . ." And then, at eleven, he puts on this smile when he walks up, fat belly all out in front of him, to open the doors, and he wears it until closing time and everybody thinks he's nice as pie. He's not. He's a big bully.'

'Well, why don't you go somewhere else? I mean, surely you could find a position with a better governor.'

'It doesn't go like that.'

'Perhaps I could help.'

'No, Arthur, it's not that. It's how you has to go about leaving. First you've to find somewhere, then you give in your notice, then you have to make sure you get the money owed before you goes. Only the governor's never got enough in the till. He always says something like, "So you come back for it next week and I'll have it ready." But you know he won't. And then if you go back he just makes you feel so small. "Here she comes, trying to tell me I owe her money," he brags out across the room, "when all the time she should be paying me for being so nice to her." Everybody laughs at this and so do you . . . and you make out you're just there for a drink – to say goodbye to the regulars – and you . . . you end up spending money you can't afford . . . That's how it ends, Arthur. That's always how it ends for people like me.'

'God. I never thought about it really. I mean, there's a man called Wilson who works for Bowden. I don't know why he springs to mind but . . .'

'Let's not talk about it. Let's . . . what's the time?'

'Eleven-thirty.'

'Let's go and have a drink. Would you like it if we did that? Of course you would. She can wait.'

'Really? I mean, I wouldn't want to get off on the wrong foot.'

'No. A half-hour won't much matter either way.'

At one thirty-five, Arthur was supporting a drunken Deirdre round the waist as she tugged at the doorbell of a small terraced house in Wandsworth. The Southern Railway ran along a bank high above the fence at the end of the back garden and as they waited, Deirdre giggling, an express passed up the line towards Victoria. Blossoms of locomotive smoke bloomed over the roof, then dispersed slowly around them, mingling with the thin rain and wreathing them in a comforting grey mist.

Still giggling, Deirdre banged on the door with her fist and called, 'Come on, Mother!'

'I've had an idea,' Arthur said.

'What sort of idea?'

'It's a secret.'

'Tell me,' Deirdre said, pressing her face to the glass of the door.

'No. I can't.' But Deirdre had lost interest so Lawler offered, 'Because then it wouldn't be a secret, would it?'

'What wouldn't?'

'The secret.'

'No, I expect it wouldn't.'

'. . . All right then. You wait there and I'll go and get it.'

'Get what? Where is she, Arthur? Where is that bloody mother of mine? I tell you, she'll be upstairs, making us wait. That's where she'll be.' Deirdre looked up towards the bedroom window, lost her balance and fell backwards.

Arthur caught her round her waist and righted her again, saying, 'Steady, Deirdre.'

'You shouldn't have got me to drink all that port.'

'You wait there then, and I'll go and get it.'

'Go and get what?' Deirdre turned and tried to focus on Arthur's face. She reached out to steady herself and as he took her hand she said, 'Kiss me, Arthur. Kiss me hard and then when she opens the door we can ignore her and just keep on and on . . . and then she'll have a taste of her own medicine.'

'In a while. I've just got to go and fetch this . . . thing. All right?'

'What thing?'

'This secret thing.'

'Oh, that. Will I like it?'

'Oh yes.'

'Is it a present?'

'In some ways. Yes.'

'You're not running away from me?'

'God, no! Why should I run away from a beautiful girl like you?'

'I wouldn't ever forgive you if you did.'

'I wouldn't expect you to. Worse than that, I wouldn't forgive myself.'

Deirdre gave him a gentle drunken shove, saying, '. . . Go on then. And don't be long.'

'I won't,' Arthur said, setting off down the narrow street.

'And when you get back just push the door – I'll leave it open for you.'

'All right,' Arthur called back, and waved over his shoulder without turning.

'No. Best not. You'd best knock. She might get funny if you just walks in . . .'

And that was all Arthur heard before Deirdre faded from earshot. Five minutes later she had faded from his mind. Within three-quarters of an hour he was standing outside Bowden's showroom, staring through the window at Royle who, with great enthusiasm and a good deal of hand-waving, was explaining something to a well-groomed young man. Arthur watched as the man handed his tweed jacket over to Royle, rolled up his shirtsleeves and established his place behind the wheel of a silver tourer. He looked across at Royle who played his part by nodding appreciatively at the spectacle of the healthy-looking, impatient gent in the red braces at the shiny wooden wheel of a brand-new car. The gent was thus allowed to see himself through the approval in Royle's eyes: man and machine inseparable. Arthur Lawler knocked loudly on the plate-glass, immediately commandeering Royle's attention. Royle apologised to the gent and walked quickly out on to the street. Before Arthur could say anything, Royle took the upper part of his right arm and manhandled him away up the pavement and out of sight of the showroom windows.

'Steady!' Arthur said. 'You're pinching me.'

'What are you doing here?' Royle said, watching the showroom door, nervous of the customer coming out to find him.

'I've come to see you, Billy.' Arthur smiled. 'It's been nearly two weeks. Honestly, you couldn't imagine the two weeks I've been through. You remember the barmaid in the Posts . . . ?'

'I told you it would be better if you kept out of the way, didn't I?'

'Yes, except . . .'

'And I meant it, Arthur. For everybody's sake.'

'I know. Except . . . except I just couldn't manage it . . . please tell me how Meredith is.'

'Listen to me.' Royle took Arthur's chin in his hand and forced him to pay attention to him.

'What, Billy?'

'Listen to me very carefully.'

'I'm listening.'

'I can't see you now. I'm busy.'

'No. I don't need to see you, I just want to explain about the decision I made. You see, I've been such a fool, Billy. I've practically asked Deirdre to marry me solely because . . .'

'Arthur. Be quiet.'

'But . . .'

'Ssh.' Royle put his finger to his lips, took another glance towards the showroom door and, as he did so, patted down the gent's tweed jacket. Feeling a weight against the blue silk lining, he reached in and removed a wallet from the inside pocket. Unfolding it, he zipped the straight edge of a thin wad of crisp new notes with his thumbnail and slipped out a ten-shilling note which, looking towards the showroom again, he handed to Arthur. He secreted a pound note in his own trouser pocket and returned the wallet to the jacket.

'Now get off and get yourself a drink. I'll come along and find you when I've finished up here.' Royle took the wallet out again, removed another pound note and, this time, replaced it for good.

'All right, Billy. Thanks. Thank you.'

'You look dreadful.'

'I feel dreadful. I feel as if I haven't slept for a year, but when I try and drop off I simply can't . . . and my stomach . . . I have this awful, awful pain in the pit of my stomach . . .' Arthur saw that he had lost Royle's attention and his voice trailed away. 'Well, look, you don't want to listen to all this now. We'll talk later, I can see you're busy . . .'

'That's right, Arthur, I'm busy. Now toddle along and try and take it steady. I don't want to arrive and find you collapsed in a heap in the corner.'

'No. I wouldn't want to let you down like that.'

'Let *me* down, Arthur?'

'I think you might be the only friend I have left.'

'Then God help you,' Royle said without smiling and Lawler set off towards another saloon bar. Disgust was translated into sadness as Royle watched him weaving away up the pavement. Something had changed. Something had come to an end and nothing had filled the void. In such periods lay possibilities and dangers. Until everything was settled again, Royle knew he must be on his guard. Arthur Lawler would have to look after himself.

'There you are,' Royle announced to the pub at large as he walked in off the street at six o'clock. The effect of his arrival in the bar was such that Arthur felt as though somebody had turned on another lamp and thrown a large dry log on to the fire.

'Billy. Billy. Thank God.' Arthur wasn't yet at ease with the figure he had now become. He felt shapeless and featureless, like a liquid which required a vessel both to contain it and to lend it form. 'I feel like . . .' he started, intending to go on to explain to Royle how he had arrived at this position, but Billy Royle was acquainted with enough drunks to know that Arthur had now crossed the line into a world where, for the most part, the booze determined his character.

'Get me a drink, Arthur,' Royle said, craning round to leer at the crowd in the bar.

'Of course. Scotch?'

'Large one.' Royle rubbed his hands together, trying to spark himself into life. The barman reached over and put the whisky on the bar in front of him. Royle planted his hands each side of the glass like an athlete mentally preparing himself for the physical exertions ahead.

'Did you sell the motor?' Arthur asked him.

'No. Young Mr Eden claims to be coming back on Friday. Though I somehow doubt he will. I didn't have him down as a time-waster but I think he just wanted an hour of being flattered into feeling like a man of means.'

'I know how he feels.'

'Self-pity, Arthur? Get a hold on yourself.' Royle took his first cautious sip and waited, wary of the liquid inflaming raw crevices, as the Scotch ignited his gullet. He breathed more easily, knowing well that the first drink of each session acted to anaesthetise the pain of subsequent ones. As the evening went on, his consumption of Scotch thus became increasingly pleasurable. 'So,' he said. 'You were telling me about a woman called Doris or something, weren't you? Some woman you've asked to marry. How did that come about?'

'She's called Deirdre. From the Posts.'

'Do I know her? Yes, I think I do. Quite pretty; eager; rather simple, takes offence easily.' Royle pictured a village church, a bride in white, a horse and trap, a country pub. 'Wasn't she involved in providing us with some food at some point?'

'Yes, that's Deirdre. Shall we sit down?'

'If we must.'

Arthur led the way to a table with an overflowing tin ashtray, two empty beer glasses and a white plate with half an arrowroot biscuit on it. While Royle settled himself, Arthur took the glasses up to the bar. When he returned he pushed the plate and the ashtray to the edge of the table. Royle watched him without seeing him.

'I can see you're irritated by me,' Lawler said. Settling back into Royle's company again was beginning to steady him.

'No. It's not you, Arthur. Well, not entirely.'

'Tell me.'

Royle, relinquishing his anger, sighed and said, 'It's the whole blasted situation. Everything.'

'Well, go on.'

'Odd jobs for Harry every evening, working all hours during the day in the showroom, and barely a penny to show for it at the end of the week . . . I can't even scrape enough together to take a girl to the pictures.'

'Tell me how Meredith is.'

'Meredith? That's a good one.'

'Why are you laughing?'

'You'd better ask Meredith how Meredith is.'

'She's all right?'

'Yes. More than all right. Depending on how you look at it.' He watched Lawler closely as he told him. 'Harry is going to ask her to marry him. He probably has done by now.'

'But . . . but, I don't . . .'

'No. I expect you don't. Nor do I.'

'I thought. I mean, the doctor . . . what was he called? I met him that day in the fog . . .'

'Pugh. Worth every penny Harry paid him. Meredith made a startling recovery and . . . well, this seemed to spur him into considering popping the question.'

'God. And she said yes?'

'I don't know. They're due back from Brighton tonight. Anyway, since Harry made the decision, yours truly has been *persona non grata*. He seems to have got it into his head that Meredith's problems are all my fault. That's the reason he's been keeping me fully occupied, i.e. out of harm's way.'

'I don't know what to say.'

'No. Neither do I. Neither do I.'

'But when?'

'The wedding? He mentioned November.'

'That's pretty soon.'

'Yes, but after the other big event.'

'What?'

'Another of Harry's outings to the East End – except this is the outing to end all outings . . .'

'I don't think I want to know.'

'He's been planning it for weeks. Him and Quinn. He's barely set foot in the showroom . . . Anticipate serious mayhem, Arthur. Heads will be broken on a huge scale.'

They drank in silence. When the barman came to clear the table he didn't stay on to banter with Royle. The despair of the two men was too much for him. But when he had hurried back behind the safety of the bar he felt compelled to watch them from a distance.

After a while, Arthur said, 'I'd like to see her. When are they back did you say?'

'Tonight.'

'They went to Brighton, did they?' Arthur said, feeling the pain as an old wound tore open.

'Yes. They went down to the Metropole for a few days.'

'I do need to see her.'

'Let it go. Let her go.'

'I can't.'

'I really don't see what you could possibly achieve.'

'She's a friend. I've known Meredith for nearly ten years. I can't just let her go like that. Besides. I want to say goodbye.'

'I think you said goodbye a long time ago.'

'Damn Bowden. This is . . . this is no good, Billy. We can't let her do it.'

'You know Meredith. There's no talking to her.'

'Have you even tried?'

'Of course. I even went as far as . . . . well, I suppose I can tell you.'

'You asked her to marry you?'

'How did you guess? Yes. And what a catch I must have seemed to her at the time. One of the rare occasions, I might add, when Meredith was stone-cold sober and I was, for reasons I won't go into, diabolically drunk. I asked her in a taxi and then had to tell the cabby to stop so that I could vomit. Crowded street – Shaftesbury Avenue, I think it was – sometime late in the afternoon. Can't remember where we were going – to the pictures, I think. So . . . heads turned towards me. Narrowly avoided by a man on a horse. Policeman trotting over to see what all the fuss was about . . . and yours truly heaving the best part of a bottle of whisky and half a veal and ham pie into the gutter . . . I put it down to the pie.'

'I presume she turned you down.'

'Turned me down . . .' Royle's chest shuddered and stilled, then shuddered again. 'You presume she turned me down!' The laugh found its way from his chest to his throat. He coughed a cigarette cough, tears of mirth sprang into his eyes and the bellow of laughter continued to build until it burst out and went on and on and on until even Arthur Lawler was infected by it. Soon, everybody in the bar was laughing too – triggered by the sight of Royle, wheezing, red-faced, trying to catch his breath, the hysteria refusing to let him rest. And at the height of it somebody lifted the lid on the piano and a woman in a black hat decorated with wax fruit hitched up her skirt and her sleeves and began hammering out a melody.

Arthur's mood lightened. Even when Quinn came in, he refused to let him dampen his spirits. For the first time in his life he understood the process of a wake. From despair to madness to hope in three short steps.

When Deirdre arrived at the pub shortly before closing time, Lawler's tie was loose, his button flies were undone, as was one of his shoelaces, his face was flushed, his parting jagged and he had lost his mackintosh. He was hanging his right arm round Royle's neck and, with his mouth close to his ear, was drunkenly trying to explain to him the reason why they should both, immediately, with no further discussion, buy a ticket for Paris, take the boat train to Dover and set off to find Kit Renton. Waving his finger like a baton, he was suggesting that a sense of purpose was what they both lacked. 'You see, Kit has a sense of purpose and Kit is the happiest man I know.'

'Happy?' Royle said. 'I don't think I'd call him happy. Would you?'

'Oh yes, I would. Yes, I'd call him happy.'

'Well, Arthur, I bow to your better judgment.' Royle said and, at this point, caught sight of Deirdre elbowing her way through the crowd towards them. 'Aye, aye. Look out!' he cautioned.

'What's the matter? What have you spotted?'

'Your Doris. Sallying forth. There. No, she's gone. Yes. There she is again. I can see the top of her head bobbing along. Like a cork in a river.'

'Doris? I don't know a Doris.'

'No? I thought you told me you did.'

'No. As far as I know, I am acquainted with nobody by the name of Doris.'

'Angry. Barmaid. Something about a proposal of marriage.'

'Deirdre! God. Deirdre.'

'That's her!' Royle said triumphantly. 'Boy Merrell has detained her. Well done that man. Time to run off?'

'Absolutely.'

'Righty-ho. Drink up and lead the way.'

Arthur drained his glass and Royle, chortling drunkenly, did the same. With one final look back towards Boy Merrell, he followed Lawler as he ducked through the half-sized door into the lounge bar. They tiptoed among the shining shoes of the genteel post-theatre drinkers, apologising noisily, and, when they reached the door to the street, Royle turned and saluted before stumbling out into the night. Outside, he found Lawler leaning against the green-tiled wall trying to catch his breath, smoke flaring from his nostrils like a horse.

'Have you seen my coat?' Lawler asked him.

'When?'

'Recently.'

'No.'

'I must have lost it.'

'Oh dear.'

'I can't afford to lose it. But I can't go back in there.'

'No. Absolutely not.'

'What should I do?'

'Well, you can't go back in.'

'No. So I expect I'll have to leave it.'

'Leave it?'

'Yes. But it was a good coat.'

'Yes, it was. You know, it was a very good coat.'

'Perhaps I'd better . . .'

'Go back inside?'

'Yes. What do you think?'

'No. Don't risk it.'

'No. You're absolutely right. Though I can't bear the cold.'

'Neither can I. But it's not winter yet. Where to now?'

'I don't know. I can't go to Deirdre's. I mean, I just can't.'

'I expect you'll have to bed down with me then, Arthur.'

'Could I?'

'I don't see why not.'

'You're a good friend, Billy.'

'Am I? Yes, I suppose I am . . .' Royle tried to take his bearings from the carousel of shops spinning around him. The spinning speeded up as he looked upwards but didn't slow when he looked down again. He reached out to the wall to steady himself. Lawler, in another room of the same dream, was also clinging on. Deirdre discovered them in the street shortly afterwards, facing each other, arguing about the shortest route back to Royle's room, which was less than a quarter of a mile away.

'Doris!' Royle announced cheerfully.

'Deirdre,' Lawler corrected him.

Arms crossed, Deirdre faced the two men. Anger, she quickly judged, would serve no purpose beyond provoking Royle into taking Arthur's side. If that happened, she knew she would stand no chance of getting Arthur back to her room where she could deal with him in private. As gently as she could, she said, 'That's right, it's Deirdre. You never could remember my name, Billy Royle. See? I always remember yours.'

'That's a wonderful . . . faculty you have, my love,' Royle told her. 'I expect the remembering of names is the stock in trade of the barmaid.'

'I expect it is,' Deirdre said, sounding as smart as she could, unsure whether Royle had complimented her.

'Though not the tart,' Royle added as the thought entered his mind and was immediately and unwisely voiced.

'I'm sure you'd know all about that.'

'Well, I'm sure I . . .'

'Deirdre,' Lawler interrupted, 'that . . . business we had,' remembering now how they parted. 'That thing I mentioned to you . . .'

'Yes, Arthur?'

'Well, the fact is that, along the way I bumped into Billy, and, well, one thing led to another and . . .'

'All those things, Arthur,' Deirdre said, smiling not at him but at Royle. 'I expect the thing you were after just got lost in all the other things.'

'Well, yes, I expect it did.'

'Never mind. Mother didn't go to much trouble on your account. She only spent the whole morning baking. But she said you shouldn't trouble yourself. She knows you're a busy man. All those *things* to attend to.'

'The fact is, my lovely,' Royle said. 'The fact is, we were just on our way to the Globe for a nightcap. In fact Arthur had only just this moment announced that we were to call on you and invite you to join us. You discovered us in the midst of a discussion over the shortest route to your garret.'

'I don't live in a garret. I lodge at the Posts.'

'Of course you do.'

'You were coming to fetch me?'

'Absolutely, absolutely, Deirdre. Back me up, Arthur.'

'Quite. Yes, that's just what we were doing.'

'You know the Globe, Deirdre?'

'The Globe? Oh, yes, Billy. I know the Globe. Not that I'm a regular visitor.'

'Then you'll accompany us to that merry barn?'

'Well, I don't know.'

'Please say you will.'

'. . . I expect I might. If you're sure.'

'Of course we're sure. We are sure, Arthur, aren't we?'

'Oh yes. Absolutely sure.'

'I expect I'd be glad to join you two gentlemen, then.'

'In that case, take my arm,' Royle said and linked his arm through hers. 'Come on, Arthur, assist me in escorting the lady.'

Lawler felt a tug of resistance as he threaded Deirdre's cold right hand through the loop of his left arm.

'On we go then,' Royle said and set the pace. Immediately he began entertaining Deirdre with schoolday stories, careful always to paint Arthur as the wise, honourable hero of all of their escapades. Deirdre enjoyed the attention. She had never before walked through a West End night, arm-in-arm with a man she considered both charming and handsome. The price she was exacting from Arthur was ignoring him entirely. As they crossed Oxford Street, she stumbled and used this as an excuse to pull her arm away from his. Grateful to have been released, Arthur dropped half a step behind and Deirdre found herself drawing Royle closer to her for comfort. At that moment she decided she would make the most of having him to herself for an hour. Whatever the reason, whatever the lies he was telling her, she had decided not to care. If she could only get rid of Arthur she knew that she would go back with Royle to his room – but she would make sure she left before he woke. She knew the spell would be broken if he found her in his bed the following morning.

These thoughts continued to go through her mind as Royle chattered happily about a school close to Brighton and told her intricate stories of bicycles and masters and dusty dormitories and a boy called Kit Renton. Arthur, dropping further and further behind, was in a position to see the growing attraction between them.

It happened when they reached the Café Royal. As they were making their way through a queue of people waiting between the ropes to be let in, Royle leaned down to say something into Deirdre's ear. It was the first unselfconscious gesture he had made. Because she didn't quite catch what he said she pulled his mouth closer to her. When he repeated the comment, his lips grazed the lobe of her ear and remained hovering close to her face. His nostrils twitched, picking up the scent of her skin, and a charge went through them both. Arthur Lawler slackened his pace further. If he ducked into a doorway now he knew it would be a few minutes before Royle and Deirdre realised he was no longer following them. He stopped, waited for a moment, then edged sideways into the shadows. He had already determined to find and confront Meredith before the night was over – wherever she was.

Royle and Deirdre had forgotten Arthur Lawler. The physical contact between them was now causing currents of desire to flow. Deirdre's long-term aspirations were soaring just as Royle's were declining, but neither was yet aware of this happening. Royle found his mind returning to the image of a country wedding, though he couldn't place the church his mind was conjuring up. Deirdre had already replaced Arthur with Billy as the man she would be happy to have at her side for the rest of her life. Of course Billy would be more of a handful, she would have to work hard to cut him away from the fast crowd he moved with, but she believed she could make him happy. More than that, she knew that if she could get Billy Royle alone she could both surprise and satisfy him. She had been with enough men to have learned how to find her pleasure within theirs, and she had chosen carefully, which meant that her reputation was safe. With few exceptions she had always taken married men to her bed. They knew more. They were grateful, cautious and considerate and they never refused her when she occasionally, tearfully, touched them for ten pounds for a visit to the doctor on Harley Street who looked kindly on girls who found themselves in trouble. She had only once genuinely needed the money and it was during the painful, humiliating experience in the cold, white room that she determined to make other men pay for her pain.

In this way, Deirdre had amassed a fortune of almost ninety pounds. However she spent her weekly day off, she always began it with a visit to the Post Office where she deposited a further few pounds into her account and confirmed the new balance in her book. She had told nobody about this account. She had always known that to escape the life of a barmaid she would need to buy herself out. She once fantasised about a rich benefactor, but the more money she saved, the more realistic her aspirations became. At thirty pounds, her dreams were of plain, good-hearted men. At sixty, she imagined herself as the neat, well-turned-out wife of a bank clerk. At eighty she began to imagine she might find somebody both good-looking, kind and with some prospects of his own. But then she met Arthur. She was drawn to Arthur because they shared similar terrors; they recognised the brutality of the world in the same way. They would stand on the same bridges watching the same trains leaving with the same sadness in their hearts. She had resigned herself to the fact that she had saved hard through seven years behind the bar at the Posts to provide a future for herself and a man like Arthur Lawler.

But perhaps she could set her sights a little higher. She chanced a glance at Billy Royle's thoroughbred profile: his strong jaw, the smooth plane of his nose, the hint of auburn in his back-swept hair, the masquerade of perpetual amusement in his clear eyes. His features shaped easily into a smile as he caught her looking at him but he checked his glib response and, instead, kissed Deirdre on the cheek. This was the moment when they both remembered Arthur Lawler and Royle turned his head, a sheepish, apologetic smile in place. But Arthur was no longer following them. Deirdre and Royle turned to face the stream of evening pedestrians making their way towards the Underground or the late trams or the West End clubs licensed to offer booze if the patrons also purchased a plate of sandwiches.

'Arthur's gone,' Royle said.

'Yes,' Deirdre replied. 'I'm glad.'

Standing on the Euston Road, looking up towards the light in Meredith's window, Arthur Lawler felt an ache in his chest which he recognised as just another pang in the long sequence of separation. The fact that the curtains were open suggested to him that Meredith was alone, which he took to be a good sign. Having spent two or three days in Bowden's stifling company she would, he knew, initially crave isolation. But, after an hour on her own and three or four glasses of gin, she would already be looking for a distraction. Having promised Bowden she would not go out, she would be hoping that Royle would arrive 'on the off chance' to share a drink, smoke some cigarettes and pass a few hours in flirtation and disparagement. Arthur saw Meredith come to the window and look up the road before passing from the frame again. She did not see him staring at her. Nor did she spot the two men standing across the street also watching her window. Arthur knew a bath would be running and that she would already be shrugging off her clothes. He had a minute or so before she lowered herself into the tub – after which point he knew she would ignore his knock on the door.

Arthur smelt the familiar dampness of the entrance hall as he passed the solid vault of letterboxes and the usual newspapers scattered on the hall table. He sprinted up the wide shadowed staircase and turned along the dark corridor. He waited, listening to the disembodied voices of the other tenants floating through the fabric of the building, before knocking at Meredith's door. She opened it immediately, pulling a silk robe round her.

'Oh,' she said, surprised but not, Arthur judged, entirely disappointed. Meredith's hair was longer and freer. The new creases round her eyes were the only indication of what she had gone through.

'Hello, darling,' he greeted her. He had decided to pretend nothing had changed between them until she told him not to. 'I thought you were down in Brighton.'

'Just this minute got back. Harry's gone off somewhere for the night . . . Well, I suppose you'd better come in.'

Leaving Arthur to close the door, Meredith went back to the bathroom and turned off the geyser. Arthur took his time following her. He was enjoying the sense of ownership of Meredith's flat. Once through the door, visitors were always allowed an equal share in her possessions. You were never Meredith's guest. For the duration of your stay, you cohabited with her.

'Take your coat off and come and talk to me,' Arthur heard from the bathroom. 'And bring me my drink.'

Meredith's gin was where she always left it – beside the ivory-inlaid cigarette box on the mantelpiece. It stood among the sticky, intersecting Olympic symbols of other drinking sessions. Arthur had always assumed that when she was alone, Meredith rarely sat down. She argued that she could only truly relax in the bath, which was why she took so many of them. Arthur draped his jacket across a chair and took the drink into the bathroom. The flat had been unheated for three days and the water from the bath had made a dense steam in the room. From somewhere within it Meredith's voice instructed him to sit down and tell her where he had been. Arthur set down the glass on the washbasin, sat on a cane chair and loosened his tie.

'I've been nowhere much,' he said into the fog, uncertain of her interest.

'Even you must have been somewhere, Arthur.'

'Even me?'

'Yes . . . I don't mean to get at you – I haven't seen you for ages. Where on earth *have* you been? Did you bring me my drink?' A pink hand appeared through the mist. Arthur inserted the glass into it and proceeded to tell her as many details as he could remember of the previous weeks, including the terrifying visit to her flat on the night the doctor was there. Meredith didn't interrupt and Arthur sensed that some of the details of that period were new to her. The only indication of her presence in the room was the chink of her glass on the tiles of the floor and the slap of water as she shifted her position in the tub.

'. . . So here I am,' he concluded. '. . . And Deirdre and Billy are – I suppose – even now dancing cheek-to-cheek at the Globe.'

Meredith didn't respond immediately. When she did, Arthur was surprised that her curiosity lay in his dilemma, not in his response to hers. 'So what will you do now?' she asked him.

'I don't know. Muddle on.'

'Very well. We'll come to that in a moment. There's something you need to know.' To Arthur, Meredith's voice was different. No petulance; the edge of hysteria and irritability gone. Instead he could hear a new directness; a woman whose decisions were now being made by her and not for her.

'You're getting married,' he interjected.

'Billy told you?'

'Yes.'

'I'm not going through with it.'

'No? You've turned Bowden down?'

'Not exactly. Pass me the towel.'

Meredith's perfect naked shape appeared before him. Arthur reached for the white towel, held it up and embraced her in it. They leaned together for a moment like exhausted lovers. When Meredith pulled away she stood still for a second, looking at him, and Arthur contemplated kissing her. But before he could she went into the living-room where she dried herself, shivering in front of the gas fire. Being with Meredith, everything felt right again. For the first time in almost three weeks Arthur began to relax. His craving for booze had diminished, his heartbeat had slowed, the warmth was beginning to return to his body.

'Could you honestly see me as Mrs Harry Bowden?' Meredith asked, watching him in the mirror.

'I could, yes. I mean I wouldn't want to see you as Mrs Harry Bowden, but I could see it.' Arthur pushed his hands into his pockets and paced lightly towards the window. Talking like this was what he imagined friends did. He felt like whistling, but when he tried his lips were chapped and ruined. He was coming out of shock and his body was beginning to break the news to him of his latest assault on it.

'"Mrs Harry Bowden." How terrible,' Meredith said, paused and contemplated the awfulness of how far she had fallen in Lawler's eyes. 'He's given me fifty pounds. He's never been mean to me.'

'Fifty pounds? For what?'

'Clothes. And what he calls incidental expenses. Oh, but not booze. He made me promise I wouldn't spend it on booze.'

'So what will you do?'

'With the money?'

'If you like.'

'I have a plan of action. You'll be proud of me. Come in here.' Meredith dropped the towel on the floor and, in a continuation of the same movement, picked up her weightless silk robe. She tied it as she skipped to the wardrobe in her bedroom and threw open the doors. The hangers were empty. Meredith waited for Arthur to take this in, then kneeled on the floor beside the bed, beckoned him down to her level and lifted the hem of the valance. Beneath the bed were two suitcases.

'You're running away!' Arthur said.

'Yes. Yes, I suppose I am. Are you proud of me?' Like a motherless child Meredith watched for his approval.

'I'm ... yes, I'm ... I,' Arthur began to reply but the emotion provoked in him by Meredith's vulnerability was too much for him to bear. He tried to swallow the tears but once they began he found he couldn't stop them. Meredith held out her hand to him and led him to her bed. Guiding him down beside her, they lay together and cried the last weeks of pain away.

'You're not alone,' Meredith said, holding Arthur tightly as he continued to sob.

'. . . Let me come away with you,' he said, when he had controlled himself again.

'Do you really want to?'

'Yes. Of course.'

'You know what will happen if Harry catches us?'

'Yes.'

She said, 'And you know it will be worse for you?'

'I don't care.'

'I can't live with you.'

'I . . .'

'No. Let me finish. I have to be clear. I can't . . . I can't afford to be nice to you at my own expense. It's very important that you understand this.'

'Yes.' Arthur reached out and smoothed the ridges around her eyes with his thumb, but he couldn't stroke the tiredness away.

'And it's not as though I don't have a clear idea of what I'm going to do.'

'Well, tell me.'

'I'm going to Spain.'

'To find Kit?'

'Yes. How did you know?'

'Why else would you be going there?'

Meredith rolled on to her back. 'I suppose it could work. When everything is over and we come back – the three of us – we could move to Hampshire or Dorset and Kit and I could live in a cottage and you could live next door and . . .'

'And when he's away I could come round and see you?'

'Yes . . . It's not a very good idea, is it?'

'Not really.'

Meredith sat up and said, 'I think we'd better go. I wouldn't trust Harry not to turn up and spoil everything.'

'You're leaving tonight?'

'Is it too soon for you?'

'Well . . . no. Not at all.'

While Meredith dressed, Arthur stood at her place by the fire and smoked a cigarette. When he had finished it he emptied the ashtray into a filthy bucket in the kitchen and washed the glasses in the sink. It had become important to him to leave the flat tidy. It was the only way he could think of to signal to Bowden that he was taking back control over his life. It didn't concern him that Bowden was unlikely to decode the message he was leaving for him.

'Ready?' he asked Meredith when she finally emerged from the bedroom. She had dressed down for the occasion and was carrying only one small suitcase. She was, however, wearing her highest shoes.

'Ready.'

'What about your other clothes?'

'I'm leaving them here. They belong to another Meredith. The old Meredith.'

'Should we lock the door?'

'No. Leave it wide open. I want my possessions to be ransacked. I don't want to believe they're all here waiting for me should I lose my nerve.'

'You won't.'

As each waited for the other to open the door they heard a loud knock. They froze. A hasty, desperate dialogue was signalled by their eyes: Bowden/he mustn't catch us leaving/no other way out of the flat/pretend Arthur is visiting/get rid of the suitcase beneath the bed/close the wardrobe.

'Just a minute,' Meredith called, then, equally loudly, improvised, 'Arthur, get the door will you,' tearing off her coat and scarf, running to the bedroom, throwing her suitcase into the wardrobe, slamming the door, lighting a cigarette, pouring a drink.

'Arthur, get the door, will you!' She shouted this into Arthur's face as he stood immobile in the centre of the room.

The game was up. He felt the cold crawling back into his bones. He needed a drink.

Seville

'Good evening, *New York Post*, this is Theodore Goss speaking from Seville. If I sound a little brisk tonight, Alice, forgive me, it has been a trying day. I'll begin:

General Queipo de Llano crosses the courtyard for his evening broadcast. This three-storeyed building in the Calle de Las Palmas has been commandeered by the rebels for their local headquarters. It is from here that the General, together with his lieutenants, is plotting the strategy of the southern Second Division as it pushes across Andalusia committing atrocities so grotesque that the battle-weary journalists who gather here are required to fight their own daily battles with their editors back home over the veracity of their reports.

A thousand cigarette butts have been stamped into the paving stones by the troops waiting to keep their appointments with the General's staff. Foreign Legionaries mix with Moors, adorned with scapularies pressed upon them by devout young girls as they marched into town. Young, blond German airmen in white overalls mingle impatiently with Carlists. One reads the *Völkischer Beobachter* as a shoe-black kneels at his feet. Embroidered on his breast, a tiny swastika. An enterprising child hawks bottles of wine chilled in a wooden bucket of iced water. The boy smiles and flirts with a group of Falangists, plotting in the shadows. They tousle his hair and take his wine but they do not pay him. A black-veiled woman chooses the moment to enquire after her husband. He was among a lorry-load of prisoners from the Rio Tinto mines driven to the headquarters of the *Phalanx* in the Calle Trajano. Nothing has been heard of them since. No shots have been reported in the vicinity but executions here are carried out at night. The men smile and shrug and when her back is turned again they laugh.

This is the rebel army at rest, united to crush the ragged forces of the Republic. And here in the courtyard they wait for orders and chits, mess passes and maps or, in some cases, just a glimpse of the man whose broadcasts they have listened to night after night. The hour-long transmissions of the man they call the Radio General reach an audience of millions across the whole of Europe. You may have heard him through the atmospherics in Paris or Berlin. If you have not, he is a master of oratory. He shouts. He whispers. He cajoles and he gesticulates. He has only his sound engineer for company. It is said that this is the only man he trusts. And around the courtyard the men listen in silence, heads bowed, to the old loudspeaker placed at an open window. I stand with them and hear him declaim, 'I don't know why we are called rebels; after all we have nine-tenths of Spain behind us. I fancy that those on the other side are rebels and that we should be treated as the legal government by the rest of the world.'

I leave, having heard and seen enough. I have been waiting for two days for an interview with the General and I suspect I could spend the rest of the war the same way. I cross the street and as I make my way back towards the Hotel Madrid I soon find myself lost in the early-evening silence of the old town; in the orange-scented, iron-balconied, narrow streets. This is the Seville travellers come to find: pavement cafés and flamenco guitars. The voice of the General is silent here. But in the silence I hear the echo of the stories I have been told: of the July mass executions – between a hundred and a hundred and fifty workers murdered each day in Seville alone. Of how the corpses were doused in oil to prevent epidemics and then left lying in the street until dark, a union card tied to the leg or arm. Of the pregnant wife of a trade-union official who had fled to Gibraltar being forced to drink castor oil and petrol and then sent to join her husband. She died the following day.

I reach the Hotel Madrid with its walls of chalky blue and red and yellow. It was in the bar here that I made the acquaintance of Maria Corrales, a sloe-eyed, olive-skinned, dignified child of the land. Maria is a woman but she is, as yet, only eighteen years old. She comes from Lora del Río, and the General's forces have already paid this small township a visit. They shot Maria's mother and then they shot her brothers. But Maria says she can recall few of the details as she busies herself between the tables of the Hotel Madrid. Perhaps this is for the best.

'Goodnight, Alice.'
'Goodnight, Mr Goss. You take care.'
'I will, Alice. I always do.'

October: The Aragón Front

Kit Renton dropped down into a dugout. It was five feet deep and lined with damp compacted mud and crusts of mouldy bread. Renton undid his cartridge belt and attached it by its brass buckle to a sheared root protruding from the wall of the trench. He lit a Russian cigarette and as he drew in the smoke he tried to control his shallow breathing. Since he had joined the battle he had craved cigarettes, his dreams had been vivid, his heart had raced. Even in his rare moments of rest he felt like a runner in the blocks waiting for the starting pistol. He ducked his head as another exchange struck up between machine-gun and rifle, each trying to shout the other down. The firefight was close by; bullets whistled above him and thudded into the dense earth. Renton squinted and imagined he could see the smudges of grey cartridge in the clear air.

Four weeks now and each day felt like a lifetime. His civilian mind no longer auditioned his responses. His civilian inhibitions no longer delayed him from diving into the mud when he heard the thud of a mortar. His London sensibilities had been blunted to the point where he thought nothing of eating from a filthy pannikin, drinking milky, stale water from a damp wooden ladle dipped into a communal bucket, sleeping fully clothed, scratching his balls when the lice began to bite. In an uncharacteristically intimate exchange the previous night, Eduardo said to him that he now felt less of the man he was but more of a man, and Kit Renton found that this accorded with his own feelings.

Antonio's face appeared above the rim of the dugout to obliterate a portion of the white sky. 'We must move,' he said. His orders, as always, were gentle, courteous and concise.

Kit Renton, obeying the command unquestionably, pinched out his cigarette, lodged it behind his ear, buckled his belt and clambered out of his shelter into the cold air. Six hundred feet beneath him, at the foot of the ravine, he saw the sierra he first crossed with Justina two weeks before. At the centre of it, a tiny town. Ahead of him, clinging to another hill, the village where they had been issued with rifles by the boy and warnings from the grey-faced militiaman. Antonio's unit and two others had fought for three days for the possession of a hill which would complete a chain of positions, enabling a line to be established. The battle had progressed, by mule tracks and stumbles, higher and higher. The hand-to-hand fighting had circled the uneven ledges and narrow tracks like a game of ring-a-roses to the point they had now reached: the prized summit was less than fifty feet above them. Flags had been planted and the positions fortified by blocks of limestone and sandbags on all of the peaks surrounding them.

Renton followed Antonio as, back bent, he led him to Wertzel, Eduardo, Justina and the others who were lying in the cover afforded by a limestone outcrop. Seeing them, hunched, tense, squinting through the sights of their rifles, Kit Renton felt proud. Despite the militiaman's prediction, not one of them had fallen. They had acquitted themselves well in the battle, quickly adapting to each other's rhythms, learning their limitations, compensating for fatigue. There had been few arguments between them. The petty squabbles of Justina and Eduardo were a prelude to romance. Renton smiled as he saw them, lying on their bellies side by side. Her muddy boot rested against Eduardo's calf. Occasionally one stole a look towards the other which was shyly returned.

Antonio knelt and laid down his rifle. Renton sat beside him. The others moved within earshot. For a moment the battle fell silent. Antonio raised his eyebrows in anticipation of another burst of gunfire, Justina laughed, and the silence was broken by the rattle of a Lewis gun.

'We must take the summit tonight,' Antonio told them, and looked around at the tired faces to establish that all of them had heard him. 'Once we have taken the summit, we may dig in and rest.'

'This will be our hill,' Justina said. She nodded, satisfied, at what she saw below them: a steep, barren ravine diminishing into a sea of mist.

'Yes. Our hill,' Antonio agreed. 'Which means we must move forward and upwards.'

'And break cover?' Wertzel asked.

'Yes. Of course. Break cover,' Antonio said, his tone acknowledging the seriousness of the situation and the inevitability of casualties. 'But we will wait for nightfall.'

This was how the pattern of their life had become established: instruction, rumination, action. Renton used the waiting time to dismantle his rifle and grease the barrel. He checked his ammunition and weighed his two bombs on his palms. On a parapet to the east of them a party was in progress. A POUM flag had been raised, a fire had been lit and the feeble glow illuminated the exhausted faces of the men taking advantage of the break in the battle to sit in a circle and eat together without their meal being interrupted by rifle fire or an air raid. They teased and tossed scraps of food to a thin black dog.

Wertzel stood sentry as Antonio and two other men built a fire, striking sparks from their tinder lighters on to bunches of dry grass. Once the grass began to spit and smoulder they laid on light twigs one by one until the fire was flaming, at which point they threw on to it the roots and branches they had foraged. Everybody but Wertzel joined in scavenging for bushes, rosemary, scraps of paper. A wooden tripod was suspended above the flames from which a small cauldron was attached by chains. A metal container of beef stew was brought up to them and tipped into the sooty cooking pot. Soon the white fat melted into the body of the liquid and shortly afterwards the stew threw up the first glutinous bubble. It broke like a fish opening its mouth. Antonio stropped his bayonet against his thigh, plunged it into the cauldron and stirred the heavy resistant mass. The smell of the stew soon pervaded the hillside and attracted them towards it like warmth.

Renton felt drawn to Justina. He needed the proximity of a woman as he ate what he thought might be his last meal. But Justina had never been so popular, she was at the centre of five men and Renton was happy to share her; to sit at her feet and gaze at her as she ate her stew.

'How are you?' she asked him, when she saw he was watching her. Renton blushed and told her how he felt. He only became aware of his feelings when he tried to express them: 'Afraid, excited, elated.' No longer the niceties of civilised society – on the front line a question asked demanded a genuine answer.

'Yes, I know,' Justina said and fixed her attention on the metal dish she was eating from.

'And you?'

'Tired, cold . . . frightened. Sometimes I feel the fear eating me inside. I want warm water. For my hair.'

'Have you heard any news?' Renton prompted.

'I have,' Eduardo interjected. 'From Antonio. He has heard that a Soviet ship has docked in Cartagena with arms for us. Perhaps tanks.'

Hearing this, Antonio leaned across and said, 'No. Not for us. The arms from the Komsomol will go to the Communists.'

'Why not us?' Justina asked.

'Because Stalin has no interest in our revolutionary struggle.'

'They can keep their tanks, Antonio,' Eduardo said, looking up at the sky. 'Tonight everything will change for us.'

'For the better?' Justina asked him.

'Who can say? But we will win or lose possession of the hill tonight. And then . . .'

'Sleep,' Justina said. 'A long sleep.' She shivered. 'I hate this cold. I can bear the filth, but the cold is hard to bear.'

'Wait for the winter,' Eduardo said. 'If we're here in two months' time . . . we will need better coats.'

When the meal was finished, Eduardo moved away from the

others and began sorting his kit. Watching him, Justina moved close to Renton, lowered her voice and asked gravely, 'Are you in love, Kit Renton?'

'What a question.'

'Are you?'

'I don't know. Are you?'

'I think so. Yes. Yes, I know I am. I think it's important that I am in love under these circumstances.'

'Because of the circumstances?'

'Oh yes. I think so. In love the circumstances are always important.'

Eduardo turned and smiled at them but he was too far away to hear the conversation.

'It's obvious that he loves you,' Renton said.

'I know. And Eduardo is not a man who comes to his decisions lightly. I knew he loved me long before he told me.'

'He told you?'

'He whispered it to me. One night when I was trying to sleep, trying to warm myself, I saw him coming towards me. I thought he was going to lose heart and walk by, but I called to him and he knelt beside me. I said, "Is there something you want to say to me, Eduardo?" And he was uncomfortable for a moment. But then he found courage and he took my hand and he told me he loved me.'

Renton said, 'Then yes, I think I am in love too. In these circumstances.'

'Who is she?'

'An actress,' Renton said, remembering Meredith's denial. 'Though she doesn't claim to be an actress.'

'On a stage?'

'Always on a stage.'

'And does she love you?'

'I think so. At least she said she did, but I don't know her well enough to know whether she meant it.'

'In these circumstances it doesn't matter. It is enough to believe that she does.'

'Yes. I suppose it is.'

'Perhaps it's always enough to believe.' Justina's enthusiasm grew. 'Yes, I would say that you have to believe. You can never know. Like bravery. I never believed I was brave until I came out here. And whatever happens to me, even if I don't go home again, I will always be glad that I came here. I wasn't living before.'

'And afterwards?'

'I don't think about after. I only think about now, perhaps the next minute. Not tomorrow. In love and war only the moment is important.'

When night fell and the cigarettes were extinguished, Antonio drew attention to himself by raising himself to his feet. Instead of addressing them as they expected, he turned his back on the unit and emptied his bladder. Justina clucked her half-hearted disapproval. Antonio, apologising for offending her sensibilities, went to Wertzel and gently shook him awake. Wertzel smiled as he saw his new friends surrounding him with their care, watching over him. Antonio patted him on the shoulder and Wertzel clasped his hand for a moment in a gesture of comradeship. Antonio whispered a few curt instructions to the group: they should proceed in silence, move with caution, assume the Fascists are round every bend. He picked up his rifle, edged past Wertzel and peered round the outcrop. Then he turned and gestured everybody to their feet. Packs were to be left at the camp. They were to travel light.

Wertzel stayed close to Antonio's shoulder. Renton took up a position directly behind him. Justina was next and the line trailed behind her into the darkness. The sound of laughter, carried on the breeze from the next hill, provoked a sharpshooter into taking a pot-shot. Only the shot was heard, the flash of fire was too far away to be seen. The sound was greeted by a chorus of catcalls and obscenities.

Antonio whispered to Wertzel and moved off, his bayonet

fixed. Wertzel followed and Renton stayed close to his back. They moved along the narrow, pebble-strewn track for twenty, thirty yards, taking careful, crouched steps. The ravine dropped steeply away to their left. If there were ridges beneath them which would break a fall, the darkness was blanketing them from sight. Another shot rang out and Renton tensed in anticipation of the knife-sharp pain between his shoulder-blades, but the pain did not come. They were moving faster now, almost at walking pace, and Antonio's boots were sending miniature avalanches of scree down the incline. In the darkness all Renton could see was the oxen back of Wertzel. He stayed as close to him as he could, matching him step for step. Behind him he could hear Justina breathing heavily, occasionally whispering to Eduardo behind her to keep back. He was trying to overtake her – to protect her. Fifty steps now, Renton had counted. Fifty yards around the neck of the hill and still no resistance. He began to allow himself to relax – perhaps the Fascists had given up their claim to the hill and had withdrawn. Perhaps, at last, they would be able to sleep for a night without the fear of a raiding party slitting their throats. But just as Renton allowed himself this fantasy he collided with Wertzel, who had stopped without warning. He turned and gestured to Justina that Antonio had halted. Justina relayed the message down the line.

Kit Renton waited, watching Wertzel's shoulders rise and fall as he regained his breath. The German turned, nodded reassuringly and beckoned Kit closer to him. He whispered that Antonio had gone ahead and told them to stay put until he returned. If he had not done so in fifteen minutes they should proceed with great caution. The soldiers in the rear were to hold back and provide cover.

Ten silent minutes passed. A gentle breeze began to play against Renton's face, drying the sweat. The exertion had cleared his nostrils. He could now smell the damp vegetation on the hill. It was only when he heard Justina whispering behind him that he began to feel concerned.

'Can you see anything?' he asked Wertzel.

'No. All quiet. Should we go on?'

Renton nodded. He cocked his rifle, tightened the bayonet and they moved off.

Wertzel proceeded haltingly. Two steps, then a pause. Three steps, another pause. Renton's ears strained for the sound of voices or footsteps. All he could hear were the voices from the next hilltop and the occasional sound of a dog. The further they proceeded the more concerned he became. He had prepared himself for a fire-fight. What he had not anticipated was the tension he now felt in facing an invisible enemy, perhaps walking into a trap, perhaps circling the hill and returning to the point they had departed from, not having encountered anything.

Wertzel paused again but this time he did not continue. He dropped to his knees and Renton did the same. Again, straining to listen, he heard movement, perhaps the scuff of boots on the track. The darkness was unbroken by line or shadow. Wertzel lifted his rifle to his shoulder. They waited. The sounds became more distinct: footsteps, not the sound of an animal or the patter of a stream on to rocks. A figure broke through the curtain of black in front of them and suddenly Antonio was back among them, his eyes sharp with excitement. The tension flooded from Renton's heart as he acknowledged his greatest fear – the loss of the boy to lead them.

'They are not far away. Perhaps a hundred yards,' Antonio whispered urgently, made young again by the anticipation of action. 'They are preparing to move off. We must act quickly. There are two sentries. They are all afraid. One of their officers is telling them to retreat to their lines before they are all shot. Some of the men have been injured. They are discussing how to get them down the hill.'

'Then let's go,' Wertzel said, shouldering his weapon.

'Wait. One moment. I have to warn you. The track is . . .'

'I can't hear you,' Justina said.

'No, we can't hear you down the line, Antonio,' Eduardo added. 'Can you please speak a little louder.'

Antonio moved into the centre of the group. Those at the back of the line bunched up and Antonio continued, 'The track drops away and it becomes very narrow thirty steps ahead. You must be very careful. And after it falls, it flattens and then becomes steep.' He demonstrated the gradient with his forearm. 'Steep for ten, twenty, steps. The Fascists are beyond the incline. The track opens into a clearing; a ledge. They have built a cooking fire and the two sentries are posted at this side of the fire. When I saw them they were sitting. Perhaps one was lying down. He may have been asleep. I could see only their silhouettes against the fire.'

'How many men?' Renton asked.

'It was difficult to see.'

'Then there are too many to count,' Justina said.

'Fifty. Perhaps more. But they have a clear line of retreat. And we will surprise them.'

'Perhaps we will surprise ourselves,' Justina whispered soberly. Eduardo took her hand and kissed it and Renton saw them say their first goodbye.

'But this is how it has always been for us,' Antonio encouraged. 'We have always faced odds such as these. It is our privilege that we are fighting a real war — a war we can at last win. Yes?'

'Come on,' Wertzel said. 'Let's move.'

Renton breathed deeply. He felt a hand reaching for his and Justina's lips against his cheek. Deftly, silently, she moved from man to man, granting each the same benediction.

Antonio took three steps and vanished into the black, Wertzel immediately followed, and Kit took his place in the line behind them. They were moving fast. Too fast. Justina cursed behind him. He heard her whisper to him to slow down but he was concentrating too hard on maintaining his footing on the track to reply. As Antonio had warned, the path had narrowed to less than a foot wide. What the boy had failed to tell them was what bordered it. Renton reached to steady himself against the cold rock at his right. For all he knew the drop to the left of him was sheer. He froze with fear, terrified to go on, unable to turn back. He fought the determined pull of the void beside him, the voice in his head calling to him to step into the darkness and finish it all. He heard Justina behind him and forced himself on. Three steps later he was moving easily again, a broad white rock, almost phosphorescent, marking the left flank of the track. As the incline steepened he dropped to his hands and knees to climb it. When the gradient became shallower he stood again and unstrapped the rifle from his shoulder. He heard Justina behind him whispering a commentary to Eduardo and he wished she had the good sense to know when to remain silent.

Afterwards, when he looked back on the action, he knew he had not been prepared for it. But Antonio had often warned them that there could be no preparation for close combat, no gentle easing into action. One moment silence; peace. The next, the first shot – and then the din and confusion of friend and foe. Antonio, with all the wisdom of his young years, told them that a soldier at war must embrace the anxiety that the first shot is always a moment away, but it is an anxiety that takes many years to shed.

That shot was fired at the moment that Renton was cursing Justina. He saw the green flash not far ahead of him: Antonio. He then collided with Wertzel, who pushed him roughly away. Antonio was crouched on one knee and firing towards the orange flicker of a small fire. Wertzel's rifle had jammed on the first shot. In panic he was trying to palm the bolt back to dislodge the faulty cartridge but the bolt was locked. In frustration he took the barrel and swung the butt against a rock. The wood splintered. Renton adopted Antonio's stance and fired towards the black shapes moving in front of the fire. A man fell backwards into the low flames and screamed in panic as the sleeve of his jacket caught alight. Antonio stood, moved a step forward and knelt again, continuing to fire. Wertzel shouted and the boy stopped firing as the German ran towards the man thrashing in the flames. He reached in and pulled his rifle from him.

Raising the barrel, he concluded the transaction by putting a bullet through the man's cheek. A ragged black hole appeared, and the man's frantic thrashing subsided as the flames engulfed him. Justina and Eduardo fanned out to the left, but remained four or five feet behind. When the others broke through into the clearing they pushed into a narrow line, some standing, some kneeling, but all firing at the figures on the far side of the fire as they stumbled away. Jesus appeared to Renton's right. He knelt and shot, then he stood to reload. Somebody called to him to drop down but he was too slow. The bullet caught him in the chin. His hand went to the wound. Then he fell.

As the firing intensified, Antonio reached into his sack for a bomb. He tugged out the fuses and tossed it underarm over the fire. The fizzing red fuse marked the arc of its trajectory and the bomb exploded just as Renton had written it off as a dud. The shockwaves from the explosion deafened them momentarily. Renton felt as if he had dived underwater, the sound of each sharp rifle shot muted and stretched and absorbed by echoes. A moment later the racket reasserted itself and the sound came bouncing back.

Antonio used the crack of the explosion as a cue to urge them forward, to press home their advantage. He was kneeling and reloading his rifle. Wertzel took up the vanguard position and strode past the fire into the uncharted territory beyond. He fired twice into the darkness. Renton went with him. The Fascists had run, leaving the camp scattered with sacks and provisions and blankets. Wertzel raised his hand and the rifles behind him fell silent.

'Down. Get down,' they heard from Antonio, and Wertzel reluctantly knelt.

'Gone,' Justina said.

'Perhaps.'

'It is our hill now.'

'Not yet.' Having reloaded, Antonio led the way down the track. Ahead of them they could hear the distant and diminishing shouts of men as they scrambled away in terror down the dark incline.

'Must we follow them all the way down?' It was a sensible question, but one that only Justina would have posed.

'No,' Antonio replied, coming to a halt. 'Why should we?'

'Well then, it is our hill,' Justina said.

'For now.'

None of them could sleep after the action. They knew that future battles would not be so easy but tonight, after burying Jesus, they lay awake watching the stars and reliving the routing of the Fascists and the heroic battle for their hill. Sometimes war is easy, and not so different from peace, Renton considered. War is surprise and darkness but mainly, just like ordinary life, it is hiding your fear. Having seen men shot dead, his appetite for life had increased. He wanted to eat and talk and make love and laugh. He felt that all of these activities held possibilities that remained unexplored.

By the light of a candle he wrote his first letter to Meredith Kerr.

London

Half-blinded by a hangover, Arthur Lawler could nevertheless make out that the figure approaching him through the morning mist was a young woman. From ten yards away she called out, 'I just had to talk to you.' Only when he heard her voice did he realise the woman walking quickly towards him was Meredith.

'I thought Bowden wouldn't allow you to see me,' Lawler called back. He was embarrassed to have been discovered wearing a pair of borrowed overalls, standing high up on a pair of stepladders and washing down the outside of Harry Bowden's car showroom windows.

Meredith peered up the steep gradient of rungs and said, 'He went out early. Is something going off today?'

'Yes. I'm afraid it is.'

'I thought so. A horrible man called Higgott came round last night and kept Harry up talking and drinking until after two.'

'What time is it now?'

'Just after nine.'

'I feel as though I've been at it for hours. Can you see any streaks on the glass?'

'Let me look . . . Yes. Hundreds of them. I think my mother used to clean the windows with vinegar and newspaper.'

'Well, I wasn't given any vinegar or newspaper. I can't seem to get the hang of it at all. Wilson showed me how to get a decent lather but the soap just seems to smear the panes.'

'Come down, Arthur. I can't talk to you properly up there and I want to show you something.'

Lawler backed cautiously down to the pavement and wiped his

hands dry on the seat of his brown overalls. 'How are you?' He asked Meredith, taking her hands and kissing her on the cheek.

'The same as you I expect.' Arthur Lawler's kisses always surprised Meredith. Convinced, as she was, that she felt nothing in the way of passion for him, when there was any physical contact between them she always felt a quickening of her heart. 'Are you all right?' she said.

'No. Not particularly.'

'Why don't you just run away?'

'I can't. Not yet. Not until you do.' Arthur looked up and down the street, then said, 'You are still intending to leave?'

'Yes. Of course. Especially now.' Meredith slipped an envelope out of her handbag. Arthur reached for it, but she held it back, smiling, telling him, 'It's from Kit.'

'Kit!'

'Yes. Isn't it exciting?'

'Can I read it?'

'I'm not sure I should allow it,' she teased, chewing a corner of the envelope.

'Come on, Meredith. Billy will be back in a moment.'

'Surely we can trust Billy, can't we?'

'Frankly, no. At the moment I wouldn't trust anybody associated with Bowden.'

'I'll tell you what he said then. Just in case Billy comes back . . . Well, get on with your work, Arthur. There's no need to slacken off just because I'm here.'

Arthur turned away to face the window. He wrung out a leather and began to rub half-heartedly at the area of glass most densely obscured by smears.

'He joined one of the Anarchist militias. That's what he calls them. And now he's fighting somewhere near Barcelona.'

'Go on.'

'Wait a minute. I want to read you something . . . here we are. "In the short time I have been here I have forged many strong friendships. When your life literally depends on the people around you, you very quickly reach a deep level of trust. There are nine of us now, and we spend our days taking turns at sentry-go, watching the skies for enemy aeroplanes and keeping an eye on the Fascists through field glasses. The Fascists spend their time occupied in a similar way. It becomes very cold here at night so we pass our idle hours scouting for firewood. Occasionally we launch a patrol across no-man's-land, generally to little effect . . ." He says some other things, then, here we are: "Meredith. I lost a good friend tonight. I was beside him when a sharpshooter shot him dead. A foot or so to the right and the bullet would have shattered my jaw instead of his. My first reaction was one of relief. He didn't fall immediately and I assumed the sharpshooter had missed. But when he went down he was already dead. Life here is extinguished like a candle flame, which makes everything seem more urgent and vivid. Food, for example, tastes so much better. We eat greedily from the canteen wagons when they occasionally arrive. We smoke as many cigarettes as our rations allow. And we dream and talk about women and how we want to make love to women and all of the beautiful women we have known. Perhaps you find this hard to believe of me. But the truth is that the man you met in Berners Street is only a shadow of the man who stands on this parapet. I barely recognise him myself. I want to tell them all about you. But you are too precious to share . . ." and he goes on a bit more. And then more. And then he finishes . . . Arthur?'

'Does he . . . I mean does he send any kind of message to me?'

'No. Perhaps he's written to you care of the hotel.'

'Yes. Of course.'

'Look at me.'

Arthur turned slowly.

'You mustn't be angry. Wouldn't you rather it was someone like Kit rather than Harry?'

'Frankly, the pain is the same whoever takes you away from me. It's selfish, I know, but that's how I feel.'

'You don't mean that.'

'. . . No.'

'I'm afraid that window looks worse now.'

'I'll have to get Wilson to show me how to do it again,' Arthur said and draped his leather over a rung of the ladder.

'Can I have a cup of tea?'

'Yes, I expect so. Wilson will complain that he has to make a new pot, but he likes you so he won't really mind.' Arthur took Meredith's arm and tried to guide her towards the door, but she resisted the gentle pressure on her elbow.

'. . . Arthur?' she said.

'Yes.'

'What did Harry say to you. To make you stay?'

'I don't exactly have a great deal of choice at the moment.'

'Shall I tell you what I think he said?'

'If you like.'

'Something along the lines of him taking it out on me if you did decide to leave.'

'Perhaps. Yes, something along those lines.'

'Well, I'm leaving in two weeks' time, Arthur.'

'Really?'

'Yes. This isn't a whim. I've planned it properly this time.'

'To find Kit?'

'I went to see a man called Pollitt. He's a Communist. He's been helping people get out there.'

'I know who he is. How did you find him?'

'It's not important.'

'He's supposed to be trustworthy.'

'He's very concerned about what Harry and his friends are up to.'

'I'm not surprised.'

'You're sure it's today?'

'Yes.'

'You must be careful, Arthur.'

'I will.'

'And Billy. He must be careful too.'

*　　*　　*

When Billy Royle returned with breakfast fifteen minutes later, Meredith had gone. As he walked into the showroom office, taking off his coat, he paused and sniffed the air. 'I'd know her perfume anywhere, Arthur,' he said. 'And so would Harry. So be careful.'

'She's had a letter from Kit. She wanted to read it to me. That's all.' Arthur was staring miserably into the unlit showroom. Behind him, sitting on the small leather sofa, Wilson was reading the newspaper.

'What did you get?' Wilson said.

'Cold mutton.' Royle tore open a white paper sandwich bag and put it down on the table.

'Any pickle?'

'No.'

'Mustard?'

'No. No mustard.'

'Not bacon?'

'No, Wilson. Cold mutton. If you'd wanted bacon you should have told me before I went.'

'We usually have bacon.'

'Yes, but not always. Look, Arthur, will you eat mutton without pickle or shall I just throw the whole lot away?'

'I can't face food this early in the day.'

'Wilson?'

'Oh, I'll eat mutton. But I'd prefer something warm inside me. That's all.'

'Take the bloody lot then,' Royle said and strode out of the office. Arthur and Wilson watched him as he crossed the showroom. When he reached the Alpine Tourer he wrenched open the door and climbed in, slamming the door shut after him.

'What's eating him today?' Wilson said. Arthur didn't answer. Instead, he followed Royle out of the gas-warmed office into the showroom, which was as cold as the street outside. He waited beside the car as Royle lit a cigarette and took three successive deep draws.

'What did he have to say for himself?' Royle finally said.

'He's joined one of the militias somewhere around Barcelona. He mentions a few understated heroics. Somebody was shot dead standing next to him.'

'Pity.'

'Yes. It was quite close, apparently.'

'No. Pity it wasn't him.'

'I'm sure you don't mean that.'

'Anything else?' Royle tapped his cigarette and dropped ash on to the showroom floor for Wilson to sweep up.

'Something about the Kit we used to know being but a shadow of the new man.'

'He'll be standing for Parliament when he comes back. It was bound to happen, I expect.'

'Yes.'

'People like Kit Renton often start out looking like eccentrics but somehow they're the ones whom you see taking a late turn towards the bosom of the establishment. You know it wouldn't surprise me if he didn't end up as a Tory.'

'I don't think that's likely.'

'I don't see why not. Look at Harry. He doesn't actually hate Jews and whatnot, he just needs some cause to believe in. Like Kit. The cause in itself is largely irrelevant.'

'I wouldn't glorify Bowden's sordid antics as a cause, and I certainly wouldn't demean Kit by associating his beliefs with Bowden's.'

'. . . I do wish Wilson would stop staring at us through the window. He looks like a trout in a display case.'

'Let's have some breakfast.'

Royle wearily climbed out of the car. When he had closed the door he lingered to rub a thumbprint from the coachwork with his handkerchief.

'By the way,' Arthur said. 'Meredith said you must take care today.'

'She said I must take care?'

'Yes.'

'Really?'

'Yes.'

'Does she still care about me, do you think?'

'I know she does.'

'Perhaps if Kit doesn't come back things might get back to normal again.'

'She might leave Bowden and elope with you?'

'Stranger things have happened.'

Neither man seemed inclined to return to the office. Instead, they waited between the cars and watched Wilson lift a triangular flap of the torn paper bag, peer suspiciously beneath it, and take out another sandwich. As he raised it to his mouth he caught them staring at him and shuffled round on the sofa, presenting them with his back. Then he went on eating.

'I've been wanting to talk to you about Deirdre,' Royle said.

'Have you?'

'Yes, I just didn't know quite what to say.'

'Well, go on.'

'I thought there was more to it. I mean I genuinely thought . . .' Royle laughed. 'I genuinely thought I was in love with her. Do you know?'

'I can see how that could happen.'

'But she doesn't want me, Arthur. She wants you . . . I mean, of all the . . . What I mean to say is, it's just my luck that the first girl I feel something for is already infatuated with somebody else.'

'Me? I very much doubt it. And you're not honestly telling me that Deirdre is the first woman you've fallen for?'

'Yes, I am.'

'But what about Meredith?'

'Meredith was different. Meredith was always . . . unattainable.'

'And Deirdre wasn't?'

'No. Far from it. Peas in a pod. Or so I thought. So there we are. Confession over.'

'You know, I haven't given her a moment's thought since that night we all went out together.'

'Well, I suggest you go and look for her, Arthur. If for no other reason than the fact that she has over eighty pounds in the Post Office.'

'Eighty pounds!'

'I found the book hidden away in the bottom of her wardrobe. Inside the family Bible.'

'Really. Eighty pounds?'

'Eighty-three pounds, seven shillings and threepence. This is a girl who won't even squander the odd threepenny bit on herself. You have to admire that kind of self-restraint. In financial matters if no other.'

At ten-thirty, shortly after Arthur had resumed work on the windows and Wilson had completed his daily exertions in the lavatory and wandered outside to offer him his advice, a convoy of black vans led by a limousine drew up outside the showroom. Bowden, in a black military jacket, grey riding britches and jackboots, emerged stiffly from the front passenger seat of the limousine. The driver, a fair-haired, pigeon-breasted youth in a black shirt, black cavalry twill trousers and highly polished hob-nailed boots, followed him to the kerb, came to attention and waited for his orders.

'Ten minutes. Tell them to switch off, then wait in the motor,' Bowden said, and the youth went to the front window of the first van to relay the order. Bowden watched him for a moment, enjoying the fruits of his authority. Then he looked up at Lawler who was straddling the summit of the stepladders, a sponge in his hand. Without any change in his expression, Bowden grasped two rungs and began shaking the framework vigorously. As the ladders toppled sideways to the floor Arthur jumped clear, managing to land on his feet. Bowden stared at him, challenging him to complain. Lawler stared back, refusing to be cowed by his bullying.

'You do the windows,' Bowden said to Wilson. 'And you come in here.'

Lawler followed Bowden to the office where they found Royle chuckling at the morning paper, leaning back in the leather desk-chair, his feet up on the desk. The debris of the breakfast remained uncleared on the table.

'What do I pay you for?' Bowden said. Royle spun round on the chair and jumped to his feet. He immediately set to tidying up the paper, and removing bread crusts and the lump of mutton gristle from the table.

'Do it later,' Bowden said, going to the desk. Royle put down the teacup he had just picked up. As he stood straight he buttoned his jacket and fingernailed his hair back into place behind his ears.

'You look smart, Harry,' he said, and Bowden couldn't entirely hide the pleasure he found in the compliment.

'New uniform. There's shirts for you two in the motor.'

'Right,' Royle said, composed again. Bowden, for all his faults, meted out punishment promptly and Royle already knew he had been let off the hook for the state of the office. 'So what's the plan?' he said.

'Over here, Lawler.' Bowden took out a rolled pencil-drawn map and spread it on the desk. Royle stood at his shoulder as he weighted the left edge with the desk-light and held down the right with his palm. 'We're meeting here at Tower Hill, at two p.m. There's another lot coming in by train.'

'How many altogether?' Royle said.

'A few thousand. Four, maybe more.'

'That's a good crowd.'

'We march up Royal Mint Street and into Cable Street and then on from there. We've got four rallies planned for the afternoon and Sir Oswald is expecting to address each one. I've just been with Higgott and he reckons that the police will be more sympathetic to us than the opposition so don't waste your time laying into them. You might just find they're on your side. Did you want to say something, Lawler?'

'Not particularly.'

'What's the matter with you? Afraid of a good clean scrap?'

'Why are you involved in this, Bowden?'

'Does he really not know?' Bowden said to Royle. 'I mean, does he not understand the game? Eh?'

Royle shrugged and smiled weakly.

'Well, you tell him, Billy. Go on. You tell him why we need to get rid of these Jew-boys.'

'You're the politician, Harry.'

'Has he been down the East End recently? No? Well, tell him to go and take a look and then come back and tell me there's room for the hundred and fifty thousand Yids who've moved in down there. If he can convince me there's houses for them and enough food to go round I'll call the whole thing off.'

'It's not the fault of the Jews, Bowden, as well you know. They've come here to get away from being persecuted by people like you. Look at the cause, not the symptoms.'

'I don't have time for this. You're giving me indigestion. Royle, what I came here to tell you is that we're providing the close guard to Sir Oswald. Me and Higgott between us. All right? A great honour as far as I'm concerned. He'll travel with Higgott but I want you around in case I need something in a hurry-up.'

'Right.'

'And Lawler, if I catch you running off there'll be trouble.'

All Arthur Lawler could see through the small van window was a square of sky the colour of a smoke-stained sheet. The men sharing the benches with him were quiet and still, like parachutists waiting for the jump. Some were smoking. Occasionally one of them coughed or cleared his throat, but they appeared to be strangers to each other and content for it to stay that way. Lawler could sense no nervousness in them, just a gentle tension and an eager anticipation of the fight ahead. Some of them, he suspected from the way they held themselves, were soldiers. One of them was wearing policeman's boots. In their silence they were conserving their energy as the van reached Aldgate and turned down the Minories towards Tower Hill.

Lawler was sickened by the humiliation he had suffered at the hands of Bowden. He sucked at the hatred he felt for him like a rotten tooth. But the rank taste of the hatred was healing, forcing him, as it did, to turn away from himself and his own blank future. Two weeks more and Meredith would be gone. Then there would be nothing to keep him in London except for Deirdre and her Post Office account. Eighty-three pounds, seven shillings and threepence. A small fortune. More than enough for a deposit on a brand-new four-hundred-pound house and furniture to fill it, a new wardrobe of clothes, a cot for the third bedroom, wallpaper for her mother's room. Sufficient to see him through a few months more on the booze before he had to face the prospect of getting himself straight. But he would never be straight and he was determined not to take Deirdre down with him. Whatever promises she forced him to make, he understood himself well enough to know that he had no real power over his destiny. His life needed an act, something bigger than a mere gesture, to set it on a new course. Perhaps he should kill Bowden. Perhaps an act of murder would be enough.

Through the van window Lawler could now see a police aeroplane. It crawled across the pane like a silver fly. The man beside him reached into the muddy, damp crate at their feet and took out a cudgel wound at the tip with barbed wire. He toyed with the handle and fingered the taped handgrip. Two rusty six-inch nails had been driven through the end. Lawler imagined planting the nails deep into Bowden's skull. How many times would he need to do it before it killed him? Would his skull cling to the nail so that he would need to employ some leverage to withdraw it, cracking the thin bone like an eggshell? Or would it relinquish the six-inch spike as easily as if it had been sunk into a lump of brawn? Lawler drew a weapon from the wooden box and the van came to a halt, the men lurching sideways against one another. They heard the driver call out, the front cab door opened, somebody banged on the side of the van, the back doors were thrown open and Lawler blinked as he climbed out and his eyes adjusted to the light.

The body of the van had shielded them from the noise of the huge crowd massed to the left of them on the bank of Tower Hill. As they emerged they were greeted by a salvo of bottles launched over the heads of the police cordon. The bottles crashed and splintered on the road and shards of brown glass scurried on towards the kerb. The jeers built in volume until they were as deafening as a Cup Final crowd. When the racket diminished, solo shouts of anger and protest could be heard. A police wireless van passed them. A loudspeaker on a house roof in Cartwright Street was broadcasting a gramophone recording of 'The Red Flag'. On the flat roof of a store, a worker was running back and forth, taunting them with a clenched-fist salute. Lawler could see that the men had disembarked from the other two vans. Ahead of them Bowden's black limousine had pulled up. More reinforcements were arriving from the direction of Mark Lane station bearing a variety of sticks and cudgels and knuckle-dusters. One man had a pistol in his belt. Three huge police horses, steaming from their flanks, trotted between them, forcing them hard against the convoy. Bowden was standing in the back of the open car waving them on. Somebody handed him a megaphone and he ordered the men to close up towards him. As he passed the megaphone down, a squadron of mounted police charged past them to reinforce the cordon holding back the crowds on Royal Mint Street. The Blackshirts were penned into a corridor and Lawler could see that the police were defending them from the protestors. He felt himself being carried along by the men surging forward. Eight or nine abreast, they were now advancing in a block up Mansell Street and as they moved somebody started calling for Mosley, and the Blackshirts around him took up the chant: 'M.O.S.L.E.Y.' Two elderly plain-clothed policemen in overcoats emerged from a police box. Seeing the size of the Fascist crowd passing them, one immediately went back inside to telephone for reinforcements.

'Here he is!' the call went up and Mosley's name was chanted with more vigour. The jeers of the workers momentarily drowned them out. The march towards Royal Mint Street halted as two motor-cycles forced a path through the ranks for a black open-topped car. Mosley was standing in the front, holding on to the windshield and saluting, his right arm stretched out ahead of him. The men around him came to attention, some returning the salute. A large Union flag was raised and swung. More bottles were thrown towards them, then a fusillade of stones. A pool of petrol was ignited and the ankle-high flames were quickly stamped out. Lawler was jostled into movement again as the advance continued.

Above the heads of the men bunched ahead of him, Lawler could see the roof of a builder's lorry rocking from side to side at the hands of the crowds defending the entrance to Royal Mint Street. To a huge cheer from the workers, the lorry rolled over.

'Look out! Clear the way,' Lawler heard, and the ranks broke wide. Two abreast, thirty policemen with truncheons drawn jogged towards the barricade. Paving stones were being torn up and smashed and a pile of them was being raised around the centrepiece of the builder's lorry. The baton charge slowed as the men encountered the thick carpet of glass on the road. Then a barrage of house bricks sent them back. A woman and a young man were dragged from the workers' ranks by three constables as they retreated. The woman was pulled into the centre of a group of policemen and Lawler saw her fall as the boots went in. The workers on the barricade also saw it and a number of them vaulted the barricade and set to dragging away the policemen surrounding the woman. Above the scrap, cudgels were raised and brought down on bare heads but the close proximity meant that the barbed-wire sticks were ineffective.

Lawler searched the crowd for Bowden and saw him thirty feet to the left, watching the beating of the woman with a smile of grim satisfaction on his face. He reached down for a brick, looked guiltily around him, and lobbed it lazily towards the scuffle. It struck a Blackshirt between the shoulder-blades and Bowden laughed and turned in the hope that he could share his contribution with Royle. But Royle and Higgott had moved away from him and were standing in the group surrounding Mosley and the Metropolitan Police Commissioner. Bowden was just thirty steps away and unprotected. With the mayhem of the battle around them and the confusion of ally with enemy, Lawler knew he would never get a better chance at Bowden. The path between them was clear. Thirty strides to an act which would change his life irrevocably.

He felt no fear as he approached Bowden, nor any plan beyond the moment of the attack. In the instant he spent contemplating it, he knew that if he was fortunate he would be able to lose himself in the crowd. If not, then he hoped his apprehension came at the hands of the police rather than the Blackshirts. Twenty strides from Bowden, who had now lost interest in the fight and was watching the group gathered around Mosley. Lawler moved quickly towards him. When Bowden saw him he directed him on like a traffic policeman, assuming him to be on his way to join the men fighting at the barricades. Only when he was within ten feet of him did Bowden register the possibility of a threat. He called to Royle and backed off a step. Royle was too far away to hear him. Bowden, seeing the cudgel in Lawler's hand, scouted the road for something to defend himself with. He picked up a brick and raised his arm, ready to throw. Lawler pushed on towards him. His conviction was such that he felt that, even if he had a man on his back, he would have sufficient strength to drive on and deliver the blows to Bowden's head. The first would be for Meredith. The second for himself. The third for Royle. The fourth for the life extinguished by Pugh on the night of the fog.

'Don't be a fool,' Bowden said as Lawler reached him. Lawler raised the cudgel, Bowden dropped the stone.

'I'm not going to waste time,' Lawler said. 'And I'm not going to offer an explanation. But if you do die today, I want you to do so knowing that Meredith has no intention of marrying you. She despises you. She's going to Spain to find Kit.'

'You think I don't know what she's planning?'

'It's too late. You've lost her.'

'She won't get far. Now why don't you bugger off out of my sight.'

Lawler swung his arm and drove the point of a nail into the centre of Bowden's skull. The effect it had was to freeze Bowden's expression. As he sunk to his knees Lawler heard a shout behind him. He tugged the spike free of the wound and Bowden pitched forward. Lawler raised the cudgel again and planted it into Bowden's exposed neck. Before he could strike a third blow he felt his arm being restrained.

'No more,' he heard from Royle. Given the circumstances, his voice was gentle. 'That's enough now, Arthur.'

'Yes.'

'You'd better run. Run. Go on.' Royle looked down at Bowden. His body was twitching involuntarily, his head jerking back with a steady pulse-like rhythm. Royle kneeled and cradled his head in his lap while Lawler lost himself in the crowd.

Lawler ran until he was exhausted and the noise of the battle was far behind him. He had come to a street where people were going about their own business. A man in a corduroy jacket was buying a garden spade from an ironmonger's. He had taken it outside and was holding up the blade to examine it by the light of the sun. A spade, Arthur thought. How extraordinary. He looked around him at the galvanised watering-cans hooked over the rail, the coils of bright chain on the pavement, the box of loose padlocks. 'A spade,' he said out loud. Nobody paid attention to him. There was no mark on him of the violence he had perpetrated. He walked into a one-roomed public house and ordered a drink, with each passing moment waiting for a hand on his shoulder, anticipating the cuffs on his wrists. He drank the Scotch, which sobered him, and his head began to clear. He didn't have much time now. He had paid for Meredith's freedom at the cost of his own. He must telephone her and tell her, then he must go to ground.

'I think I've killed Bowden,' he said. The first words he spoke to Meredith. No preamble, just: 'I think I've killed Bowden.'

'Arthur, what are you talking about?'

'You must go to Kit now. Leave before they come after you.'

'They? Who are they?'

'We didn't go to Brighton, did we? He took you to Brighton.'

'Brighton? I don't understand, Arthur. Slow down. You said you think you've killed Harry? How did you kill him?'

'There was a rally. Mosley was there.'

'You were at the rally?'

'I simply walked up to him and I . . . I whacked him over the head.'

'But you're not sure he's . . . ?' The practicalities beginning to press in on her: railway ticket; clothes; currency.

'Meredith, this is important. You must listen to me. You must leave as soon as you can. You see, Bowden knew all about Kit. He knew you were going to leave. I'm sure there's somebody watching you now. I can't . . . I can't quite . . .'

'And what about the police, Arthur, surely they'll . . . ?'

'One day, my love. When all of this is over, we'll meet . . .'

'Arthur, please, you're frightening me now.'

'. . . And we'll dress up (yes, this is important). We'll dress up in our best and finest clothes and we'll walk into the Metropole as man and wife (I'm sure Kit won't mind). And we'll take a table by the window and we'll gaze out at the sea and we'll . . . we'll talk, Meredith. That's all. We'll talk and I'll tell you everything that happens to me from this day on and you'll tell me all about your adventures in Spain. And by then everything will be fine again and Bowden will be gone and, yes, everything will be calm again . . . Meredith?'

'Yes, Arthur.'

'I do love you,' he said, and the line was cut.

Meredith was standing in the kitchen now, looking across the narrow yard to the rear of the building facing her. Her heart was racing but inside she was calm. The chain of events set in course from the moment she first saw Kit Renton had led to this moment. She had known there would be a time when she would have the opportunity to leave and she had been waiting for a sign. Poor old Arthur had played a greater part than she had anticipated. He had laid down his life for her and she couldn't let him down. It was time to go now. Time to run.

The Aragón Front

Standing sentry on the hill, Justina was singing and her gentle voice sugared the chill of the morning. Kit Renton was listening to her from the shelter of his dugout. The short trench beside him had been used as a dump for discarded tin cans; he found the odour of rot and decay emanating from it to be marginally preferable to the smell of excrement which pervaded the area to the rear of the position. To the front of him, ahead of the sandbagged wall and coiled barbed wire, the debris of the occupation was strewn down the side of the steep ravine.

Renton was hugging his knees to his chest to try and warm himself. He was wearing all the clothes that he had with him but, wherever the mist touched his bare skin, it chilled his body and from each of those points the cold radiated deep inside him. At night the temperature fell sharply, freezing the earth and the rocks. For the past week the heat of the sun had been insufficient to burn off the mist until midway through the afternoon. When the earth thawed it became a greasy layer over stone, like flesh over bone, making movement treacherous.

Justina's singing stopped mid-phrase, alerting the men who had been listening to her to reach for their weapons. But, as happened most mornings, the alarm the sentry called was 'Fascist planes!' and the heads of a number of bored militiamen appeared from their rat-holes, their eyes automatically searching the skies to the east. Renton spotted the specks of five Heinkels approaching in a V formation, returning from a raid on Barcelona. The pilots were flying low over the hilltops but above the mist layer, the sun pouring a precious gold warmth on their shoulders. The sound of their engines lagged for a moment until a clattering whine overwhelmed the silence and the dots filled out to shark-nosed, screaming vectors which passed deafeningly close overhead. The streaks of silver looked like molten metal poured into the wind, the racket of them so loud that Renton felt that the rivets would loosen, the belly of the fuselage tear open and the acid cargo of undropped bombs fall harmlessly on to no-man's-land. He glimpsed the pilot of the leading plane, helmeted, goggles down, hunched over the controls like a huge fly. Belatedly, the anti-aircraft gunners sent a barrage of shells harmlessly after the formation and the sky became spotted with the new clouds of shell bursts. Not to be outdone, the men tending the heavy guns positioned in the foothills joined in and the metallic roars of the heavy shells drowned the *back-back-back* call from the a.a. batteries. This, in turn, provoked a half-hearted response from the enemy lines. A few rifle shots were heard, a mortar shell landed in the sierra. When the action stopped, each side willed the other to mount a suicidal daytime attack across the plain. Anything to alleviate the boredom.

When the planes had disappeared over the enemy lines to muted cheers from the Fascists, Justina went back to filleting the mud from her fingernails with a small knife. Renton called her name, catching her attention. 'How are you today?' he asked her.

'I am ill,' Justina called back. 'I have another cold. My nose feels like pepper. I can't breathe.'

'I'm sorry to hear that.'

Justina shrugged away his concern.

'. . . Any more action today?'

'Yes. Antonio said we will have our cigarette rations at last.'

'Good. And what about food?'

'Food soon, he said.' Justina had no interest in prolonging the conversation. She closed it off by leaning to peer through a loophole in the sandbagged wall. Despite Eduardo's attentions, her enthusiasm for the struggle had diminished. Her laughter was now rarely heard and she no longer joined the rest of them in their eager speculation about the progress of the war. She refused to be drawn into their flirtatious conversations about love and barely seemed to notice when they degenerated into discussions about sex.

'Psst,' Renton heard from behind him. He twisted round and saw Wertzel's large round head peering from his dugout.

'Good morning,' Renton called.

'Good morning, mister. And how is your family today?'

'Very active.'

'The same with mine. But I intend to send them away on a long holiday.'

'Good. I hope you won't mind if mine join them.'

'Of course not. If you won't miss them.'

'Not at all.'

'Very well. But I need your help.'

'Gladly. I'll do anything I can.'

'Anything?'

'Of course.'

'Come, please,' Wertzel said, and disappeared back into the hole. Renton, his boredom threshold high, and having assumed the conversation to be another meaningless, time-wasting diversion, was now intrigued. He climbed quickly out of his dugout and, shivering, crossed the thirty feet to Wertzel's. Justina watched him with neighbourly curiosity as he backed out of view down into the German's hole.

Wertzel, unlike the rest of the unit, took pride in his dugout. It was deeper and wider than those of the others, who considered their temporary homes to have been completed when they had shovelled out a tunnel long enough to lie in. The German approached the project methodically. He had surveyed the ground and dug a number of test holes in the limestone cliff-face. It soon became clear to the rest of them that by adopting this process he had chosen an area of the hilltop where the limestone was softest. He began by excavating a narrow tunnel. Ten feet in, he widened it out into a circular, flat-floored chamber with a diameter of seven or eight feet and a height of five. Stepped up the wall were three hollowed-out small holes and, in each one, he had set a tallow candle. Only one of the candles was lit but, in the enclosed space, the flame gave the illusion of heat.

'Do you like my home?' Wertzel gestured to the neatly rolled bedding, the four books stacked on the tin box, the shaving kit and soap, the tin cup and the bucket of clear water.

'Yes. It's remarkable,' Renton said.

'Your family and mine . . .'

'Yes.'

'I have a solution.'

'If you have a solution, Wertzel, you will be the most popular man on the front line.'

'But I need your help.'

'That's why I'm here.'

'Very well.' Wertzel reached to lift the water bucket and tipped a little into his tin cup. He took a bar of shaving soap, dipped it into the water and began to work up a lather in his palms. 'Now,' he said, 'you must look the other way.'

Renton turned to face the candle. He could hear the German grunting behind him as he manoeuvred in the cramped space. Then he heard a rasping of soap on skin and, finally, 'Very well. I'm ready.'

Renton turned back to find Wertzel naked from the waist down. The dense thatch of light hair surrounding his balls was lathered, and the soap extended down the inside of each of his thighs. The area of soaped skin was red raw. On Wertzel's left leg blisters had broken out where his frantic scratching had broken the skin.

'Now you will understand why I need your help,' he said, handing Renton a cut-throat razor.

'Yes. Of course.'

'If you remove the hair then the family have nowhere to live.'

'Except in your clothes.'

'Yes. But I can deal with them in my clothes. I can't bear them on my balls.'

'Quite.' Renton kneeled in front of Wertzel. 'You'll have to keep very still. I'll try not to cut you.'

'I'm ready.'

Renton took a deep breath, grasped the razor between his finger and thumb, folded the handle into the snug of his palm and set the blade just beneath the fold of Wertzel's belly. As if he were shaving his own cheek, he applied a little gentle pressure and tugged the cold metal against the edge of the German's pubic hair. He was looking so closely he could see the movement of the tiny lice in the lather. The stiff hair resisted and would not give.

'It's no good,' Renton said. 'The razor is not sharp enough.'

'Please, I can bear the pain.'

'Perhaps we should try and heat the water.'

'No.'

Only by disassociating himself from the act could Renton continue. He tried for a second time, increasing the pressure of the cold blade. Again it had no effect but Wertzel's anxiety had raised his body temperature and the soap-matted hair now looked as though it was alive. Fascist lice, Renton thought. Fascist lice colonising territory they have no rights to. Thinking of them in this way he conquered his squeamishness. He reached out his left hand and stretched taut the skin of the German's thigh. He found the conviction to apply the blunt blade with greater force and the resulting stroke cleared an inch-wide thicket of hair. The raw flesh beneath it was soft, like a baby's. Several pinpoints of blood appeared on the surface. Renton wiped the blade clean on his trouser leg and, keen to maintain the momentum, he immediately returned to his task, etching the blade in from a wider angle and clearing a more substantial swathe of skin. The blood from the previous sweep had now pooled, lubricating the cleared surface and turning the soap pink.

Wertzel lay prone and still as Renton completed the task. Only when he announced that he had finished did the German lift his head and the pain was evident on his face. Wertzel's upper thighs were red and exposed with a pink sheen of blood, but the skin below the fold of his stomach was white and new. The blisters had been scored flat and only the crater circles remained. He reached his right hand down and with a broadening smile, tentatively explored the area. He declared it to be cold and not at all unpleasant. What's more, the itching had stopped. Renton turned away again as the German found his trousers and put them on. Then the men sat, facing each other, embarrassed but gratified that they had achieved what they chose to see as a small victory in their heroic struggle against the Fascists.

When night fell, Wertzel proposed to Antonio that they launch a patrol across the plain. It had been two weeks since any of them had experienced any action and he suggested that the activity would improve morale. When Antonio asked for volunteers, Renton was the only one to put up his hand. Justina announced that suicide was more easily achieved in the comfort of one's own dugout with a single bullet in the temple. Renton saw Eduardo go to her and try to talk to her but she pulled away from him and went back to the parapet where she sat alone, drawing a blanket round her shoulders and staring at the ground. Renton watched Eduardo return to his dugout and clamber inside. He scrambled across the ground to her and sat beside her.

'Are you all right?' Renton said. It was ineffectual, he knew, but he could think of nothing else to say.

'Two months ago the Fascists came to our village,' she said. 'Last night I dreamed about that day for the first time . . .'

'Tell me,' Renton said.

'You want to know?'

'Of course.'

'Eduardo doesn't want to hear my story. He says we must put all of our horrors behind us. Only then can we move forwards.'

'That's Eduardo. I don't know Eduardo's story, perhaps he has good reason to close off the past. I don't.'

Justina looked across towards him, then she began rocking forwards and back. 'I was in the village visiting my mother when the first refugees came. Hundreds of them fleeing the Fascists. I saw a man holding a baby. He was running after a cart transporting his wife and the rest of his family. An old lady in black sat in the cart watching him. She seemed to want him to fall and be trampled by the column . . . most of them were on foot carrying blanket bundles of possessions. Cooking pots. A young boy stopped to squat and shit on the road. The woman following him – his mother, I expect – picked him up and the boy's shit messed all her dress but she didn't care. As they began to pass through our village I saw the Fascist planes coming out of the sun and machine-gunning the road . . . I ran towards the screams but my mother held me back. Then my father and my two brothers ran from the fields and everybody who had a weapon gathered before the old mayor who stood on the step of the Ayuntamiento and said, "Good people of the town, have courage." I think he believed we could defeat the Fascists with courage. But, soon after, the Moors arrived. Huge men: black men with gold teeth you could see when they smiled. They were shouting "Viva la Muerte!"'

'And how did you get away?'

'We were taken to the village square. The men were drinking. To give them courage. All of the men and the boys were soon drunk. They stood in a line. The Moors took their weapons from them – their old rifles and their pitchforks – and threw them on a pile. The women and children waited behind their men. If any of us got too close to them a Moor would come and push us back. One woman was struck on the head by a rifle. Then a few Legionnaires came along and they took command. An officer with a moustache walked up and down the line of our men; he stared into their faces. When he reached my father, he stopped. I think it was the pride he saw in his eyes that made him take my father's arm and pull him forward . . . The two men stood face to face and the officer told him to dance. He wanted to show us all how important he was. My father smiled, he had a very gentle smile, and in the silence he began to dance slowly. He encouraged the men in line to clap in time and they joined in. He twisted in the dust until his soles had worn the ground away to reveal the stones beneath it. Then the Legionnaire commanded him to stop. My father froze – he had a smile on his face. The Legionnaire snapped his fingers and two men with rifles marched over to him. He issued an order that nobody but the two men could hear and they took my father – one on each side of him – under the arms. As they pushed him against the wall they turned him so that he was facing the crowd. His eyes found mine and he smiled. Despite everything, I smiled back my goodbye.

'There were two shots. They scattered the birds that had settled on the buildings. My mother screamed. Through my tears I saw my father pitching to his knees and falling on to his face into the dust. I fought with the crowd to go to him but my eldest brother held me back. He seemed to have such strength in his arms because I had never felt an impulse so strong. When I finally pulled away from him I ran away and I left the village without saying goodbye either to my mother or to my brothers. Nobody tried to stop me when I boarded the bus for Barcelona . . .'

Renton took Justina's hand and held it. After some minutes of silence they began to talk about the night ahead and the patrol. When he left her, Eduardo came to take his place at her side.

Renton prepared for the raid by dirtying his bayonet, wiping mud over his face and greasing his cartridges. As he allowed himself a few minutes of silent contemplation, the void behind his eyes clouded, he looked within himself and floated away into the warm salt pool. No pain there or cold, no creaking bones or tiny lobsters tormenting him. No hunger or fear. He lay back in it for a while, folding in on himself. Just a moment longer and he knew he would immerse himself in sleep. But then he heard the sentry calling a challenge and the password being shouted back.

Antonio was talking to a man too clean to be engaged on

the front line. His red neckerchief was pressed and his grey hair was springy and clean. The man's cheeks were free of stubble and beneath his eyes there were no crescents of black. His well-being repelled the members of the unit who stayed clear of him, concerned by the contagion of health. When Antonio dismissed him he did so with a disdain Renton had not seen before, and only when the man had dashed away like a goat down the steep track did they emerge from their dugouts and gather round the boy.

He waited for them all to join him before he said, 'I'm sorry to report that yesterday morning the Government left Madrid for Valencia.'

'So Madrid has fallen?' Eduardo said.

'Not yet. General Miaja is presiding over the defence junta . . . I am told that Prime Minister Largo Caballero's passage from the city was impeded by our comrades at Tarancon. He was turned back but later continued by plane.'

'What now?' Justina said.

'Nothing changes for us here.'

'That's what I was afraid of,' Justina said and walked away into the shadows.

Renton stumbled as he crossed no-man's-land, and when he fell he chose to rest on the cold earth listening to the stealthy footsteps of Wertzel and Antonio fading away. If I lie here, he thought, how long will it be before I die? Perhaps I could scavenge sufficient to survive. All I need are a few roots each day, a vegetable or two. A pot to cook in and some water. I could live like a hermit between the lines and watch the bullets sail back and forth over my head. He remembered a railway bridge and the light latticed through the black metal and he began to contemplate why the past was so much preferable to the present. When he eventually scrambled to his feet again he could no longer hear Antonio or the German. He was experiencing his first moments of solitude in almost two months and he enjoyed the sense of liberation.

He leaned against a wall. There was no moon, just the gentle luminescence of night; too dark for the sharpshooters to see him. He was safe. He smoked a cigarette without urgency and heard, from deep behind the enemy lines, the sound of church bells as clear as fresh water falling on stone.

The Fascists were talking on a hill. He could hear them as he approached their line. He felt the weight of the grenade bombs in the sack bumping against his thigh and it anchored him again. Crouching, he looked for cover but he was exposed and he knew that if either side threw up a flare he would be cut to pieces by machine-gun fire. He knelt and strained for a sight or sound of Antonio and Wertzel but he assumed that they would already be back safe in the position. He had been in no-man's-land for almost an hour. Perhaps for ten minutes of that time he had been conscious of time passing. For the rest of it, he'd been elsewhere: beneath the bridge at Shoreham, standing with Arthur in the pub, kissing Meredith, longing for the mundanity of his old life, his ideals safely stacked away on the bookshelves.

Hearing footsteps cracking through the bushes to the right of him, he raised his rifle. He heard another sound behind him and he swung round. At that moment he felt the force of a body thrown against his back and he fell flat, losing his rifle, the wind knocked out of his lungs. He fought and squirmed on to his back. A hand went over his mouth. He smelt the onion breath of the assailant and then he heard: 'How are your family, mister?'

'Wertzel?'

'We thought you were captured. We were set to return to our lines when Antonio saw you walking towards the Fascists.'

'What were you thinking?' Antonio whispered.

'I don't know. I wasn't thinking.'

'No.'

'I'm sorry.'

'We must go back to the line quickly.'

As Renton stood again he felt a sudden damp heat on his right shoulder. Beside him he saw the shapes of his friends diving to the ground. He dropped beside them and cracked his knee on a stone but all he was aware of was the warmth in his arm which became an ache. Once acknowledged, the ache transformed itself to a needle-sharp pain. Renton reached up and tested the wound. The crater was deep but he could not resist the urge to probe it with his fingers. He felt the edge of a splintered bone, a sticky rag of cloth and skin and then the pain became too much to bear.

The Golden Arrow: Folkestone

'Would you like a cigarette?' the man said as his bulky shadow fell across Meredith's table.

'No, thank you.' Meredith was looking out at the silver tracks which were picking up the red light from a distant signal lamp. Tantalisingly, the harbour station lay only fifty yards ahead.

'Are you sure?'

'No. Perhaps I'm not.' Meredith slipped a cigarette from the man's case and studied his short ugly fingers, his well-manicured nails, the bright gold wedding band. She had been aware of the stranger's interest in her from the moment she arrived in the parlour car for dinner. While she ate she watched the man in the mirror of the carriage window. He stared at her with a sly, unconcealed hunger. Only when the train passed through a station did the yellow lights outside purge his reflection from the glass and replace it with a fleeting snapshot of a lonely platform.

'Thank you,' she said and tamped the end of the untipped cigarette on the table.

'I don't understand the reason for the hold-up. Do you?' Having lit Meredith's cigarette, his arm still outstretched, the man manoeuvred himself into the seat facing her.

'No. I have no idea. We were due in at ten past six, weren't we? I hope they hold the boat for us.'

'This is the boat train, so I expect they're unlikely to leave without us.'

'No. I expect not,' Meredith said, delivering a gentle reprimand to the man's sharpness.

He stood again, grunting with exertion and poked his head

through the window to look towards the front of the long train. They had come to a halt on the railway pier. Through the rain the silhouette of a crane on the East Pier was just visible swinging a crate from the deck of a mail boat. The warm yellow lights of the Pavilion Hotel speckled the black water of the inner harbour.

Meredith had not intended to eat alone but when she'd come into the parlour car she had taken the decision to sit at an empty table. The tweed suit she had carefully chosen to travel in seemed suddenly to belong to a woman who would insist on dining alone. By the end of the meal, during which time she had entertained herself by listening to the sound of her own thoughts, she was as happy as she would have been had she struck up a new acquaintance. Kit Renton and the future featured prominently in the conversation she had held with herself while Bowden and the dead weight of the past she dispatched as quickly as her first glass of wine. She recognised that she had felt a certain pity for him when she had gone to the hospital to see him, and tears came into his eyes when she kissed him goodbye. But Harry Bowden, paralysed, was no less menacing than he had been before the attack and Meredith knew she couldn't risk confiding in him that she was going for good. When she left him, Royle went in for another stint at his bedside. As far as Meredith was aware, Bowden's empire was still intact, even if the day-to-day running of it had been passed on to his lieutenant.

'There's a red light up ahead of us,' the man said.

'Perhaps we're waiting for the Channel steamer to dock. I heard somebody say it was going to be a rough crossing.'

'No. She's there. I can see her just beyond the station.' The man settled into the seat again and Meredith felt an obligation to smile at him. 'You'd think they'd let us into the platform, wouldn't you?' he said. 'Perhaps we're waiting for customs or some such thing.'

'Perhaps. Are you going all the way?'

'To Paris, yes. And you?'

'Yes,' she said.

'Business or pleasure?'

'Business.'

'Should I guess what that might be?'

'If you want. Though I doubt you will.'

'I like riddles. Don't tell me.'

'All right.'

'First let me get you another drink. What will you have?' The man raised his arm and the attendant approached them. A large beetroot-coloured birthmark eclipsed his right eye, giving the impression that his face was half in shadow. Without it, Meredith thought, she would have found him immensely attractive.

'A gin and french, thank you,' Meredith said to the attendant.

'I like a woman who know what she wants,' her companion said.

'All women know what they want – whatever they pretend.'

'Gin and french.' The man lifted his whisky glass. 'And I'd better have another one of these.'

'So . . .' Meredith said. 'Pleasure or business for you?'

'Oh, pleasure.'

'I wonder why that doesn't surprise me . . .'

The conversation proceeded easily. Neither of them had to try very hard or think very much about it. The man offered his name as George Monroe and used it as an excuse to take Meredith's hand and hold on to it for longer than necessary. Meredith was weighing up how long it would be before he invited her to share his private cabin on the short crossing to Boulogne.

' . . . No, please don't tell me, let me guess . . .' Monroe, eyes narrowed, continued to parade the limitations of his imagination. 'Not a singer or a dancer, or a . . . what did I say?'

'Spy, wasn't it?'

'No. Not a spy. Then are you, perhaps, a member of the medical profession?'

'No. Not that either. You're rather hopeless, aren't you.'

'All right. I give in. Tell me.'

'I'm not going to tell you,' Meredith said. 'I don't think you deserve to know.'

'I do.'

'Oh, I don't think so.'

'Oh yes I bloody do.' Monroe took her knee beneath the table and squeezed it hard.

'What a charmer you are,' Meredith said.

'I'm known for it.'

Meredith lashed out with her toe and connected with Monroe's shin. He pulled away his hand and winced at the pain.

'You're a flighty one,' Monroe said, rubbing his shin. 'I was warned . . .' he started but broke off as the train jolted into movement and began to lumber forward towards the platform.

'Flighty? God.' Meredith laughed in Monroe's face. She knew immediately that she had pushed him too far and she cursed herself for the misjudgment. She couldn't afford anything to distract her from reaching Kit. But then she felt a chill as his words struck home. 'What do you mean you were warned?' she said.

'Warned?'

- 'You said you were warned.'

'Yes, I did.'

'Tell me what you mean.'

'All I mean is that I was warned about girls like you.'

'Yes? By your mother, I expect?'

'Yes. Who else?'

'Very well. You want to know so I'll tell you what I'm doing. I'm going to Spain.' Meredith had discussed her journey with Arthur Lawler and Harry Pollitt, but only now – poised at the English Channel – did it become real to her. The admission was also a test. If Monroe had been sent after her by Bowden he would doubtless already know her destination.

'And why would you want to go there?' Monroe asked her, offering no clue in his response.

'My business.'

'. . . Are we still friends?'

'No.'

'Oh. That's a shame.'

'But we never were, nor would we ever be.'

'But we could be close?'

'Oh, yes. I'm sure we could be close.'

'I'm sorry I hurt you.'

'No, you're not.'

'Well, my dear, you must at least let me carry your cases on to the boat.'

When the train drew to a halt in the station, passengers from the rear coaches began to stream past the window towards the customs shed.

'I'll get a porter,' Meredith said, seeing a young man tugging an empty handcart towards the baggage van. A newsboy trailed after him carrying a sheaf of final editions over his arm like towels.

'There's absolutely no need.'

'You don't know how many cases I have with me.'

'If there are too many to carry I'll find a porter. They're rather scarce round here nowadays.'

'Do you fuss like this over your wife?'

'Yes.'

'I expect she enjoys the attention.'

'Of course she does.'

'All right. You can carry my suitcase. Wait here while I go and fetch it.'

Meredith stood and immediately Monroe stood too, insisting, 'It's no trouble. I'll come with you.'

'You're a very persistent fellow, Mr Monroe.'

'I'm not going to let you out of my sight.'

'Are you afraid you'll lose me to somebody else?'

'Yes. Lead the way.'

Meredith acknowledged the mechanical smile of the attendant with a nod and then realised that the man was looking for a tip. She had always left the responsibility for tipping to others. Finding a half-crown in her purse, she pushed it with some embarrassment into the man's hand. As she did so she had a sudden longing to make the moment last. 'Thank you,' she said to the careworn man with the birthmark and the gravy-specked jacket, but before he could reply Monroe took her elbow and pushed her towards the door.

As they walked back through the Pullman car, Meredith found herself wondering what orders Monroe had been given. Would she find herself pitched into the sea from a secluded part of the steamer deck or would they not get that far? Would there be a car waiting for them outside the station ready to take her straight back to Bowden? She examined the options in a matter-of-fact way. This is just another part of the test, she told herself. If I have the strength to get through this stage, then Kit Renton will be my reward and I will be at peace. Perhaps all of my life has been a test leading to this moment.

'Here we are,' Meredith said when they reached her seat. Somebody had left an *Evening Standard* folded neatly on the table beside an empty china teacup.

'Just the one case?' Monroe said, tugging it down from the rack.

'Yes. And what about you?'

'In the next carriage. Hand luggage only for me.'

'Good,' Meredith said. 'Then we won't need a porter, will we?'

Good, Meredith thought. If Monroe has brought luggage with him then at least he's expecting to board the boat. With each further mile she travelled from Bowden the stronger she became. Perhaps at the centre of the Channel, released from the shackles of England, she would find the strength to confront Monroe with her suspicions. What could he possibly do to her on a crowded steamer?

The new companions stood side by side on the promenade deck watching the dark quay slip away from them. As the turbines churned and propelled the *Maid of Orleans* slowly past the lighthouse and out into the open Channel the deck pitched and Meredith lunged to take hold of the handrail. A wave slapped the bow and she tasted salt on her lips. The harsh south-easterly wind was driving the rain horizontally towards them and making shifting valleys of the sea. Monroe was staring back towards the lamps of the marine garden with an expression which suggested he had left something behind but he couldn't quite remember what it was. Meredith, clinging tightly to the cold rail, was looking ahead, her eyes bright with hope as she strained vainly for a first glimpse of the distant lights of Boulogne. By midnight she would be in Paris. If she could only get through the next two hours she would be safe. She felt Monroe's hand on her arm again as he manoeuvred her towards the shelter of the saloon.

'You don't have to manhandle me,' she said, raising her voice above the noise of the engines and the wind. 'I'm quite capable of walking a few steps on my own without being led along like an old lady.'

'I'd hate you to lose your footing. If you went over the side in this weather they'd never get you out.'

'You seem to have taken it upon yourself to look after me.'

'Yes. I have. I've secured a private cabin for us.'

'That was quick work.'

'We'll take some drink down with us, shall we? I don't want to spend the voyage waiting for the man to answer the bell.'

'Whatever you like.'

The bar was busy with a noisy crowd thrown into enforced proximity and intent on making the most of it for a couple of hours. A group of French schoolgirls were sitting cross-legged on the floor tossing a ping-pong ball around the circle. Monroe bullied his way to the bar and called for a bottle of champagne and two glasses. When the crowd of damp overcoats closed around him Meredith glimpsed an opportunity to escape. It came to her that if she could find somewhere to hide away until they reached Boulogne, she could then book herself into a room in the town for the night. Monroe would assume she had boarded the Flèche d'Or and he would spend the three-hour journey to Paris searching for her on the train. With no further thought of the consequences, Meredith moved quickly to the exit to the promenade deck. The ship lifted again and plunged and the schoolgirls squealed in delight as their ball went rolling away under an armchair. A glass crashed to the floor from the bar and a woman shouted in alarm. Meredith regained her balance and when she trusted that the floor was not going to fall away again, she continued towards the door. An elderly woman, a black shawl draped over her knee, looked at her with sympathy as she passed. 'Tonic water and a slice of lemon, dear,' the woman said, assuming seasickness.

'Yes. But first I need some fresh air.' Meredith smiled, marking her down as a potential ally in the battle ahead. It had been so long since she had enjoyed the companionship of women.

'You be careful on the deck,' the woman's nurse said. She turned to her charge and asked, 'Why do they let passengers outside in conditions like this?'

Meredith walked out into the raging elements. She turned towards the bow and felt the wind pushing her back towards the comfort and shelter of the saloon. Through the thick oval windows she could see the mime of laughter and gaiety of the party she had left behind. Ahead of her, white foam was sluicing from the deck like a roll of lace unravelling over the starboard side. The ship tilted, waited, paused for an agonising moment, then plunged. Meredith planted her feet squarely down and, with her right hand outstretched, edged with deliberate, exaggerated steps towards the handrail. The black sea rose and fell beyond it. The marine sky was distinguishable only by a faint green glow. Above her the lifeboats creaked and swung out on their chains. The two tall funnels of the steamer valiantly vented white smoke into the night sky. On the bridge the barometer continued to fall. Meredith heard a voice behind her and turned to see a steward at the distant saloon door waving her back inside, but she faced the rail again and by the time she had reached it the man was out of earshot.

What now? she wondered. Her suit was soaked through. The deck was lifting and falling twenty or so feet. She looked towards the bow but the promenade deck was cordoned off from the foredeck and it seemed to Meredith that in the battle the foredeck had been sacrificed to the sea. She turned back and saw, halfway towards the stern, a fixed metal ladder which led up to an open walkway above the saloon where the lifeboats were suspended. In her rapidly improvised plan of escape it seemed as good a step as any, so she edged towards it along the safety rail, hand-over-hand. She heard another shout behind her but chose not to turn. The ship's hooter sounded, stalling her heart for a moment and setting it off again at double time. When it had slowed she continued along the deck. Twenty more carefully won steps and the ladder was directly behind her, just ten or so feet away across the deck. A gull swooped and laughed at her before rising into the black. Somebody called her name. Meredith released her right hand and twisted round, putting her back to the rail. A dark figure was approaching her along the deck. She watched, fascinated, as a white wave reared up over the rails and broke over the man. He waited, then continued to pull himself along towards her, using the handrail like the rope in a game of tug-of-war. Meredith drew breath, then let go of the rail and dashed the distance across the slick deck to the ladder. When she reached it she peered up towards the lifeboats, the funnels and the sky beyond. The absurd image of Arthur Lawler came to her mind. She smiled at the memory of him ineffectively daubing the windows of Bowden's showroom with a wash leather. The picture diminished her anxiety as she took hold of the sides of the ladder and, using the strength of her arms, hauled herself up to the first rung. She climbed another and another. With each step she found the rhythm and confidence to climb the next. This is easy, she thought, I'm safe now. She chanced a look below her and immediately regretted doing so when she saw just how far the drop was. She moved her right hand to the next rung of the ladder but just as she lifted her foot to follow she felt a hand clamping her ankle. Looking down the right side of her body, she saw Monroe staring up at her.

'Come down, you stupid bitch,' he called, but 'stupid bitch' was drowned in the wind and the hiss of the sea.

Meredith kicked out a heel but the grip on her ankle tightened. She could see that Monroe was hampered by concerns for his own safety. If he used both hands he could drag her off the ladder with ease, but then there would have been nothing to anchor him to the ship. Meredith lashed out with her left heel and caught him hard on the chin. She felt the bone give and immediately her right foot was freed. Before Monroe could recover and take hold again she climbed to the top of the ladder and hauled herself on to the walkway. Meredith reached out to a lifeboat to steady herself, then chanced a look back down the sheer face of the ladder. Monroe was holding a handkerchief against a gash in his cheek. He pulled it away and with anger and curiosity examined the blood on it. Then he looked up towards her, and began to climb.

The upper deck had not been designed for the comfort of passengers. Meredith saw that there was no shelter, no safety rail, nothing above her. The nearest of the funnels was huge and terrifying, and only the lifeboats offered anything in the way of handholds. But she knew that if she waited for Monroe to reach her then she would have done his job for him. Her only option was to keep moving, to maintain as much distance between them as she could. She moved on towards the stern. When she risked her next look back towards the ladder she was four lifeboats away from her pursuer. Monroe was smiling, no urgency now. He knew that she had nowhere to run and he beckoned her towards him by wagging a podgy finger. Meredith turned her back on him and lunged for the next lifeboat. One more, then there seemed to be a low rail and, beyond it, a sheer drop to the deck below.

In the moments that Meredith waited for the hand on her shoulder, for the shove or the hug, she contemplated which she dreaded the most. But as she resigned herself to her fate her fear left her.

Monroe was closing on her. He was finding it as hard as she had done to maintain his balance. Meredith willed him to fall but all she could do was watch him edge closer and closer, feeling his way along the lifeboats. And then, behind him, she saw another man. A saturated, small man in a white jacket whom she recognised as the purser who had called her back towards the saloon. Monroe continued towards her. But as he reached her and took her shoulders the purser called. Monroe composed himself. The man called again and Monroe found a smile. 'Thank God,' he said, turning to face the man. 'You got here just in time.'

'Are you all right, miss?' the purser said.

'She is now,' Monroe said. 'Aren't you, darling?' He relaxed the grip on Meredith's shoulders and began massaging them.

'Yes,' Meredith said. 'I am now.'

'Just a stupid argument,' Monroe said. 'You know how it is.'

Meredith knew that the purser saw through Monroe's story. All three of them tacitly acknowledged the lie, but she was safe now, and that was all that concerned her.

'Perhaps you could help me down,' she said to the man. 'I think George is exhausted after all this excitement.'

'Of course,' the purser said. 'We'll follow on after you, sir.' And as Meredith and the capable man watched Monroe walk away from them, the purser took her arm and she felt safe again. Behind the ship she could see the white rails of the ship's wake narrowing into the night. She imagined the snug warmth of the Pullman car back in Folkestone and wondered if somebody had picked up the *Evening Standard* that had been left on her seat. She wished she had taken it for herself; Kit Renton would have appreciated the bulletin from home.

November: London

'What is it?' the woman said.

'Just a letter,' Royle told her and continued to read. Taking his response as a challenge, the woman walked behind his seat where she trailed her hand across the cushion, her fingernails making contact with the back of his neck. Royle shrugged off her touch.

'Well, it must be a very important letter,' she said, coming round to stand in front of him. He looked up and saw her watching him, her arms crossed, with an expression of superior boredom. She had controlled him with the desire he felt for her from the moment he saw her. Royle had employed the woman to nurse Harry Bowden, which she achieved with a minimum of tenderness. Bowden was sleeping behind her now, his wheelchair positioned so that he could look out of the tall windows and down through the wrought-iron railings into the private gardens behind the mansion block. He was shrouded from neck to toe in a green blanket. His head was angled to the right and his eyelids flickered.

It wasn't long into her employment that Royle discovered that the woman was incapable of tenderness. Their lovemaking was functional and wholly physical. She contained whatever spiritual interest she had in him behind a petulant indifference, barely seeming to tolerate his body's intrusion into hers. However hard he forced himself into her, he felt that she was holding him at bay, wanting something from him that he was incapable of giving her. When he complained that she didn't care for him, only for the wages he paid, she adopted her other strategy: she babied him. But because she did it without derision, he tolerated her treatment of him.

Behind Royle's desire, muscling it away to the edge of his mind, was an impatience which coloured his response. 'It is important,' he said. 'It's from Spain.'

'You have a friend in Spain?'

Royle looked towards Bowden who was still sleeping. 'Yes. An old friend. He's in prison.'

'And what does he want you to do about it?'

'The letter is not to me.'

'Then why are you reading it?'

'Because the woman he's written it to has gone to Spain to find him.'

'And she doesn't know he's in prison?'

'I doubt it.'

'Can I see it?'

'No.'

'Why?'

'Because it's private.'

'Between him and her. Yes, I suppose it is.'

'I take your point.'

'Then read it to me.'

'No.'

The woman approached Royle, hitched up her skirt and straddled his waist. 'Read it to me.'

'Or what?'

'Read it to me.' She pulled his face into the crevice of her small breasts. 'Read it to me,' she said, pushing Royle's face away again.

'And then?' Royle said, his passion ignited by the warmth and weight of the woman pressing down on him.

'We'll see,' she said, standing. She crossed to the settee and sat, tugging up her legs beneath her.

'"My darling Meredith,"' Royle began, hearing Renton's voice more clearly in his head than he had done when he had read the letter in silence.

'"My darling",' the woman echoed.

'Yes?'

'He loves her, doesn't he? He doesn't write, "Darling Meredith", which is a phrase you write out of habit, he writes, "*My* darling, Meredith". It's a new love.'

'Shall I go on?'

'Please.'

'". . . Perhaps you will have heard by now that I have been captured and wounded. The wound is beginning to heal. My pride is not. I am ashamed to say that I was responsible for the capture of two of my colleagues who had come to look for me after I wandered off alone during a patrol. What was I thinking? I was thinking, in part, of you and my life back in London. We have all experienced moments of weakness, unfortunately mine came at a time and place which cost me my liberty . . ."'

'Who is he, this man?' the woman said. 'And how do you know him?'

'He's a schoolfriend.'

'Describe him to me.'

'I thought you wanted me to read the letter,' Royle said, and continued. '"If this letter does reach you, my pesetas will have been well spent. Bribery is an accepted part of the economy of the prison here. I receive my board and lodgings free, but I pay dearly for writing paper and shaving implements and tobacco. I occupy a peculiar position within the hierarchy of the prisoners here. I think I am the only Englishman and as a result the Fascists treat me with some caution. Shooting me would serve no purpose beyond drawing further attention to the plight of the Republic back home. Needless to say, I welcome any efforts you might make on my behalf.

'"Perhaps I should describe to you something of my time here. Rumours are the daily newspapers of prison life. You can subscribe to any number of them, but there are few you are prepared fully to believe until the source has earned your trust. The boy who brings me my food three times a day I tend not to trust because he tells me what he imagines I want to hear.

When I ask him about the progress of the war he smiles and tells me the end is in sight. The National Army, as he has recently taken to calling them, is set to pardon all the political prisoners and the Republicans are, even now, negotiating a surrender which will enable Spain to return to peace again. A question to my jailer about the night-time screams and the chilling sound of boots along the corridor elicits the ingenious response that one of my fellow internees was suffering with agonising toothache. A doctor was called. The man was taken away in the middle of the night and his tooth was pulled. But why did he not return? I ask. The boy tells me that he is convalescing in hospital.

'"I have paced this cell so many times that I know the exact distance between the door and the wall. It is fourteen and a half feet. Feet, in this case, being a literal measure. Let me describe this cell to you. There is an iron bed-frame which is hinged along the base and folds away flat against the wall. There is also a washbasin, a WC, a steel table, a steel chair and a straw palliasse on which to sleep. My woollen blanket is changed each week. On my first day in residence here I was instructed in how to scour the flagstoned floor with a broom and damp rag. The floor is cleaned each morning after the first bugle call of the day has roused us from our sleep at six forty-five. All of the cells bear a name plate and a number. Mine is 65. I estimate there to be close on a thousand prisoners in this particular establishment. We live along the endless corridors of heavy doors, each of which has a spy-hole. When you are escorted along these corridors for interrogation or to visit the doctor, you see an eye pressed against each spy-hole. It is like living in some sinister fairy-tale world."' Royle paused and looked up, anticipating an interruption, but the woman impatiently waved him on.

'"... As to the view: a barred window is recessed at head-height deep into the thick wall. Through the mesh across the bars I can see out to the courtyard where the majority of the men spend their mornings and late afternoons, and take their meals in the evening. They pass the time kicking a soccer ball which has been improvised from packed rags. Others play leapfrog or trade tobacco. The atmosphere is good-natured and leisurely. Few would suspect that these men face the imminent prospect of standing before a firing squad. Perhaps the elders have taken it upon themselves to protect the younger boys – some of whom seem no older than twelve or thirteen – from the truth.

'"One can hear the breakfast coming long before it arrives. The boy and one of the warders shove a huge galvanised metal tub of coffee along the corridor. Another warder follows along with a ladle and a basket of stale hunks of bread. When the bolt is thrown and the door bangs open the ladle is dipped into the tub and passed to the inmate. The inmate drinks his morning ration of black coffee, careful not to spill any of the valuable liquid. A hunk of bread is broken and given to him. The door is slammed shut again. When it comes to your turn you greet the three faces at your door gratefully. When you live in enforced isolation you crave human contact. You have no argument with these men, only with the regime that employs them. There is little differentiation between the jailers and the jailed. When the warders patrol the courtyard, occasionally they join in one of the huge games of football.

'"In this hotel lunch is served before the afternoon siesta. Most of us sleep between one and three p.m. and then the men are let out again into the yard. Those of us kept incommunicado watch them with envy. The afternoon mood differs from that of the morning. Perhaps it is due to the length of the confinement which precedes it – two hours, not twelve or thirteen. It may also be due to the heat: the sun is by now high above the white walls and there is scant shade. But what there is is sought-after. As the afternoon goes on, the men sit together and discuss the latest rumours. They roll thin cigarettes and indulge in the peculiar prison habit of tossing handfuls of dust into the air and watching the sudden patterns the dust makes. Across the wide yard, dozens of tiny fireworks of dust. There is no breeze so the dust falls back swiftly to the ground.

'"At seven p.m. the final meal of the day is taken outside. Afterwards the men drift slowly inside again. By eight o'clock an eerie silence pervades the courtyard and the prison around it. A thousand men here but little sound from them. The last post is sounded at ten and the nightmare hours begin.

'"When you hear the sanctus bell at night, however deeply you sleep, you are soon awake. Your heart is already beating hard. You sit up quickly and search for your cigarettes, which you have left within easy reach. The reason for this is that if your name is called there is little time to prepare yourself. You have rehearsed this moment many times, nevertheless you feel a profound terror. You look around your cell for what may be the last time, at the names and dates inscribed on the wall together with the initials of political affiliation. The names are now as familiar to you as the faces of friends. You prepare yourself for the final goodbye.

'"Outside in the corridor, when the march of the warder halts, you can hear the sound of paper being unfolded. Then the calling of names and numbers begins, sometimes alphabetically, sometimes not. On alphabetical days, once the R's have passed, I breathe again, lie back on the mattress, perhaps smoke the cigarette I have been saving and fall into a relieved sleep. For those whose names have been called, the final journey begins. Up and down the corridor, cell doors open, the warder and the guards bring the men out. Remember they may have been playing soccer together only a few hours before. Obligations of civility are fulfilled on behalf of jailed and jailer. Occasionally a man breaks into song, though a voice is rarely raised in defiance. Only once did I hear a man pleading to be left in his cell.

'"Within ten minutes the prison is silent again.

'"Two nights ago my name was called. The door to my cell was soon opened and I found the boy facing me. It was such an occasion that he had decided to come for me himself. Whether this was out of some sense of love or hate I could not tell. Perhaps he anticipated a final tip from me as he led me down the corridor.

The warder was with him, and so was the priest. I joined a queue of men waiting by the office. They were silent, filthy, tired. All were staring into space. For the first time I encountered one of my colleagues. Perhaps I have mentioned him to you before. His name is Antonio, he is barely more than a youth, but he led our small unit with great courage. We shook hands and I felt ashamed that if it hadn't been for my foolishness then Antonio would have returned safely to the Republican lines. But there was no blame in his face and we exchanged only a few words. I asked him about the fate of our other colleague, a German, but Antonio told me they had become separated on their arrest and he feared that Wertzel had already been shot. We embraced. The prison gates were then unlocked. Outside, a number of covered trucks were waiting. The first men were led out. In the searchlights I could see that a wooden crate had been placed behind each vehicle.

'"As I walked through the gates into the blazing light I felt the boy tugging at my arm. Believing it to be a fellow inmate seeking some final human contact, I tried to shrug off the hand. But it would not let go. When I turned the boy smiled and beckoned me back into the prison. We walked silently along the corridor to my cell. After a sleepless night I asked the boy why my name had been called. He shrugged his shoulders and told me that perhaps it was a mistake, or perhaps I have a powerful friend. Bowden's face came into my mind. Though if his influence extended as far as this prison, I have no doubt I would have been shot by now.

'". . . And then I thought of you and found myself trying to picture you. Despite the time we have been apart the image of you is not fading. I recall the brief time we spent together and I look back with regret at my behaviour towards you. We could have had a night together. Instead, I sent you packing. I ask you to excuse my behaviour in the hope that I can make it up to you when I get out of here.

'"If they do release me, which they may, I will come home to you. Until then, I will think of you each hour.

'"I send you my love. Kit."'

'. . . I'm sorry,' the woman said.

'For what?'

'For making you read it to me.' She stood and, needing something to hide her discomfort, went to turn Bowden's chair so that the afternoon sun was angled away from his face. The movement woke him and the woman wiped the spittle from his chin with a corner of the green blanket. Bowden stared mutely towards her. She said, 'He loves her. You can't ask much more than that.'

'I suppose not.'

'Will she find him? I mean, if she does find him, will she be able to get him out?'

'I can't honestly say. Meredith is . . . single-minded.'

'I hope she finds him.'

'Yes,' Royle said. 'So do I.'

With Kit Renton's voice still in his head, Royle left the flat and went out to get drunk. As he walked down the stairs he heard a noise from a landing above him. He stopped and craned his neck to see. A huge chandelier hung from the ceiling four floors above him. Wreathed in cobwebs, it looked poised to drop on to his shoulders like a huge spider. Royle hurried on. He emerged into the street pursued by the ghosts of Renton, Lawler and Bowden. Of the three, he considered he had a genuine responsibility only towards Bowden, but there were parts of him he felt he had lost and, somehow, they would remain lost until the three schoolfriends were reunited.

Barcelona

The American journalist, Theodore Goss, was sitting alone at a table beside the fountain in the courtyard of the Hotel Continental. The thin musical trickle of the water soothed and cooled him but provoked a constant nagging in his bladder. The noise of the Anarchists packed into the hotel echoed down to the courtyard from the open windows above. The racket from the voices competing for attention in the reception area spilled through the French doors. Goss's walking cane was leaning against a palm, his white Panama hat lay beside the glass of anise on the table. He was smoking a cigar and watching a tall young waitress attend to a table of three men just outside the French doors which led into the hotel bar. The courtyard of the Hotel Continental was a marketplace for information and the men were also journalists. Goss recognised the first as Paul – he could never remember his surname, from *L'Intransigeant*. The other was a short, bull-necked man called Grand from the Havas agency. They were buying drinks in return for information from a Spanish journalist who lived in the hotel and worked for the *Solidaridad Obrera*. The Spaniard, pleading deadlines, was trying to leave, but Grand and Paul detained him by ordering another bottle of wine. Grand, catching sight of Goss as his eye roved the patio, raised a glass to him. The Spaniard took the opportunity of a momentary break in the conversation to stand, bow to the French journalists, collect his papers, and walk away.

The sun had already gone down and the stored heat now radiated from the hotel walls. Goss's attention strayed to the waitress as she carried her tray across the courtyard towards him.

She moved slowly, as though she was wading through thigh-deep water. A gecko flicked up the wall behind her and froze like a crack in the stucco.

'Join me. Please,' Goss offered when she reached him. Remaining seated, he leaned over and pulled the other chair out from beneath the small square table. 'Please . . .' He gestured at the seat, took a silk handkerchief from his top pocket and made a show of dusting it. 'Take a break.' Goss stood, light-headed from the anise on an empty stomach, and tugged up the waistband of his linen trousers. 'Give me your tray.'

Seeing Goss get to his feet, Grand looked across and nudged Paul in the ribs to draw his attention to the ludicrous spectacle of the large, red-faced American trying to pull a flimsy tray from the hands of the tall, angry waitress. After briefly resisting him, she gave in and the Frenchmen were then confronted by the sight of Goss striding across the patio towards them. His white jacket flapped on his haunches; his limp was barely discernible. The metal in the heels of his brogues cracked like horseshoes across the stone floor.

'She won't let you into her bed, Theodore,' Grand said as the American drew level with his table. 'If she won't do it with Paul, she won't do it with you.'

Goss leaned down towards him and asked, 'Where's your friend Brue this evening?'

'I don't know.'

'Drinking beer with his Germans, I imagine,' Paul said in his high singsong voice.

'And why do you imagine that?'

'What do you know?' Grand said, relinquishing his smile.

Goss shrugged and walked on to the bar. Grand watched him push through the men standing there. He took a bottle, then another, then another from the rack, inspected each label, and finally selected an Amandi he seemed satisfied with. He collected two clean glasses, pushed a dollar into the barman's pocket with scissored fingers, and came back out.

Goss paused again at their table. 'He was taken away last night. You'd better speak to your ambassador if you can find him.'

'Why was he arrested?'

'Ask the Communists.'

'Don't they understand we're on their side, for God's sake?' Paul said. He tried to take another drink but his glass was empty. He inverted it, head back, over his tongue, waiting for the last drop to fall.

'That rather depends on how they view your reports,' Goss said.

'You're not immune yourself, Goss, and, incidentally, don't try and pretend you're simply interviewing the pretty waitress.' Paul turned away and raised a hand to attract the waiter.

Goss said, 'I look forward to the day soon when Blum wakes up – and believe me he will – to the imminent possibility of France being surrounded by Fascist states. Perhaps then we'll see some genuine support from him for the Republic. What is it I hear they're writing on the walls in Paris? "*Mieux Hitler que Blum*." Excuse me, gentlemen, I mustn't keep the lady waiting.'

The waitress was sitting still and silent at the table. Her knees were a little splayed, her hands resting on the drum-tight apron of her long, full skirt.

'*Salud*,' he offered. The greeting hung in the air, unanswered.

'Why don't you take a drink,' Goss suggested. A voice called the waitress to the bar. Goss gestured it away impatiently. A figure approached the table. Without looking up, Goss said, 'Go away, Paul.'

'I need some wine. Or anise, perhaps. Get me some wine.'

'I said, go away.' Goss stood. His chair-back clattered against the wall where it rested, half-tilted. He grasped the arm of the Frenchman tightly, and marched him back to the bar. Paul gave off a sweet sandalwood smell of shaving soap.

'You're a pathetic man, Goss. You're like all Americans. You don't understand anything,' Paul said, moving to the French doors, turning and looking back before stumbling away towards the hotel entrance, rubbing the bruise on his arm.

Grand was still at the table, steadfastly working his way through a third bottle of wine. 'Don't mind my friend, Theodore,' he said. 'He's drunk and a little afraid. He needs a woman.' He picked up a cheap cigarette which had been burning in the ashtray. The loosely packed tobacco spilled out and cascaded on to the table. The burning coal fell into his wine glass and was extinguished.

Goss leaned his weight on the back of Grand's chair. He could see the waitress stand and leave the table and make her way back to the bar. Paul's attack had unsettled him. As a journalist he was always afraid of misunderstanding the motives of others; as an American he was afraid of his own motives being misunderstood.

Grand said, 'Last night he accused Haig from *The Times* of reporting the war solely in terms of his own domestic concerns. Did you not hear him ranting? "It's nothing more than a mirror to you!" Then he passed out.'

'Well, I expect to some extent that's true. You could make that charge against any of us.'

Grand said, 'I'm not sure. Perhaps. But I have a difficulty in cases such as this. I can always see both points of view. I'm very easily swayed . . . I'm never sure if this makes me a good reporter or a bad one.'

'It's the mark of a good agency journalist.'

Grand tried to fish the debris of ash and tobacco from his glass. This served only to break it up further. In frustration he dashed the contents of the glass towards the French doors. Goss saw the Daliesque flash of a rainbow of red wine frozen in the air. The clock stopped. Everything was still. The world was healed.

The pendulum swung again when Grand reflected, 'I much prefer writing about villains than heroes, I think.'

Goss's light-headedness had returned. He was afraid he was

going down with a fever. He said, 'One must accept that a hero to one side is a villain to the other.'

'I'm not sure that's entirely true. There are few villains who consider themselves such. Heroes, however . . .'

'I can see we're not going to reach agreement on anything tonight, are we?'

'Perhaps. Perhaps not.'

Goss smiled, and said, 'Join me?'

'No, Theodore. Thank you, but I had better go and find Paul. Having paid for the wine tonight, I feel a certain responsibility towards him.'

Goss crossed the patio again, righted his chair, drew it away from the table and sat down again in his favourite seat. He had chosen it because it gave him a view of the tide of humanity flowing past the French doors and in and out of the hotel.

Listening to the night-time voices around her, Meredith Kerr felt that if she could just clench her ears as she clenched her eyes then she could bring the words into focus and understand everything that was being said. She was hungry and exhausted, relying on the final reserves of energy that had driven her on the interminable journey from Paris to the Spanish border. There she had found the two impish French boys who had taken her through steep seas in their father's fishing boat and delivered her to a Spanish quay late at night. From there she had gone on by train to Barcelona. She had found that by breaking down the journey into stages in her mind it had become manageable. A peacetime journey of three days had taken her as many weeks. But now she was on the final leg – a tram ride to the Hotel Continental which was where she would seek information about Kit Renton.

She took her place in the long tram queue behind a lean, unshaven man in a greasy, tightly belted, grey overcoat who was passing the time examining the remaining contents of his lunchbox. All that differentiated his uniform from that of a bank clerk on his way home from work was the Mexican rifle which was resting against his leg like a crutch. Meredith tried to snare him with a smile. She longed for some human contact. But the man was distracted. He returned his tin lunchbox to his shoulder-sack and then, from an inner pocket of his coat, flourished a newspaper which he shook out and began to read. The front page had been given over to celebrating the nineteenth anniversary of the Russian Revolution. Heroic figures were depicted, dark against the white snow, hurrying to attack the Winter Palace. Soberly the clerk digested the words; smiling, he inferred the parallel. Behind him, pasted at an eccentric angle on to the shutters of a shop, a coloured poster showed a leather-jacketed worker tossing a hand grenade towards a white tank advancing on Leningrad.

The queue stirred as a tram cut round the curve towards them with a jaunty triple ring of its bell. Meredith watched the passengers shuffling together to make room. The line threaded slowly in until the last man to climb on to the platform dropped a step back down again to the street. As the tramcar pulled away the passengers packed inside swung in unison, picking up the rhythm of its surge. Meredith turned to look at the length of the queue behind her and saw, beyond it, a woman shovelling sand into a sandbag which was being held open for her by a young boy. The woman's movements were fractious. She was impatient with her poorly dressed son, imploring him to hold the heavy sack higher. Behind her, a group of vagabond boys was engaged in crowbarring cobblestones from the road. Their vandalism validated, they were eagerly building a pile of ballast to add to the city's barricades. An elderly man with a single medal on the breast of an old army greatcoat was chaperoning them, his hands anchored behind his back, some nervous condition causing his red-rimmed eyes to twitch.

Twenty minutes and two trams later, Meredith finally forced her way on. She grabbed for a rail as the tram accelerated. The electrical whine of the motor rapidly rose in pitch before it steadied to waver around the chosen note. They were soon passing a cinema, half-demolished in an air raid the previous afternoon.

A cloth banner advertising continuous showings of *Battleship Potemkin* flew as ragged as a battle standard. Workmen were standing on a makeshift wooden scaffolding, swinging pickaxes at the teetering walls. Bricks scattered dust as they bounced down the piles of rubble to the street. A refugee stood, watching the men work. Undeterred by the dust ghosting his clothes, untroubled by any sense of purpose, he leaned against a farm cart which had two goats roped to it. The starving animals were nosing hopefully among the rubble for food. Meredith regarded the moments of city life as she would have watched a film, with a similar sense of distanced engagement.

She stumbled at the next corner as the tramcar turned sharply along a street of abandoned tenements. The doors and windows of many of the tall buildings were open. Scattered on the ground in front of them was further evidence of a hasty evacuation: splintered furniture and wooden toys, a broken cot, torn sheets, smashed china. A chandelier thrown from an upstairs window had smashed elegantly on the street below, forming perfect concentric circles of crystal glass. Towards the end of the row, an ambulance was stationary a little way away from the kerb with its back doors open. Two pale stretcher-bearers, smoking cigarettes, stared briefly towards the tram as it passed. On the pavement behind the vehicle a row of department-store dummies lay covered in tarpaulins. A weeping man, kneeling on the ground, had lifted the corner of a sheet to look inside the tent. Meredith glimpsed the models of two tiny children dressed for school. The tram was silent but for the driver singing cheerfully, having no concern for the ghost-train horrors of the journey.

At the next bend there was the sound of a rifle shot and the tram stopped suddenly, throwing the passengers hard against one another. The tram came to a standstill in an empty street and the driver began shouting for a doctor. A rifle bullet had webbed a side window and hit a man in the shoulder. Fifth Columnists were being blamed by the noisy huddle around the victim, but, beyond apportioning the blame, nobody seemed capable of doing anything to help him. The man, impatient and in agony, called to the driver to take the tram to the terminus, deliver the passengers and then get him back to the hospital as quickly as he could. His bravery was rewarded by a spontaneous burst of applause. Meredith did not join in, she was nervously craning her neck to survey the windows of the buildings around them for any sign of the sniper. None of the other passengers seemed concerned by the danger. As the tram continued to wait, her anxiety grew. She felt claustrophobic and the air around her was becoming foul and hot. Meredith apologised to the man in front of her and pushed past him off the tram and out into the street. A moment later the tram pulled away and she was alone.

But where, she wondered, was the rifleman? Meredith turned and looked methodically along the rows of windows of the dark apartments. Nothing on the top floor. A filthy curtain flapped from a shattered pane on the floor below, then three sets of shutters and, next to them, an open window, noticed because all of the other windows were closed.

'There,' Meredith said quietly. She wanted to run but something held her back. Some instinct for survival had sharpened since she had escaped from Monroe on the Channel steamer. Kit Renton was with her in her heart and they were facing the journey together. 'What should I do?' she had asked him on many occasions, and in the silence that followed she would always receive the answer.

The woman standing alone on the street below had been immobile for so long that the assassin in the apartment had fallen into a trance watching her. He knew that she had seen him because he found himself caught by the sweep of her eyes, but something was holding him back from pulling the trigger. It would have been easier for him if she had begun to walk away. Easier still if she took fright and ran. He could not kill in cold blood because he was not the slow-hearted murderer he boasted of being. He had, nevertheless, despatched thirty-five people in the past week alone. Eighteen men, ten women and seven children.

He was keeping the tally in a small black pocket notebook so that when victory came he could provide a detailed account of his endeavours. He enjoyed the notion, tasted the thrill he would feel when he was introduced to women as 'Narciso, the cool killer'. Of course, he wouldn't mention that like an animal he made his mark in every empty apartment he broke in to. And that he felt a sexual pleasure in wandering through abandoned bedrooms.

'Fat Narciso', bullied Narciso, with the slabs of meat for thighs, the face that was always perspiring. The taunts mocked him in the moments between activity. But blushing, awkward Narciso now had a beautiful woman in his sights.

'Run,' Meredith heard in her head. And she did.

The sound of the report surfed off the buildings. It chased her, echoing hard against the hard stucco, and repeated again and again until the final echo was a whisper. When she could run no more she stood panting in an alley. She dropped her case and slumped to the ground. For the first time she allowed herself tears of frustration and exhaustion. She closed her eyes and tumbled into a shallow sleep.

Meredith woke shortly afterwards to the sound of a wireless being turned up loud. She stood and followed the sound and, at its source, found a number of men gathered round a loud-speaker which had been placed at the open window of a small backstreet bar.

Meredith touched one of the men on the shoulder. Impatiently he waved her away, gesturing for her to wait until the broadcast was over.

'I'm looking for the Hotel Continental,' she said as slowly and clearly as she could. The man ignored her. She approached the unshaven younger man beside him. He seemed more weary, listening only with mild curiosity. She repeated the request for directions and offered the man the small piece of paper she had used on a number of occasions. It had been given to her in Paris. In a few scribbled lines of Spanish, the paper explained her mission. The man read it and nodded wearily.

'English?' he said.

'Yes.'

'Wait, please. Then I take you.'

'Thank you.' Meredith waited and then whispered, 'What are they listening to?'

'Madrid radio. The Fascists are advancing on the city. Yes. He is saying ... "People of Spain! Put your eyes, your will, your fists at the service of Madrid ... Accompany your brothers with faith, with courage, send your possessions, and if you have nothing else, offer us your prayers. Here in Madrid is the universal frontier that separates Liberty and Slavery. It is here in Madrid that two incompatible civilisations undertake their great struggle: love against hate; peace against war; the fraternity of Christ against the tyranny of the Church."'

'Can I help?'

When Meredith turned from the clerk at the Hotel Continental desk she was confronted by Theodore Goss. The American was holding his Panama hat by the brim so that it shielded most of his chest. Behind the congeniality Meredith saw a familiar hunger. Strange, she thought wearily, how men were incapable of masking this hunger. Once she had seen it, the moves were laid out ahead of her. All that changed from man to man was the pace of the pursuit.

'I don't know. Can you help?' Meredith said. She allowed a little flirtation to colour her voice, but she felt suddenly bored by the old game and her face hardened again.

'Well, that rather depends on what you want,' Goss said. He had read the change in her and his approach became more formal. He laid his hat on the reception desk and offered Meredith his hand after wiping it dry on his thigh. 'Theodore Goss, of the *New York Post*.'

Meredith laughed. Now she had placed him. Goss had the mannerisms of Oliver Hardy and, by the look of it, the same unpitiable self-regard. 'Hello, Mr Theodore Goss,' she said.

'Why are you laughing?' Goss said, feeling it would serve him better if he joined in.

'I'm tired. Exhaustion always makes me mildly hysterical.'

'I see,' he said. 'Would you care for a drink?'

'Yes, why not.' Taking her case, Meredith followed Goss through the reception and out into the courtyard. She looked with hope into the faces of the men they passed. Could a miracle have transported Kit Renton to her in the hotel lobby? She felt closer to him there, imagining he might have had contact with any of the people crowding the hotel. Goss directed her to the table by the fountain and went to the bar to fetch the drinks. Meredith waited beside the circle of stones and the captive black water which endlessly circulated. Her attention was caught by a party of stout Italian men in formal dress coming noisily into the bright bar. With their arms around each other's shoulders they breathed alcohol and love into each other's faces. As they passed through the room they straightened up; once out of sight, their raucous laughter broke out again. Two prostitutes with shawls loose on their bare shoulders followed sedately a moment later.

'Tarts,' Goss said. Arriving at the table with a bottle and two glasses in his hands, he watched the women go. 'Prostitution is now back on the streets of the city, having been for some time removed.'

'You sound disappointed.'

'No. No. Not at all,' Goss said hastily. 'I'm not here to judge. Only to report.' Something seemed to concern him for a moment. He shook his head to rid himself of it and sat down. He struck a match and touched it to the wick of the tiny oil lamp at the centre of the table. The wick fizzed and caught and the cheerless flame glossed a patch of moist skin on Meredith's face. The light was echoed in her eyes, which were fixed on the damp green stones surrounding the fountain.

'There,' Goss said, as the darkness backed a step away. 'Drink, and then we can talk,' he said, pouring her a glass. 'Or, if you don't care to talk, then we won't. Or I will. Whichever you'd prefer.'

'Thank you,' Meredith said. 'You're very kind.'

Goss smiled and watched her relax as the wine loosened the tightness of her shoulders and released some of the tension in her chest.

'Can you believe it?' she said.

'What?'

'All this. Here. Transported from my comfortable life to a Spanish hotel. In the middle of a war. Finding myself on a tram that somebody was firing bullets at . . . And then being shot at in the street.'

'Extraordinary times,' Goss said.

'I expect you're used to it.'

'No. You never get used to it. I've faced death on three occasions, in three separate countries, and I can assure you you never get used to it.'

'Would you mind if I had another glass?' Meredith said.

'Of course not.' Goss poured and said, 'Tell me what's on your mind.'

'I was just thinking . . .' Meredith said, thinking how easy it was being with Goss. Large men always made her feel safe. She had even felt safe with Harry Bowden, at least in the beginning. But all that was behind her now, safely away on the other side of the Channel. '. . . I was thinking about a man I met, when? What would it be? Two, nearly three weeks ago? He tried to pick me up on the boat train and we ended up together on the Channel steamer . . .'

'Yes?'

'Well, you see at the time I was convinced he'd been sent to get me . . . Get me. I mean, that probably sounds ridiculous to you. It's a long story. But I was, actually, in fear for my life.'

'And you got away from him?' Goss laughed. 'What I mean to say is that clearly you got away from him.'

'Yes. Except that now I wonder if I was just imagining it. The threat, I mean. He came after me when I went out on deck. There was a storm and I assumed . . . I mean, I . . . I mean, he seemed to be . . .'

'By the sound of it, you've been through a great deal,' Goss said.

'Yes. I feel as though I have. But it's all for entirely selfish reasons. I mean, I'm not here in pursuit of some cause. I'm here to find somebody.'

'That's a fine and honourable motive.' Goss raised his glass. 'Would that we all had honest motives.'

'So what are your motives, Mr Goss of the *New York Post*?'

'My motives? My Lord. Well, I expect my overriding motive is to tell a good story each day. A story which is somehow true. And if people take something away from that then I'm happy. So I guess you'd say that my motive is ostensibly to shed light on the dark places of the world.'

'Then I also salute your honourable motive. Cheers.'

'Yes, indeed.'

'Tell me how you became a journalist.' Despite her exhaustion, Meredith managed to sound genuinely curious.

'Very well. If you're interested.'

'Of course. Why shouldn't I be?'

'Because in my experience a woman asking questions is not a woman who's interested in giving answers.'

'That's what people do, isn't it?' Meredith said. 'Ask questions. Answer questions. That's all talk is.'

'Yes. And how meaningless it all is.'

'I'm sorry, Mr Goss. Perhaps I've caught you at the end of a bad day, but I don't consider it to be meaningless. I mean, if it's meaningless then . . . where does that leave us all?'

'Do you know something?' Goss said, leaning forward. 'Shall I tell you why I hate the theatre?'

'If you like. Though I don't think we were talking about the theatre, were we?'

'The reason I hate the theatre is because it's all questions and answers. Questions and answers are what polite folk engage in when they have no interest in each other.'

'But if I say to you, just to pick a question at random: "Do you love me?" surely you can't argue I'm not interested in you.'

'Yes, I can. If you need to ask such a question then you must already know the answer. People always know the answers to such questions.'

'Very well, and that may be true. But perhaps I do know the answer, and perhaps I'm seeking reassurance from you.'

'Then that's not a genuine question.'

'Isn't it?'

'No.' Goss smiled.

'How did we get to this?'

'You asked me how I became involved in journalism.'

'Of course.'

'But what you really wanted to do was to tell me what you're doing here and find out whether I could be of any help to you.'

'Why should you help me?'

'Because you need me to. Because there may be a story in it. How many reasons would you like?'

'I'm looking for a man called Kit Renton,' Meredith said.

'Then you'd better tell me everything you know about him.'

When Paul and Grand staggered back to the hotel an hour later they called in at the bar for a final drink before going to bed. Grand ordered, but was interrupted by Paul drunkenly calling him to the French doors.

'A vision,' Paul said, looking out at Meredith.

'A dark angel,' Grand said, and stumbled back to the bar.

'I must speak to her. I must declare my love for her.'

'Paul,' Grand said.

'Yes, my friend?'

'Do it tomorrow.'

As she lay in her narrow bed listening to a commotion in the hotel, Meredith sorted the sequence of events that brought her to the Hotel Continental. Every decision she had taken since the night she went to Kit Renton had led her towards her simple goal – to find him. She was angry for revealing so much of herself to the fat American. But he had been plausible and kind. She had even gone so far as to call him 'My dear Goss' when they said goodnight at the door of the room he had found for her. She knew that she must now guard herself from such sentimentality. It was the American's voice she thought she could hear now from one of the rooms below her in the hotel. She went to the window which looked down on the courtyard below. The smell of the oranges growing against the wall of the patio floated up to her. Two soldiers were smoking cigarettes, sitting at the table she had occupied three hours before. When they were called to the vestibule they threw away their cigarettes, adjusted their caps and vanished into the hotel. Other voices echoed up to her. The American's was the clearest of them. He was protesting ('in the strongest terms') the rights of one of his colleagues. Meredith decided to go and see for herself. But by the time she got downstairs the troops were gone and the only evidence of the arrest was the smell of fresh cigarette smoke at the check-out desk and the American's Panama hat on the floor. Meredith picked it up and dusted it and put it on the counter. It was cool in the bar so she pushed two chairs together and resumed her night's sleep.

London

'Goodbye,' Arthur Lawler said to his landlord's sister as he walked past her and out of the lodging-house.

'Don't bother yourself coming back before six. The door won't be open.' The woman slammed the front door shut and the draught blew off Arthur's hat. When he stooped to pick it up he felt the winter sun on his back. It was lighting up the frosty roofs of the canvas-covered barrows in the street market and the card in the filthy lodging-house window advertising 'RooMs for SinGle mEn'. Arthur had never seen his destiny as that of a single man. Nor had he envisaged a run of luck that would result in him hiding out in 9d-a-night lodgings. But, for under a shilling a day, he had found a quiet contentment; a roof over his head, warmth, and a hard short bed. The sweat-scented sheets no longer detained him from sleep. He had also become used to the men stumbling around him in the dark to piss in the communal pot; to the rhythmic canvas tug of men masturbating; to matches flaring in the dead of night and cigarettes being lit. And he had become expert at washing from head to foot in the filthy cellar sinks and drying himself on a saturated roller towel. The orange heart of the coke fire in the basement kitchen was always glowing. Without it there would have been neither heat nor light in the damp room where the single men fried their horsemeat steaks in hissing yellow fat and hung their grey washing to dry. The stevedores and news-paper sellers, screevers and labourers, many patrolling the borders of sanity, congregated at night by the low fire for cigarettes and games of nap or draughts, and Arthur Lawler was grateful to be a part of their community. 'Good old Arthur', they called him and often laughed at his appearance. One evening, as he lost his footing on the stairs and fell headfirst into the kitchen, somebody shouted, 'Drunk as a lord, Arthur?' And for the rest of the night they deferred to him and waited on him hand and foot.

Negotiating the street-market slurry of rotten vegetables, Arthur walked past a man dragging a canvas sheet from his green barrow. He was tugging the sheet towards him like a laden fishing net and as it dropped in lengths to the floor he folded it into squares by karate-chopping in creases. Finally he nudged the cube of canvas under the barrow with the toe of his boot, coiled a rope and tossed it on top. With that, the man dusted off his hands and looked around to satisfy himself that the world had not changed in the minute that had passed since he had begun his labours. As he did so he caught sight of Arthur standing behind him.

Arthur considered asking the man for work. It could, perhaps, have rewarded him with sixpence for very little trouble. With jobs like this – a few pennies here and the odd shilling earned from giving out handbills – he had found a way to survive. But he had saved hard for today and he decided he would see it through without grafting. He was going to find Billy Royle. If Royle gave him up to the police then so be it. He could no longer bear the life of a fugitive. The seven shillings in the breast pocket of his one remaining un-pawned suit should see him safely drunk. Whatever the outcome, he would be cushioned from it.

'No, I don't think I will,' Arthur said to the man by the barrow, declining an offer of work that had not been made. 'But thank you.'

He took a nip from his flask and went on. A little further up the road something resembling a pine cone caught his eye in the gutter. He knelt down and looked closely at what proved to be a tiny frozen sparrow. This provoked a few easy tears; for the sparrow, for himself, for humanity. Still weeping, he passed out of the market and set off up the short, gentle gradient in the direction of Oxford Street.

Since he attacked Bowden he had kept himself south of Oxford

Street, which had put Meredith's flat, the car showroom, the Posts, the Fitzroy and most of his other regular haunts off limits. Crossing Oxford Street now, Arthur caught sight of a clock in a jeweller's shop window. It called to him, tick-tocking silently within the vacuum behind the glass. Like a squat brass owl, the clock engaged his attention and he watched the brass pendulum swing for a while – his head, not just his eyes, following the hypnotic movement – until the hands showed exactly five past ten. At his current speed he estimated he would reach Royle's flat above the showroom within five minutes. Too early. The service was due to start at twelve, which meant that if Royle wasn't in then he would have nearly two hours to waste. The service. (Of course!) He had forgotten the other reason for his visit to Royle. Another nip from his flask triggered an idea: why not call in on Wilson first and see how the land lay? The worst that could happen was that Wilson wouldn't let him in. Which was precisely (he congratulated himself), precisely why (one of the reasons, anyway) he had gone to so much trouble over his suit. No, there were no flies on Arthur Lawler today. Fleas, yes (what a chuckle!). Flies, no.

Good. The whisky, his old friend, was back with him, warming him and lifting him up as it never failed to do. Now he must have a cigarette. Cigarettes, like nothing else, were truly a perfect food for the soul. Unlike the booze, they never left him feeling more wretched than he did before. And of course (he reflected), a good smoke suited all moods, commiseratory or celebratory. Yes, he really must have a cigarette. He scouted around but there were no decent-length butts on the ground so he reached into the store in his jacket pocket and pulled a handful out. He examined the mess of charred paper, the few cork filters, filthy-smelling ash, yellowing, spit-stained papers. Arthur was in no doubt that his right-hand pocket smelt like an ashtray but since he had fallen down the stairs he seemed to have lost all sense of smell, which, under his current circumstances, he considered a blessing. In compensation, his hearing had become more acute. He could now hear conversations from what seemed like hundreds of yards away. The odd thing was that most of these conversations seemed to concern him in some way. ('That chap over there,' he heard one man say to another, 'don't play cribbage with him, not for cash. He's a dab hand.')

'A blessing,' he said out loud as a horse and cart went by. He could hear the bell of a fire engine ringing from the direction of Piccadilly. 'There,' he said. 'You'll have to do.' He pinched a one-inch butt from the mess and returned the residue to his pocket, blowing his palm clear of the ash. All he needed now was a light for it and a potential solution was suggested by a smart man walking towards him smoking a pipe.

'I wonder if I could take a light from you?' Arthur Lawler called from the jeweller's doorway. He leaned slightly forward from his waist, presenting the cigarette butt (now in his mouth) in the man's direction.

'Yes, I expect so,' the man said impatiently, taking his lighter from a coat pocket and striking the flint. He held the flame steady, twelve or fourteen inches from Arthur Lawler's face. Arthur ducked towards it and missed. (Damn!) He blinked, shook his head and leaned in again. The cigarette caught and Arthur took the first draw of filthy smoke. 'Thank you so much,' he said, coughing heartily. But the man didn't hurry away as he had expected. Instead, he asked, 'I say, are you all right?'

'Yes,' Arthur assured him. 'Quite all right, thank you.'

'You're not chilly?'

'Absolutely not. Not at all.'

'Well, here, buy yourself a shirt on me.' The smart man gave Arthur a pound note from his mahogany-coloured wallet.

'That's very kind of you. But I can't take charity.'

'Please.' The man replaced his wallet in his pocket. 'I insist.'

'Then consider it a loan,' Arthur said.

'Yes. I will. Well, goodbye.'

'You must let me have your address.'

'Why?'

'So that I can repay you.'

'No. Please. That won't be necessary.'

'But I insist.'

'I pass here most mornings. If you feel you must return the money, wait here for me.'

'Good idea. I won't detain you. Goodbye.'

'Goodbye. And good luck.'

'And to you.' They shook hands firmly and the smart man set off. He had never given money to a tramp before, but then today had been the first time he had seen anything of himself in the sad figures shambling along the streets.

Arthur sat on the pavement, took off his right shoe and slipped the note inside. When he put his shoe back on he could feel the folded note against his bare sole. No shirt (of course not!). The chambermaid never returned it (where had she appeared from?). Which would explain the man's reaction to him. He really must get hold of a shirt before he met Royle. Again Wilson came to mind. In the cocktail party of life, the solitary guest standing in the corner often served as a necessary companion until someone more suitable arrived on the scene. Wilson, of course, fell firmly into this category. However (and Arthur found this unsettling), the solitary guest in the corner often proved the most content in all the room. He didn't circulate because he had no need to – so where did that leave everybody else?

Where did all this start, all this talk of parties? With Wilson of course. So Arthur walked a short way towards Oxford Circus and then turned up Great Portland Street. Soon he was standing outside the car showroom, looking at himself in the reflection of the plate-glass windows. He could see the dim figure of Wilson moving about in the sales office, but the lights had not been turned on, which would seem to suggest that the showroom would be closed for the day. On further inspection, Arthur saw that there were no longer any motor cars inside, just the sand-filled trays speckled with black oil. He banged on the glass with his palm but the sound didn't appear to have travelled through the vast space to penetrate the sales-office windows. He banged again, but Wilson was now settled, sitting on the sofa reading the newspaper and eating a sandwich. Just as

Arthur began to contemplate giving up, Wilson stood and went to the telephone on the desk. As he answered it, he turned and saw a peculiar figure waving his arms around on the pavement. Wilson stared at the figure as he continued his conversation with the caller. Arthur saw a slow recognition dawning on his face. Recognition and a certain amount of confusion, or perhaps horror.

Nevertheless, when the call was complete and he had latched the earpiece back on to the stand, Wilson came immediately to the showroom doors and unbolted them to let Arthur in.

'Hello, Wilson,' Arthur said and held out his hand.

'Yes,' Wilson said unsurely. 'Hello.'

'I've come to borrow a shirt from you.'

'A shirt?'

'Yes. You see I made the mistake of coming out this morning without putting one on and it struck me that you might just be the person to help me out.'

'I see. Why?'

'Because. Because you were in the vicinity.'

'Well, I don't know that I can,' Wilson told him.

'Oh.'

'I haven't got one here.'

'All right. It's no matter, really. I have a pound note in my shoe which I can use to buy one.'

'In your shoe?'

'Yes.' Arthur winked. 'Needs must.'

'Well,' Wilson said, regaining some of his composure, 'why don't you come through and have a cup of tea?'

'Yes, I'd like that.'

Tyre-track Ys were printed into the dust of the showroom floor; a complex diagram of manoeuvres indicating exactly how the vehicles had been evacuated through the back doors.

'Where are the motors?' Arthur said.

'Mr Royle got rid of them.'

'He sold them?'

'You'll have to ask him about that.'

'Yes. I will.'

'All I know is that he expects me to be here to keep an eye on things until decisions are made.'

'Decisions?'

'Yes. I'm not party to them.'

'Oh. Well, perhaps you should be.'

'I offer my opinion if I'm asked for it, otherwise I consider it not being required.'

'That's a good policy. And Billy still lives upstairs, does he?'

'No. He's moved to Mr Bowden's place. The flat's empty.'

'So there's no point calling for him then?'

'I wouldn't have thought so. Like I said, he doesn't live there.'

'No. I see.'

'You'd better come into the office.'

'Yes, I will. Just like old times, isn't it?' Arthur said happily, but Wilson didn't answer.

Arthur scorched his lips on the tea. The pain was intense and aggravated the longstanding ache in his bottom jaw. His tongue probed the serrations of the two broken teeth and the jelly of clotted blood over his missing incisor.

'Your head,' Wilson said.

'I'm sorry?'

'You should get that cut seen to.'

'Oh, that. No, it's nothing.' Arthur reached to feel the hefty scab above his right ear. He had tried not to scratch it because when he did it slipped off and opened the wound again. ('Your head/your shirt/aren't you cold?' – why was everybody so interested in his welfare all of a sudden? And what right did they have?)

'How did you do it?' Wilson asked him. He was leaning against the desk, maintaining the distance between them as though he expected Arthur to pounce on him.

'I fell down some stairs, Wilson. If it's any of your business.' ('Bugger me,' he whispered noisily. Then another voice in his head joined in, asking, 'What right does he have?' 'No right at all. None whatsoever.' All of this in his head and out of it.) Wilson edged a little closer to the telephone.

Falling down the stairs. What a palaver that caused in the lodgings. Anybody would have thought (mistakenly) that somebody there actually gave a damn about him, the fuss that was made. ('Here, fetch a cloth/give me your shirt/I'm not giving you my shirt, I've just washed it' – 'Bugger me')

'What's that?' Wilson said.

'The fuss that was made. When I fell down the stairs.'

'Oh, you fell down the stairs, did you?'

'Look here.' Arthur stood. 'I'm sorry, Wilson, but I can't waste all morning passing the time of day with you. I have things to do.'

'I'm sure you have, sir.' (Was that a slur? Odd how the working classes always used that title as an insult – but it only wounded when you had fallen to their level.)

'Well, thank you for the tea, and if Billy asks for me you can tell him I'll be at the Posts where I'll be happy to have him buy a drink for me. I'd be glad if he'd invite me, at any rate.'

'Invite you where?'

'To the Posts. For a sandwich and a . . . God, I don't know.' ('Bugger me, I don't know.')

'If you're sure.'

'What do you mean by that?'

'If you're sure you want to leave.'

'Well, I am sure.'

'Well, why don't you take a sandwich with you?'

Arthur laughed and said, 'I have a pound note in my shoe, Wilson. Don't you listen? I'm not a charity case.'

'I didn't mean to . . .'

'Bugger me.' ('I'm not a charity case. Just down on my luck. That's all. Just down on my bloody luck.')

Clapping his hands as he passed through the showroom, he paused and listened to the echo. He clapped his hands again and listened for a second time. Wilson waited by the office door, watching him, fearing that Arthur would be clapping in there all day.

'Hear that?' Arthur called.

'No.'

'Then you must be deaf.'

'What am I listening to?'

'The fizz. The . . . fizz. Just listen.' Arthur clapped. 'Did you hear it that time?'

'Well, I'm not . . .'

'I really don't have time for this. If you want to listen you'll have to come in here and do some clapping yourself . . . Well, come on, Wilson.'

Wilson sighed and came to stand beside Arthur. 'You do know how to clap?' Arthur said and found that Wilson did.

'There,' Arthur said and patted him on the shoulder. 'Easy when you know how. Don't forget to tell Billy where I am.'

'No.'

Puzzled, Arthur looked round the room. 'What happened to all the motors?'

'They . . . they were taken away.'

'Righty-ho. Well, goodbye, Wilson.'

'Goodbye.'

'Get clapping, will you.'

As soon as Arthur had wandered out to the street, Wilson dashed across the showroom and slid the bolt into place. He suspected that already Arthur had no memory of the visit; his interest had been caught by something in the gutter which he seemed now to be discussing with himself. Arthur's temper flared. He looked behind him, but saw nobody there. Then he wandered away towards the Posts and Wilson went to the office to call Billy Royle.

'It's for you,' Bowden's nurse said, holding out the phone.

'Who is it?' Royle said, emerging from the bedroom fastening his cuffs.

'It's your man from the showroom.'

'Tell him I'm busy.'

'Tell him yourself. He says it's important.' She shrugged in the petulant way Royle had come to expect of her, laid the earpiece down on the marble table top and went back to her magazine in the drawing-room.

'Yes, Wilson?' Royle said into the device. He saw the woman lick her fingers and turn a page of the magazine, but the magazine already bored her. She went to the window and looked down into the garden below. The gardener was forking a pile of leaves into a barrow while his boy raked the gravel path. Royle was jealous of everything the woman saw, every moment of her attention that wasn't awarded to him. Was this love? Because the feeling was certainly different from that which he had felt for Meredith and even the barmaid. But Wilson's voice was droning in its limited range into his ear. Something about Arthur showing up.

'Lawler?' Royle said. 'What do you mean? . . . Did he? . . . Yes, well, I expect we'll bump into each other one way or another . . . Thank you.'

Royle went into the drawing-room and presented his right cuff to the woman, saying, 'I can't fix it. Can you?'

'If you give me the cufflink.' She took it from him and looked him in the eye as she threaded it easily through the double fold of thick fabric. Royle reached his left arm round her and drew her close to him.

'That's not part of the service,' she said, pulling away and helping herself to a cigarette from a box on the coffee table.

'Well, what do you think?' Royle asked, turning and presenting himself to her.

'You look very good in black. Most men do. What did Wilson want?'

'Arthur Lawler's surfaced. Today of all days.'

'Will you tell the police?'

'No.'

'Why not?'

'Because . . . because there's no need. If he's back he's not going to run away again. If I know Arthur, he's probably come to face the music.'

'Do you think he knows about Harry?'

'Perhaps.' Royle went to the door and said, 'See you at the church.'

'Yes, I expect you will.' The woman slid back on to the sofa and picked up her magazine again.

Royle dashed down the stairs, glad to be away from the flat. He turned as he left the block and looked up at the wedding-cake layers of red brick. Why shouldn't he enjoy it? He surely had as much right to it as Bowden.

The woman he had left in the flat picked up the telephone. Life was so dull with Royle and his friends. And, God, funerals were turgid. Particularly if one was there solely out of a sense of duty. A visit from the police would liven up the proceedings. And who was Arthur Lawler, anyway? From what Royle had told her about him, he deserved everything he got.

The Posts. What was it about the Posts that provoked such a salt tang in Arthur's memory? Arthur looked up at the bright hanging sign and tried hard to remember the last time he visited there. Yes, it was the day of the fog and the doctor and the dreadful ache in his chest. Not the beginning of it all. No, he'd never get to the root of it. But certainly the day when he just seemed to lose control of himself. And then, of course, there was the barmaid. Deirdre. Yes, she was the salt in the wound. He owed her money and she wouldn't take it and therefore he was still in her debt. Never mind. There was nothing he could do about that now. With any luck she'd be in one of the other bars, or on her day off, or somewhere he wouldn't have to talk to her.

Good. No sign of her in the public bar. Just the dim-looking lad in the apron staring into the middle distance behind the freshly polished bar. The pumps were gleaming too. The ashtrays were empty. The fire had been lit. Perfect. Perfect. Breathe in deeply, Arthur. Breathe in the smell of yesterday's cigarettes and Jeyes fluid from the lavatories and then, then as you walk to the bar –

beer. Beer. Nothing like it in the whole wide world. A rich man could keep his toys. All Arthur needed was this. The smell of beer. The bar. Cigarettes. Whisky to up the tempo. Faster, faster, until he couldn't keep up. Then tiredness, nausea, despair. But that was all for tomorrow. And bugger tomorrow.

To the bar, savouring the steps across the new sawdust. He saw the dim lad sliding back down the rope into the present and looking at him so disdainfully he seemed almost grateful to have been confronted by someone from a lower station in life. Even so, the lad was not so confident that he could risk rudeness. After all, the shirtless, unshaven tramp might just be a friend of the governor. And as far as the governor was concerned, he would take money from anybody. The filthy notes from the public bar were worth no less at the bank than those from the saloon lounge.

'Yes?' the boy said with as much rudeness as he could risk.

'Yes?' Arthur said back.

'What can I get you, sir?'

('"Sir" again. Bugger me.') 'A pint of best. And a Scotch.'

'Certainly, sir. Any particular brand?'

'Johnnie Walker.'

The boy tugged the beer pump; his bicep flexed under his shirt. He pushed the handle back and pulled it again. The beer gushed into the glass and raced to the rim. He lifted the full glass up to the light. A clear chestnut-brown, the overspill like spit sliding slowly down the side. A translucent head. 'There you go,' the boy said and put the glass on the bar, and as Arthur weighed it up a glass of Johnnie Walker was set down next to it.

'One and sevenpence,' the boy said.

Arthur sat down on the floor and removed his shoe. The pound note inside it was hot and damp. He unfolded it and hoisted himself back to his feet and gave it to the boy. The boy opened a wooden drawer and his lips moved as he calculated the sum. He turned and tried to give Arthur his change. But Arthur was distracted.

'Your change,' the boy said.

'Yes,' Arthur said, taking the money. It was four days since he fell downstairs. He reached up to feel the scab on his head. ('Here, fetch a cloth, give me your shirt, I'm not giving you my shirt, I've just washed it' – 'Bugger me'. 'Get him up.' 'What's the matter, Arthur?' 'Look at him. Just look at him.' 'Leave hold, Arthur. Leave hold of that newspaper.' 'Tripped.' 'Bugger me.')

'She'll be down,' the boy was saying.

'I'm sorry?'

'Deirdre. She'll be down soon.'

'For the party?' (What party? Where did that come from? And had he asked about Deirdre? He supposed he must have done.)

'I don't know anything about a party. She's off out somewhere,' the boy said.

'What time is it?'

'Nearly eleven.'

'Where are we?'

'Who?'

'You and I?'

'In the . . . in the Posts.'

'That's right. Of course we are.' (Didn't he come here for a reason? Wasn't he on his way to see Royle?) 'Of course. You see I'm on my way to see an acquaintance.'

'Very good.'

'I must leave, you see. I have to go to church.'

'He's at the church, is he?'

'What church?'

'You said you were on your way to church.'

'Don't you damn well try to tell me where I'm on my way to.'

'What about your drinks?'

'Oh, those. Look after them for me. Put them under the bar, will you.'

As Billy Royle warily approached the church it began to rain. Just as the sight of his old school induced anxiety, churches provoked guilt. In front of the black railings the Fells twins were in lively conversation with a heavily perspiring Johnnie Quinn. Boy Merrell was walking jauntily down Margaret Street towards them smoking a cigarette, whistling, and tapping an umbrella dandyishly on the pavement. A number of Bowden's men were loitering in the courtyard waiting to be given instructions. Royle knew that he was now the ringmaster of this circus and, one way or another, they were all there because of him. From the distance he saw another noisy group approaching, making an armadillo of umbrellas as the rain fell harder. Behind it, the sinister hearse, drawn by a heavy horse, black-plumed, followed a top-hatted man marching in long strides along the centre of the street. Despite the rain driving into his face, his expression was frozen. Like the guards outside Buckingham Palace. Royle felt that nothing would break the pattern of his march.

'Quinn,' Royle said, prompting Quinn to turn away from the twins and shake Royle's hand.

'Full house. Standing room only,' Quinn said.

'Wilson telephoned. Apparently Arthur Lawler's broken cover.'

'I'll deal with him.'

'I don't want him hurt. If he turns up tell him I'll see him in the Posts afterwards.'

'Leave it to me.'

'Margaret's on her way. See to it she finds somewhere to sit.'

'Right.'

'Anything else I should know?'

'No.'

Walking behind the hearse, the moment went round in Arthur's head. Why was it sticking? Why couldn't he find any peace? Each slow step, each revolution of the heavy cartwheels, each shallow breath. Each miserable glimpse from every passer-by ('Here, fetch a cloth/give me your shirt/I'm not giving you my shirt, I've just washed it' – 'Bugger me' – 'Get him up.' 'What's the matter, Arthur?' 'Look at him. Just look at him.' 'Leave hold, Arthur. Leave hold of that newspaper.' 'Tripped.' 'What's he looking at? What's he reading? Here, Arthur, leave hold. Bugger me.')

'Leave off.'

'What?'

'Leave off of the carriage.' It was an acned junior from the funeral company following on at the rear of the procession.

'I only wanted to touch. That's all. (Bugger me. I only wanted to . . .)'

('What's he reading? Here, Arthur, let the dog see the rabbit. He's reading the obituaries. Perhaps he's found himself in here, what do you reckon? Is that what you've seen, my old mate?')

'Just leave off,' the youth said.

('Here we are: Harold Bowden. Died peacefully in his sleep. Is this the one, Arthur?') 'And now I'm a murderer. Murderer. Made something of myself at last. Bugger me. Of course the joke is, I thought he was dead all along.'

'He is dead, dad. That's why he's in there,' the youth said. 'Now leave off.'

(Is there some sort of party? Why are they smiling outside the church? Why is Boy Merrell laughing? Why is Royle talking to Quinn? What possible right does he have to be there?)

'I said leave off,' the youth said.

Shoved hard in his chest, Arthur fell back on to the street and lay there watching the matt black carriage roll away. A woman came up and stood over him.

'Arthur?' she said. She was holding a sheet of newspaper over her hair to protect it from the rain.

'What do you want?'

'My God. It is you. Arthur? My God.'

'No. You've got the wrong man.'

(Her. Can't deal with her now.)

'We're the same, you and me. You know we are, Arthur. There's no getting away from it.'

'No. You've got the wrong man.'

Inside the church, Royle passed the huge stone font, the stained glass colouring the light like redcurrant cordial. A few eyes were turned towards him. The rich, low-pitched whisper of conversation accompanied the sound of his leather soles scuffing the worn stone of the floor. Royle heard a commotion outside but he walked on and into the cool harbour of misery. When he saw the man in the back row, his arm in a dirty sling, his jacket sleeve hanging empty, he stopped dead.

'It's done,' Quinn said from behind him. But Royle didn't hear. 'It's done,' Quinn said again.

'What?' Royle was looking at Renton and Renton was looking back: seeing and knowing. Kit Renton, with an anger in his eyes instead of the old hurt. A fully grown man now.

'It's done. Lawler is.'

'What did you do?'

'I saw to him.'

'I told you I didn't want him hurt.'

'He'll live,' Quinn said. At that moment Bowden's nurse walked in. Men's heads turned and they stared. She could never enter a room without attracting attention to herself.

'Hello,' she said, signalling her claim on Royle by kissing him on the cheek and linking her arm in his.

'Hello.'

'There's a man being sick outside.'

'That'll be Arthur Lawler.'

'Shall we sit down?'

'In a moment.'

'What's the matter?' she said.

'Over there. That man with his arm in a sling.'

'Yes?'

'It's Kit Renton.'

'The letter man?'

'Yes.'

'She must have got him out. "My darling Meredith".'

'I doubt it.'

'Well, we should sit down, shouldn't we? Isn't it bad manners to stand around chatting in a church? . . . Billy?'

'What?'

'I don't think you're listening to me.'

'What?'

'I said I don't think you're listening to me.'

'Just be quiet, will you.'

'I'm sorry?'

'I said, just shut your silly mouth.' Royle turned to Quinn who was smirking behind them and said, 'Find a seat for her.' Then he went outside and Kit Renton followed him. On the street, the coffin was being lifted from the back of the carriage. The pall-bearers were standing shoulder-to-shoulder, preparing to take the weight. Royle and Renton stood side by side watching the manoeuvres.

'What happened to Bowden?' Renton said.

'Arthur did it. He's around here somewhere.'

'What do you mean, Arthur did it?'

'I'll tell you later. It's a long story.'

'I find that hard to believe.'

'Believe it . . . How are you, Kit?'

'Alive.'

Royle turned to Bowden's nearest man and said, 'What happened to the man Quinn dealt with?'

'Over there.' The man made a back toss of his head in the direction of a bench. Behind the bench there was a figure prostrate on the cold, wet stones.

It was Kit Renton who reached Arthur first and when Arthur saw Kit's face he believed he was in heaven and he was glad that the pain was over and everything he had hoped for had come to pass.

'Have I been hanged?' Arthur said. 'Have I?'

'All right, old chum. Let's get you up,' Renton said, but he didn't have the strength in his left arm to bear Lawler's weight. Instead, Royle took over and lifted Arthur up by the waist.

Arthur said, 'I wish somebody would tell me what is going on.' (Billy Royle, too. Surely they couldn't all have passed away! But if they had, then where was Meredith? Perhaps she was back at the flat waiting for them, gin poured. With the radiogram turned too loud. The best of Meredith; cheerful after the first two drinks of the day.)

'Up you come, Arthur.' Royle tugged him to his feet. The scab on Arthur's head had broken again but the membrane of skin behind was holding the blood at bay.

'We're not dead then?' Arthur demanded of Kit.

'No, Arthur. Not yet.'

'Well, I'm glad,' Arthur said and the two men embraced.

They heard the distant sound of a police bell. 'Take him,' Royle said. 'Take him to the Posts and wait for me there.'

When they reached the Posts, Kit sat in silence while Arthur told him as much as he could remember of the past weeks. He had constructed a carefully edited version of events. Where his motives had been suspect or his actions less than honourable he diverted round them, which led to a few surreal moments in his narrative, but Kit recognised that to Arthur they all carried equal weight.

Renton's interest was triggered when Arthur said, '. . . I telephoned Meredith and told her what I'd done.'

'After you attacked Bowden?'

'That's correct. Absolutely correct.'

'And what was her reaction?'

'You know, I really can't remember. I think I mentioned that Bowden knew she was going out to Spain to try and find you, and she should get out as quickly as she could.'

'To find me?'

'Yes. Am I not making myself clear now?'

'But I don't understand. You're telling me . . . ?'

'It's really quite straightforward. She was coming to find you, Kit. That's what she'd decided. Did she not tell you? No, I expect she didn't. I mean there was no stopping her. You know what Meredith's like once she has an idea in . . .'

'And you didn't try to stop her?'

'Quite the contrary, I encouraged her to go. I mean . . . yes, I absolutely encouraged her to come and find you.'

'And she went?'

'Well, yes. Yes, as far as I know, she went.'

'My God,' said Renton.

'Go on! . . . No . . . Go on!' A very drunk woman was listening to Boy Merrell telling a story at the bar of the Posts.

'Well, let me finish, my dear, and I will, as you suggest, "Go on"!' Boy Merrell said to her.

'What did he say?' one of the Fells twins asked the other.

'He's tellin' Netta to let him finish. Let me finish and I will go on. That's what he's tellin' her.'

'I can't hear anything in this racket.'

'Poor dear.'

'We'd better have a drinky. Another drinky, dear?'

'If you don't mind.'

'I don't mind, dear, you know me.'

Arthur felt a hand on his shoulder. He smelt cheap perfume and turned to face Deirdre.

'I lost my sense of smell,' he told her. 'And now it's come back.'

'That's not all you lost, Arthur, by the look of it.'

'Would you mind if we didn't talk,' Arthur said. 'I don't much feel like talking at the moment.'

'I'm not letting you get away, Arthur. Not this time.'

'Where's Kit?'

'Kit?'

'Kit brought me here and now he's gone and I want to know where he is.'

'Well, that's all very well, I'm sure, but I don't know who Kit is. And I'd ask you to take your temper out on somebody else in future.'

'Well, there he is. He's over there, talking to Billy.'

'Oh, the man with the bad arm. That's Kit, is it?'

Instead of replying, Arthur forged a path through the crowd towards Renton and Royle who were deep in conversation in a space they had made for themselves by the piano. When Arthur reached them, Renton was asking about Meredith and Royle was telling him all he knew.

'I did it for her,' Lawler said, remembering now and forcing his way into the conversation. 'That's why I attacked Bowden! I knew she wouldn't get away from him otherwise. Did I mention that at all?'

Royle and Renton looked at him with pity. Renton reached out his left hand and patted Arthur on the shoulder.

'But where is she?'

'I expect she's still out there, Arthur,' Renton said.

'So you didn't bring her back?'

'No. No, I didn't. Look, I think I need to get out of here.' He turned to Royle and said, 'I'll try Pollitt, though I doubt there's much he can do from this end.'

'Yes. Of course,' Royle said. 'But don't underestimate her. She's a survivor. I mean, she survived us, didn't she?'

'Yes, she's a survivor all right,' Arthur said. 'But the war, Kit. I presume it's still going on?'

Arthur didn't want Renton to leave. He was one of the few people in whose company he didn't feel alone.

'Yes, it is.'

'And . . . and you were going out there to . . . help, weren't you? You said something about Miss Canary Islands? I'm sorry, since I hit my head it's all rather . . . Bombers, was it? Going into the sea?'

'Look,' Renton said to Royle. 'I have to go. You'll look after him?'

'Yes, Kit.'

'Come and see me. In a few days' time. When the dust settles.'

'I'm glad . . . I'm glad you're here. Alive. I mean,' Arthur said.

'So am I.'

'Was it terrible?'

'Goodbye, Arthur.'

'I mean, the Republic, how did all that side of things go? Did you . . . ?'

'Please. I'm leaving. Now you take care.'

'Yes. You too,' Arthur said. Nobody seemed to have moved aside to let Renton through, but suddenly the door was swinging shut on the grey street and he was gone.

'You see,' Arthur said. 'I thought Meredith would find him and everything would be all right for them both.'

'I know you did.'

'Well, what happened?'

'He was captured. Then they released him. He was lucky. You'll have to talk to him about it.'

'But he looked so . . . changed.'

'Yes.'

'And what about Meredith?'

'I don't know. Who can say?'

'And why did he say goodbye like that? I mean, it was almost as though he thought he'd never see us again.'

Billy Royle put his beer glass down on the bar and faced Arthur head-on, trying to block the rest of the room from him. 'Arthur, listen to me.'

'Yes. I'm listening.'

'No. Listen to me properly.'

'Of course.'

'You have to leave now. The police are looking for you and you need to go away. And not come back. Do you understand?'

'Yes.'

'And Deirdre, fool that she is, is going to take you. Do you understand?'

'Yes.'

'And now you must go.'

'So this really is goodbye.'

'Yes. I'm rather afraid it is.'

'I see. Well, goodbye, Billy.'

'Goodbye, Arthur.'

Barcelona: The Following Day

The hotel's morning delivery of bread did not arrive in time for breakfast. When Meredith Kerr came into the dining-room, she paused by the doors and listened to Goss protesting loudly about it to a young girl who was standing at his table. He was sitting with another man – the Frenchman, Grand. Grand was hungrily smoking a cigarette. He was unshaven and dishevelled. He looked as though he hadn't slept. In contrast, the skin of Goss's face shone; he had just returned from his ritual morning shave in the hotel's barber shop. Wherever he went in the world, whatever his circumstances, Goss couldn't face the day without a shave and a cup of hot weak tea. The shave prepared him mentally, the tea quelled his digestive system. Goss had also paid to have the creases pressed into his suit, though the light cloth still bore some stains.

Grand seemed to sense Meredith's presence in the room before he saw her. Immediately he had done so, he nudged Goss and Goss stood and waved her over. If he hadn't she would have turned and walked away. Meredith had woken on the chairs after three uncomfortable hours of fractious sleep, then she had returned to her room to re-pack her bag. Despite being deprived of sleep, and although she was physically exhausted, her mind was clear. She was now convinced that she couldn't trust Goss. There was no particular reason for it, just a hunch that his boorish behaviour in the dining-room seemed to confirm. She was now contemplating what her next move would be. Not so long ago, this would have thrown her into confusion. But it didn't, she felt liberated. She was free, free of Bowden and the ties to London, free of the doggedly persistent Arthur Lawler, free of Royle's pawing hands, and most importantly, free to find Kit. After considering it for some time she now believed she could do this without Goss's help.

The atmosphere of the room was more akin to a canteen than a dining-room. As far as Meredith could tell, apart from the two young girls who were pouring coffee and swinging their hips expertly to avoid the men's hands, she was the only woman in the room. As she moved through the waist-high field of heads, chairs were pulled close to tables to make way for her. In her wake, conversations started up, hungry looks followed her, a few obscene gestures were made.

Goss was relishing his role as her protector. He looked proud and proprietorial as she approached him.

'Good morning, how did you sleep?' he called when she was just too far away from him to answer without raising her voice.

Two steps closer to him, she said, 'Badly.' With the delivery of that single word, Goss's hopes were dashed. The tone told the story of her change of heart, of her new strength, of her regret at having said so much the night before. Goss swallowed; he rarely misjudged women. Grand, meanwhile, blinked tiredly and his eyelids briefly adhered. He could, he felt, easily have fallen asleep sitting down. Under normal circumstances the arrival of the woman would have brought him to life, but he had been awake for much of the night worrying about Paul. When his colleague arrived back at the hotel at dawn, he had been too anxious to sleep.

'I'm afraid there's no bread,' Goss said, trying to make light of it to Meredith.

'No? Never mind.' Meredith sat down and helped herself to one of Grand's cigarettes. Grand stirred and offered her a light. Goss fell silent. He felt he should have introduced Grand, but suddenly he had no heart for anything.

The nicotine nudged Meredith towards a fleeting optimism. Perhaps she had been too brutal. After all, Goss had found her a room, he had listened to her for hours, he had looked after her. 'I doubt anybody gets much sleep here, do they?' she conceded.

'Very little,' Grand said, after waiting for Goss to pick up the cue. 'Particularly when one's colleagues are taken away in the dead of night.'

'Yes. I heard the commotion.' Meredith managed to inject some sympathy into the response. 'Is he all right?'

'He's asleep,' Grand said. Meredith sensed that Grand seemed to be seeking her opinion as to whether sleep was a good or bad sign. She had always found Frenchmen hard to read. While Englishmen were always boys and Americans adolescents, she had always considered Frenchmen to be born adult with the wisdom and world-weariness that entailed.

'I'm sure that's the best thing for him,' Meredith pronounced, and Grand nodded as if she had imparted some great wisdom.

'As promised, I made some enquiries on your behalf.' Goss had recovered sufficiently to manage a businesslike tone.

'That was very kind of you,' Meredith said. She gave little away, but Lawler, had he been there, would have seen the change in her, the sudden stealth as she waited to pounce on the information. Enquiries, just bland interrogations, the fruits of which could change her life.

'I'm a man of my word.'

'Yes. I rather thought you would be.' Meredith was being won over by him again. He held the gift of news about her love and, for as long as he did, some of that love was gifted to him. She had always been in thrall to polite men. Perhaps it was something to do with her father, who had been unerringly polite to everybody until the shellshock manifested itself and one day he started swearing at her from a bedroom window. She ran away from him as far as she could across the yard and then into the fields. But soon she came back, trailed by the family terrier, and went up the creaking stairs. The house was otherwise empty. Her mother was out. Meredith found her father crying on the bed. He said, 'I can't fucking stand up straight without holding on to something, my darling.' Three days later he caught the flu and within two weeks he was dead.

'According to our friend on the newspaper,' Goss deferred to Grand, who nodded and said, 'A reliable source.'

Goss continued, 'The unit returned from the front last week. Three or four of them were missing, including the Englishman – the presumption is that there was only one Englishman – and the belief is that he is in enemy hands.'

'Well, well, yes,' Meredith said. 'Yes, I see.'

'That's all they know.'

'Or perhaps, I expect, he may not be in enemy hands.'

'. . . That could be the case. But I should say that – for the time being at least – the Fascists are acting rather cautiously in their approach to non-nationals. If he has been captured then I think he has a good chance of remaining alive.'

'. . . Well, thank you for your trouble, Mr Goss,' Meredith said, standing. The room had become a cone of sound. The perspectives stretched and shortened. She fought the feeling of faintness. A man at the far end of the room laughed and slapped another man on the back; the laugh was bright in her ear.

'It was really no trouble,' Goss said. 'Please have some coffee at least.'

'No. I won't. Thank you.'

'If there's anything else we can do, please don't hesitate to ask.'

'I think I might go back to my room for a while, if you'll excuse me.'

'Of course.'

Meredith ran through the dining-room and pushed through the crowd at reception. She ran up the flights of stairs and into her room where she slammed the door behind her and leaned against it, catching her breath and sobbing.

Half an hour later she heard a tap at the door which she ignored and closed her eyes. The door opened and the face of a girl peered in. The girl saw the woman lying curled on the bed and the door closed again. Meredith kept her eyes clenched shut. Her mind was a raucous, hellish funfair; each of the stalls offering bright horrors. A rifle was handed to her; Kit's head had been skewered and the target drawn on his face. A woman gave her a mat for the helter-skelter, but the slide ended in a fiery pit and men were screaming as they rushed into the flames. There was a circus horse tugging a cannon from the mud, a dwarf was beating it. She saw a veiled tent billowed by the breeze, and she made towards it. Inside it was silence and she slept.

She awoke just after midday. Exhaustion still burdened her limbs, but not her mind, which now allowed her to proceed towards the comforting prospect of Kit's imprisonment. She couldn't, however, stop herself from testing the wound: what if Kit was dead? First feelings, nausea, terror as she tried to put herself in his place as he fell. A bullet? An accident? What? How does a bullet feel? Out of the tent and back to the funfair. She went to her bag and opened it and took out a small pair of scissors. Spreading her left hand on the bedspread, she knelt on the mattress, clenched the scissors in her right hand and held them high.

How does a bullet feel?

She drove the closed point through the centre of her hand. Metal met bone, but the scissors were blunt and the point slipped and came to rest just short of penetrating her palm.

She must have screamed, because not long afterwards, as she lay on the bed, the scissors still buried in her hand, the door opened and Grand walked in. Following him was Goss, which, even under the madness of the circumstances, she felt was strange. Surely Goss should have come in first. But, no, Grand was more in control. In times of crisis she would always have turned to a man like Grand.

They carried her through the streets. Her hand was bandaged in a filthy room. She kept her eyes fixed on Grand's face throughout. Afterwards Grand, then Goss, told her she should go home. There was nothing more she could do in Barcelona and she should get out of Spain while she still could.

The following morning she began her long journey back to London.

A Week Later: Ferring, West Sussex

When the train pulled away from the small station the bewildered refugee figures of Arthur and Deirdre were left behind on the platform, standing beside their luggage. They had brought with them a large new suitcase and an old one roped round the middle, both of which were stacked on top of an old steamer chest. Beside it was a leather shopping bag. Arthur was wearing a new off-the-peg suit in a dark blue serge and Deirdre her Sunday-best coat. She had given their appearance careful consideration. Nobody knew her in Ferring, which meant that she had an opportunity to reinvent herself. Hence the accessories which, along with the new suitcase, included a freshly shaved husband at her side and a lounge-bar haughtiness which she had already employed against two ticket collectors. After all, as she told Arthur, you could well be travelling in the same compartment as your new neighbours without knowing it.

'You'd better find a porter,' Deirdre said, but Arthur was transfixed, listening to the novel, genteel silence of the small seaside village. Perhaps he would be happy here after all. The peace might be just what he needed to quieten the chaos of his thoughts.

'Arthur,' Deirdre said, hardening her voice.

'Yes?'

'You'd better find a porter.'

'Very well.' Arthur was still weighing up how best to deal with Deirdre's new persona. He knew he couldn't tackle her head-on but if he didn't say something about her rudeness soon then he knew he probably never would.

He walked slowly up the steps of the footbridge; he couldn't seem to catch his breath nowadays, and paused when he reached the centre of the span. The two sets of silver tracks ran perfectly straight for as far as the eye could see. A few weeds had taken root at the edge of the ballast. He caught sight of Deirdre watching him and waved down to her. From a distance he could always feel compassion for her, and from there he knew it was a short distance to caring and, ultimately, he hoped, to love.

They had come to Ferring because, a few weeks before, Deirdre had visited the village with her mother. Her mother had spent a holiday close by in Worthing as a child and one day, for a treat, had been taken along the coast by her father. Since then she had always felt herself drawn to the small, hard-to-find village with the hidden paths to the shingle beach. It seemed an appropriate place for her daughter to begin her married life. When Deirdre and her mother returned to London, it seemed to have been decided that this was where the newlyweds were to set up home together. The precise setting had been kept from Arthur 'as a surprise'. All he had been allowed to know was that she had secured the house with a small deposit and that they would have paid it off within a year.

Fifteen minutes after their arrival at the station a telephone call by the stationmaster fetched the village's only motor taxi to transport them to their new home. Sitting close together on the back seat of the cab, Deirdre slipped Arthur a ten-shilling note, whispering to him to give the man a generous tip. A moment later she whispered that this was a luxury they would not be able to afford in the future. She then attempted to engage the driver in conversation, lying fluently about their circumstances, and building (to Arthur's ears) a bizarre portrait of the pair of them as runaways from London, pursued not by the law but by unsuitable suitors. Arthur, it seemed, was fleeing an heiress. Without comment, the taxi driver left Deirdre to fill the silence.

At a crossroads the driver hauled round the large steering wheel to turn them into a long straight road of bungalows which were under construction. Only the two closest to the road junction were completed. Each had a wide sweep of green-tiled roof which dropped down to throw a deep shadow along the front of the squat dwellings. The large windows in the sitting-room were metal-framed and wrapped around the right edge of the buildings. A circular window was set into the wall beside each front door and to the left of each door was a smaller bedroom window. The gardens at the front were long and wide and laid to turf. Free-standing garages were set back behind the bungalows, half-hidden by the buildings. The unfinished road was lined with crates of shining green roof tiles and wooden pallets of house bricks. A solitary bricklayer was working, placing each new brick on a stiff ledge of mortar, leaning down to check its position against the string line, then tapping one end with the wooden handle of his trowel. Another man was shovelling dusty grey cement on to the top of a small volcano of sand. A woman in a suit of Lachasse tweed with a cigarette in her mouth was banging a dusty doormat against the wall of one of the finished buildings which was labelled 'Show office'. A billboard on the front lawn depicted a happy couple, arm-in-arm, strolling along the sea front, the red sun half-submerged into the sea behind them. A bungalow was shown in silhouette. Beside it, the silhouette of a two-seater car.

Arthur tested his feelings about his future life here; an existence in a single-storey house a few hundred yards from the Channel. But he found he could not find anything to feel about it because he couldn't yet find anything within the experience to associate it with the life he had already lived.

However it seemed that their life together was not to be in a bungalow. The taxi went on until, beyond the marked boundary of the new road, they passed a crude wooden sign hammered to a post with '1 to 8 Railway Carriage Row' painted on to it. The post stood beside an open five-barred gate. Beyond the gate was a track which led across an island of scrubland towards the shingled beach. After the taxi had bounced across a number of potholes they came to the first railway carriage, which was supported by piles of bricks. A blacked stovepipe protruded from the roof; white curtains with a blue cornflower pattern were tied neatly back with blue ribbons at each compartment window. Outside the front door was a rusty mangle. Beside it, a laundry tub. A line of washing was strung from the roof of the carriage to a wooden post. The woman taking in the washing turned and regarded them with suspicion.

'Al,' she called out to a man inside. 'Al!' A dog barked. Deirdre waved regally to her.

'Just here,' Deirdre said, three carriage-dwellings later. The driver drew up and pulled on the brake. He and Arthur peered out at the ramshackle third-class railway carriage. Above it, a wireless pole was visible.

Deirdre broke the silence. 'You get what you pay for, Arthur,' she said and got out.

'Well, yes. Yes, you do,' Arthur said, following her after settling up with the driver.

'I never did like travelling by train,' the taxi driver said as he reversed away after helping Arthur out with the luggage.

Deirdre went to the door at the end of the carriage, climbed on to the wooden sleeper which served as a step, found the key in her bag and let herself in. Arthur walked round to the back and discovered that Railway Carriage Row ran along the top of the gently shelving shingle beach. He looked out at the sea. The horizon was empty. Arthur turned back and faced the carriage. Perhaps it was the fact that it was a carriage, with its tantalising promise of flight, that depressed him so much. He walked along the line of windows and peered in. All but two of the inner compartment panels had been removed to provide a wide, dingy living area. A black wood-burning stove squatted at the centre of the room like a splay-footed, fat-bellied imp. From the top of it, a rusty pipe, tied up with rope, went up through a damp hole in the roof. The carriage seats had been re-attached as benches along the carriage sides. A wooden table had been made of them to the right. Motley kitchen apparatus took up one end. A bed was stretched widthways across the other and, beyond the bed, a curtain which Arthur assumed must lead into a bathroom. Deirdre was standing at the centre of it all, talking quite animatedly. For one happy moment, Arthur was tricked into believing that a neighbour had wandered in and his wife had already struck up an acquaintance. He then realised that Deirdre was alone and was talking to herself. Partly to stop her, partly to re-establish contact, Arthur rapped on the thick window and Deirdre waved to him to come and join her inside.

He completed his slow tour of the perimeter of the carriage. From where he assumed the bathroom to be, a waste pipe extended some twenty feet across the shingle. Looking down the line of carriages, he saw that this was common to all of them. At the end of each pipe was a stagnant green pool of waste water. This, he surmised, went some way to accounting for the sewer stench which was wafted towards him on the breeze.

'It's a roof, Arthur. It's a roof over our heads,' Deirdre said, coming out to find him.

'I suppose it is.'

'And it won't be for ever. When you get yourself a job we can buy one of those bungalows. But for now, well, we'll just have to make do.'

'Of course.'

'You'd rather stay in a lodging-house, I expect?'

'No. This is . . . this is just the job.'

'Come inside, Arthur, and help me get straight.'

On the landward side of Railway Carriage Row was a ploughed field. Beyond it was another one which rose towards the coast road a mile or so inland. When night fell, the lights began to show to the east and Arthur asked permission to go in search of a pub. Deirdre told him to wait for her to get ready and then joined him. Arm-in-arm, they retraced their morning route, picking their way through the unlit building site until they came to a crossroads. After a short argument they turned left along a road of coastal mansions. Between the houses, the occasional cuts through to the beach were labelled 'Private Beach. No Entry'. In one of the few inhabited houses they saw a man in a coat and scarf sitting in a glass gazebo in the front garden reading a newspaper by the light of a storm lantern. He watched them until they had passed beyond the boundaries of his property. Shortly afterwards, Deirdre broke the awful silence to say, 'I'm going back.'

'Why?'

'I'm freezing cold, Arthur. And I don't want to spend all night wandering round in the dark.'

'Well, if you're sure.'

'Yes, I am.' As Deirdre began to walk away she said, 'You could come back with me.'

'Should I?'

'Do you want to?'

'Well, no. Not yet. I thought I'd have a quick drink and then come back.'

'Don't be too long.'

'No. I won't.'

'I mean it.'

'Of course.'

After a further ten minutes' walk, Arthur arrived at a row of shops: a greengrocer, a post office, and a baker's. Beyond the baker's was a car showroom and in front of the showroom a single petrol pump stood beside a small wooden hut which looked like a sentry box. The pump was unattended but there was a bell next to it and instructions to the motorist to ring it should service be required between the hours of six and ten p.m. The shops faced on to a playing field. Beyond them was a level crossing with a signal box. On the other side of the line was a pub, an afterthought to the row of Victorian houses that stretched away from the railway towards the coast road.

Arthur walked into the hallway of the public house and stamped the mud from his shoes. He realised only when the door closed behind him just how cold he was. A half-glass door led through to the lounge bar. The landlord was standing behind the counter talking to a man sitting on a stool. A log fire burned in the open hearth. The horse brasses gleamed. But Arthur could find no will to go in. Like a child playing hide-and-seek he had opened a cupboard door and found nobody inside. But who had he been looking for? he wondered. Meredith? Yes, he didn't really need a drink at all; he had gone out looking for Meredith. By the time the landlord looked up to greet him, Arthur was already gone.

As he returned to Railway Carriage Row it began to snow. The first flakes dropped weightless from the sky and the sea breeze caught them and tormented them before finally letting them rest. Arthur opened his palm and when a flake found it he closed his fingers and felt a tiny charge of cold. The snow thickened and Arthur reached out and snatched more. Soon the polite intrusion had become a blizzard. The white whirled and settled on the carriages, laying down a crystal carpet of white across the pebble road. Arthur walked to the beach and looked out at the horizon. The flat grey sea was idling between the wooden breakwaters. A herring gull stood one-legged on one of the tarred piles and looked back at Arthur. Half a mile to the west he could see a wooden café which looked like it had been thrown up on the beach in a storm. Above it, an illuminated flagpole which flew the Union Jack.

Arthur turned away and saw Deirdre leaning down to load wood into the stove. When she opened the square door the orange flames flooded her face with colour. The lanterns suspended from the roof were also lit and the carriage looked inviting and warm. To the right and to the left of it, Arthur saw the lights showing up and down the long static train. Wood smoke curled from the chimneys. He went to the door of his new dwelling, opened it, walked inside and slammed it shut behind him.

London

Two weeks later the snow was falling on London and when Meredith Kerr turned the corner into Berners Street the familiar landmarks were already being made magical by it. The hotel doorman in his maroon coat, blowing his hands warm, was smiling and the smile, Meredith was convinced, was provoked by the novelty of the weather. Meredith had taken a taxi from the station but had asked to be dropped off at Oxford Street. She wanted a few moments to compose herself as she approached Kit's flat. She knew that a heart could be prepared for anything by the gentle pace of footsteps. Since arriving at the station, which was the first time she had allowed herself to think about it, she had known that the first sign of Kit's presence could well be the light through the thin curtains. Of course, if the flat wasn't lit, then that didn't necessarily mean he wasn't home from Spain. He could easily be out. So, either way, she decided that she wouldn't allow herself to draw immediate conclusions from a light showing in the window.

She stood in front of the building, not allowing herself to look up at the second-storey window until she had prepared herself. She drew a breath and slowly tilted her head back. Her eyes swept up from the door, slid up a pane of glass, a number of courses of red bricks, finally resting on Kit's window. The room was dark. Out then. Out, or perhaps asleep. She wouldn't allow any other possibility to bully her optimism. If the front door was unlocked, she would wait in the entrance hall, perhaps make a seat for herself on the large table. She would light a cigarette and when Kit came back, she would be swinging her legs, and she would say, 'Hello stranger.' Or perhaps she would have worked up a better line by the time he arrived.

Meredith pushed at the door. It opened and she walked into the hall. Kit's hall. His presence was almost palpable. Perhaps some of the newspapers scattered on the table were his. Perhaps all of them were his. No, that certainly couldn't be, because if he hadn't collected them then that would signal that he was still away. The door behind her slowly swung shut, robbing the hallway of light. She reached for the light switch beside her but nothing happened; the new electric circuit had yet to be connected. The darkness, however, was not complete because there was a large window on the first landing. Slowly Meredith's eyes adjusted sufficiently for her to find her way to the table. Without the draught from the front door to stir them, the smells of cooking from the flats above her began to accumulate in the pit of the hallway. Meredith felt them beginning to taint her, the fumes glossing her skin with a fine film of stale oil. She began to resent the presence of the others in the building. Soon she had worked herself up into a fierce anger with all of them. Why couldn't her meeting with Kit be perfect? Why couldn't he walk into the hall, smell her perfume and wrap her in his arms? Her anger faded as she sat on the edge of the table and smoked a cigarette. Halfway through it she decided she should strike a pose so that if he did arrive, he would see her silhouetted in the dim light, her legs crossed, elegantly finishing her smoke. She adjusted her position and helped her right knee across her left. It wasn't so easy to cross her legs with neither of her feet on the floor. Two minutes later she had cramp in her left leg. She jumped down and stressed her heel against the floor, stretching her hamstring muscles. The pain worsened until it was almost unbearable, then the cramp passed. There followed an interval of silence and bleakness during which the cold of the hallway began to find its way through her clothing and into her bones. She was tempted to go out on to the street again and stand beside the cheerful doorman under his striped awning. At least light gave the illusion of warmth, and the hallway was as cold and dark as a vault. But she didn't want to stumble into Kit as she left. He must come to her. That was how she saw it in her mind.

Meredith went to the foot of the stairs and looked up towards the landing. She heard a door open above her and waited for somebody to emerge. Instead, there was a clink of bottles and the door closed again. Now she needed the toilet. Why hadn't she thought of it before when she had had the opportunity? Well, she told herself sternly, she would just have to wait. But for how long? She stepped away from the foot of the stairs and paced up and down the worn stone floor, from the table to the wall, five times. On the sixth, the idea struck her that Kit might be inside his flat resting, which was why the gaslight hadn't been lit. She should at least go upstairs and check. But what should she do with her case? Leave it downstairs, of course. Damn the case.

Meredith walked up to the first landing, feeling herself choked a little by the stench from the lavatory she passed. Pausing by the window, she looked out at the street and watched the snow falling. It had already gathered in the valley of the canvas awning above the doorman. Motor-car tyres had scored silver lines in the white on the road and within them were the tracks of a horse and cart. Meredith went on up the next flight of stairs, passed the first flat and then came to a stop outside Kit's door. She reached out and tenderly touched the cold wood. Then she straightened her hair and knocked. She waited. There was no sound from inside. Or perhaps the shifting of a chair. She knocked again. A moment's longer wait before she began to retrace her steps towards the stairs.

Behind her, a door opened. Meredith stopped. She couldn't turn, she could barely breathe. She heard a voice in the darkness calling, 'Hello?'

'Hello,' she said back.

'Did you knock?'

'Yes. I knocked.'

'Who are you?'

'I'm a friend of Kit's.'

The door closed. It was not Kit, not even Kit's flat. Only the voice of an older man hungry for company.

Meredith went down the stairs and back across the hall. She couldn't bear the darkness any longer so she opened the heavy door. The street was bright with snow. The sight of it lifted her spirits and warmed her. As she walked across the pavement her footsteps made sudden stiff craters in the new fall. All she wanted was a cigarette and a friendly voice. The doorman would meet these simple needs.

But as she crossed the road she saw the figure of a man turn the corner. The man moved slowly, as if he was afraid of slipping on the snow. The right sleeve of his grey coat hung limp and empty. He was using his umbrella as a walking stick. Meredith waited in the centre of the street for him to notice her. She had tried so hard to predict what she would feel on meeting Kit Renton again, but she knew now that, like shock, nothing could prepare the soul for a pure flood of happiness. She went back to the pavement, her path being marked by a semicircle of footsteps in the snow. When Kit saw her he stopped dead, which was not how she had planned it. But it no longer mattered. She saw gratitude and love and relief on his face, which was all that she had hoped to see when he finally found his way back to her.